Adam Zameenzad was born in Pakistan and spent his early childhood in East Africa. His first novel, The Thirteenth House, won the David Higham Award for best novel of 1987. He is also the author of three other highly acclaimed novels: My Friend Matt and Hena the Whore, Love, Bones and Water, and Cyrus Cyrus. He lives in Kent, England.

MY FRIEND MATT AND HENA THE WHORE

ADAM ZAMEENZAD

Ziji

PUBLISHING

Published by Ziji Publishing Ltd. in 2018
www.ziji publishing.com

First published in Great Britain by Fourth Estate Limited 1988
First published in the United States of America by Penguin Books 1993

Distributed by Turnaround Distribution Services Ltd
www.turnaround-uk.com
Telephone 020 8829 3000

ISBN: 978-1-908628-13-8

Printed and bound in Great Britain by Aquatint Ltd

MY FRIEND MATT
AND
HENA THE WHORE

CONTENTS

Part I
THE SPIRIT DANCE (a beginning of sorts)

Part II
GOLAM'S COW (two years later)

Part III
HENA THE WHORE (one year later)

In memory of Little Mama Walters and her five children: the un-named, BB, Benjamin, ET, and Chu Chu, all of whom died within six months of her death. Also for Itsy and baby Charlotte. May their bodies make the Earth more fertile for the hungry.

In the hope that at some stage in the life of this planet no man or woman will have to experience the shame of writing another book like this one again.

Part 1

THE SPIRIT DANCE

(a beginning of sorts)

One

Meet Matt, Hena, Grandma Toughtits and Golam

My friend Matt is a real smart-ass. He knows everything. Everything: why birds fly and men don't – their shit is deadly for the ones below; how mama rhino punishes baby rhino – by hiding its hide; when is the worst time to pick your nose – after you've picked your ass; how to tell the size of a man's dingus without looking – by holding it; where the Spirits of the trees and the Spirits of mountains meet for their nightly dance – at each other's bases. He also knows when cows will and when cows won't; which water-holes are deep and which water-holes are shallow; where the dead go when they die; which clouds are rain clouds and which raise dust... The list is endless. The list of all the things Matt knows. I just mention some of the more important ones.

And, he's only young! Of course he is a year older than me, which makes him ten. Not exactly what I'd call a child, but still fairly young.

Fairly young for a smart-ass, that is.

He's always right, too. Well, nearly always.

Even when he isn't, he ends up making you feel stupid. Like it was your fault for believing him in the first place. Like he was joking and having you on and you got took.

But we don't mind. At least not so's you'd notice. For no longer than three bats of an eyelid, as he is a true pal and will lay his life down for a friend. And when all's said and done, that's what truly counts. Ask Grandma Toughtits if you don't believe me.

She is another one who knows everything. Only more as she is old. About four hundred and seventy-three years old. Mam says it's only seventy-three. But I like to think it's four hundred and seventy-three.

I like to think that for I never ever want her to die.

Neither does Matt nor Golam nor Hena nor any of the other children in the village, as we like to pull her tits.

They hang so, Grandma Toughtits' tits, and flap so, like living leather. She refuses to cover them up in what she calls 'modern fashion'. 'Vulgar' she calls it; hiding what the spirits have made and 'lifting it up' to look like what it's not.

She runs after us when we pull her tits, screaming and shouting and threatening to strangle us with her waist scarf. We run for a while and then pretend to fall over so she can catch hold of us. Which she does. Then she hugs us hard and rocks us in her arms and gives us her best made sweets and tells us stories of good Spirits and bad Spirits and good mountains and bad mountains and good men and bad men and good rains and bad rains and good animals and bad animals and loves us to bits. We never ever want her to die.

Matt says she will. Smart-ass. I hate him. But I'm also his best friend.

Golam is his other best friend. The three of us are best friends. Matt says that's how it should be, for all the best things in life come in threes. One head with two eyes, one nose with two nostrils, one dingus with two balls, one mouth and one asshole with two cheeks each – and so on and so on.

One Matt and two friends. Golam and Kimo.

Kimo is my name.

Hena is also our friend but sort of different from a friend. We like her and we don't like her.

No-one knows how old she is but I expect she's at least nine, nine and a half.

She don't know everything, like Matt and Grandma Toughtits, but she knows quite a lot. More than Golam and me put together.

She always knows what anybody is thinking whether they let on or not.

Most of all she knows what she wants and how to get it. No matter what, no matter how. Of course it's easy for her on account she is rich. She can eat as much as she wants whenever she wants and no questions asked. And she has lots of things. I can't tell you what most of them are for I don't know myself what most of them are.

Her Dada won't let us near them.

We do most things together. Matt starts us off, usually; Golam and me follow, usually. Hena turns up somehow – if she wants to.

Like the other night, not long ago, when Matt comes running to me. It is long after sundown. Nothing new in that. No one knows when Matt sleeps, if ever.

It's not sleeping that makes him so thin and small, says Grandma Toughtits, but Matt don't care.

He likes to wander at night finding where birds nest and where animals sleep. He sees the pathways of the stars and meets other wandering Spirits and learns from them. And comes to conclusions.

'Let's bunk school tomorrow,' says he.

Now that is new.

Unlike the rest of the world, Matt loves going to school. He's such a smart-ass he loves to show off in front of the Master – and the rest of us!

He knows the language of the North and he knows the language of the South; he can read and write the language of the South; he can read and write the English language and he speaks another language of the white man. He can add, take away and multiply; and he knows all there is to know about science.

Of course he can't sing or dance half as good as me. And that, says Grandma Toughtits, is the best learning of all. But she don't like flash talk so I best not go on about it.

'Let's bunk school,' says Matt, all out of breath for having run all the way to my house.

'Why?' go I.

'Why!' he goes, 'why – because we're going to Gonta, you knuckle-head, that is why.'

Just like that.

Not, 'Will you come to Gonta with me?' or 'We could go to Gonta, maybe tomorrow,' or 'I hear Gonta looks good this time of the year,' or something polite like that. No sir. But straight out, 'We're going to Gonta, you knucklehead.'

Now Gonta is the next village, some twenty hours walk to the west of us. I've heard of it, but no more. It's near enough to the big city to be quite famous. Or so I've heard. The thought of going there is truly exciting, but I try not to show it. I try to show my strength. Like I have a mind of my own.

'Maybe I don't want to go to Gonta tomorrow,' say I, trying to hold my excitement from showing. 'I've got history in school tomorrow and I like history.'

And that is the truth. History is the only lesson I like at school. All those stories. I like them. I don't believe them, but I like them.

Matt believes them but don't like them.

He finds them scary. He finds them scary, because, he says, they're real. Me, I find pretend stories more scary. Stories about ghosts and ghouls and monsters.

Matt's more afraid of real people. He won't admit it to no one. But he is. I know it for I know him.

'You don't want to go to Gonta tomorrow?' says Matt with that naughty note in his voice which makes me prick up my ears, wondering what's coming next. 'You've nothing to worry then, have you,' he carries on, still with the same voice, 'for we are going to Gonta tonight.'

'Tonight?' I shout.

I mean, I know he roams around like a nameless Spirit most nights, and many is the time I've walked with him – but going to Gonta in the middle of the night!

'Why that's many days' walk away,' say I, making it out to be further than it is. Just so it sounds more impossible.

'No it isn't,' goes Matt. 'We'd be in the heart of Bader if we walked that far.'

Bader is the big city further west.

Matt carries on. 'Gonta can't be more than a day or two away.'

'That's far enough for me,' I reply, trying to be difficult.

I can walk if Matt can. After all I am twice his size. Nearly.

But I am being difficult.

'If we take the path,' Matt carries on, 'and leave the big road, we can cut it by a good few hours.'

Now that truly puts the wind up me. The path goes through thick copses before the desert, then up the mountains. No one goes there these days on account of the strange stories we hear.

'But...' go I.

Before I can think up of what to say Matt puts in, 'I thought your legs were the strongest in the village!'

Now I should know better than to rise to such talk, but I do.

Just like he hopes I will.

But so what. After all, I do so want to go.

'What do we tell Mam and Dada?'

'I don't know about you, but I told Ethlyne to tell Dada not to worry. That I'll be back Monday. Tuesday at the latest!'

Ethlyne is his kid sister.

'Tuesday!' I pipe back. 'But that's days from now.'

'We only miss a couple of days of school,' he says.

It is Thursday.

It is also the least of my worries. Missing school, I mean. But I let it pass on account I do so want to go.

'You still haven't told me why we're going to Gonta.'
After all that's not the sort of thing one does every day. I reckon not many elders have been to Gonta in all their born days.
'You'll find out,' is all he says.
I am so annoyed I nearly decide to stay back.
But I go. I go but I sulk, which suits him fine for I don't ask no more questions. I never do when I am sulking and he knows it. Smart-ass. I hate him.
I write a note saying I have to go out 'exploring' for a school topic – pretty clever I think – run a string through it and put it round little brother's neck. I've to pull his head up sharply to do it, but nothing wakes him so there's no worry. He reads well so he'll tell Mam and Dada. How they'll take it I'll learn when I get back.
I pull my trousers on and throw my shoes in my sling bag, just in case. Even though it is summer. I fling my shawl across my shoulder – it can get a bit chilly at night, especially over the mountains – and tiptoe out of the sleeping hall into the open air; one step ahead of Matt just to prove my legs are bigger, and stronger, than his. He don't mind. Or if he does he don't let on.
We get to the little tree at the back end of the village behind the little hill. Our regular meeting place.
The little hill is hardly taller than a house but once behind it no one can see us there. And if we crawl up to the top we can see almost everyone and everything down below for the village is flat as bread. It is extra black. There are clouds in the sky which

cover the light of the stars with oily grey shawls. That and the cold silence between us make the short walk long. It's hard to believe we go that way every day at least once. It is like walking through a stranger's house.

When we get to the little hill Golam is already there waiting for us. That cuts me even more. It means Matt spoke to him before he came to me. Then I think. It also means he left Golam to make his own way. Me, he brings with him. This cheers me up, but I still decide to keep to myself.

Golam grins from one end of the jaw to the other. He has big white teeth and the happiest smile you ever saw. When he smiles his whole face changes. Changes from a simple clay mug to a lovely china cup. In the dark all you see is the teeth and the whites of the eyes but you can feel the happiness. I can't go on having the hump after that.

But before I have the chance to say a word, a sharp voice says, 'You took your time, didn't you!'

Spirit of Shit. I nearly jump up the hill.

I should've expected it but I haven't.

It is Hena.

She has a large bag by her side and she is sitting in the most comfortable part of the slope where there's a little dimple in the earth to hold her bumsey-wumsey. She is resting her arm on a curvy rock that sticks out on one side.

We don't like Hena on long travels. We don't like Hena at all for long times. We end up running around doing things for her. Doing everything for her. Of course she does things too. But she does things she likes to do. We've got to do things she likes to do. We can do what we like when she's not bothered about what we're doing. But if she don't like what we're doing or needs something else done we've to stop doing what we like doing and do what she likes doing. Even Matt can't do nothing about that.

Sometimes we're doing what we hate and she wants and don't even know it. We even begin to like it. Sometimes. Sometimes we pretend we like it and end up believing we like it. Mostly we don't but still we do it.

My bad mood returns.

'What's she doing here?' I ask myself but get no answer.

'What's she doing here?' I ask the tree. He just waves his arms about helplessly.

'We're not taking her?' I ask the Earth. It spits dust in my eyes.

'Are we?' I ask Golam. He shivers from head to toe, his lips move but I hear no words. Only a sigh.

'Are we?' I ask Matt.

'You tell me.' He turns on me. 'She has the hots for you.'

'Then how comes she's always around you lot?'

'Children, children, don't fight on my account,' rises the shrill voice of Hena at its sharpest.

It pierces my ears like a needle of north wind.

Something in the way she speaks, and the word 'children' – in front of Matt at that – tells me she is at her worst.

She gets up, practically falls down as she lifts her bag from the ground, steadies herself and starts walking towards the village.

I act relieved but my Spirit tells me she has something up her sleeve.

She hasn't. Not up her sleeve. She has it in her bag.

Matt has it figured out.

'You wait,' he nudges me in the rib, left side third from the bottom where some people have their waist. 'You wait,' he goes again and nudges me again with his thin sharp elbow. It is like getting an injection in the bone. 'She'll stop before she's twelve steps gone and pull something out of her bag and squeak.'

I don't count the steps but he isn't far out.

Hena stops, pulls a torch out of her bag, lights it up and flashes it around. 'Useful, this,' she goes, 'especially when walking further than the bat flies.'

She waits for a reaction.

We are impressed but say nothing.

'Especially on a night as black as this,' she carries on. 'Especially through the woods.'

I am about to waver and speak but Matt squeezes my arm. It is surprising how strong his bony fingers can be.

Hena puts the torch in the bag, fumbles about inside it and comes up with a big round clock. Its numbers almost glow in the dark.

She comes closer to Golam and says, 'Can you see what time it is? I've got something in my eyes.'

She knows how Matt always wants a watch.

He has a thing about time. It charms him like a flute charms a cobra. To have a watch round his wrist and to know the time at the turn of a hand is one of his dreams.

Of course you can't wear that heavy thing round any part of your body. But still, it does the time.

'It has an alarm bell, too,' adds Hena as we're still shut up.

This time Matt takes in a breath as if about to say something but I squeeze his arm.

A torch and a clock. She is rich that girl. And cunning as the Spirit of the Left-Sided Beast.

But we stand firm. We don't want Hena with us for three days and nights. We'll end up slaving or fighting.

She pulls a bundle of shawls, a flask filled with goat's milk, flat bread, dried meat, half-ripe mangoes, a pineapple, a coconut, a cigarette lighter and a battery radio. It don't work but it's still a battery radio.

You can't argue with all that.

'How did you know we was going in the first place?' I ask Hena as we start walking towards the trees standing dark against the dark sky, half the night away.

She says nothing, she likes to be quiet and mysterious.

To my left Golam misses a step. I bet she has a hold on him, or bribes him or both.

My back is breaking under the weight of her bag.

While Matt plans and Hena schemes and Golam grins, I get landed with the heavy jobs. Always.

Matt says that's how it should be.

He's got a great brain so he uses it.

Golam's got a lovely smile so he uses that.

Hena's got a twisted mind so she uses that.

I've got a strong body so I've got to use my strong body.

I kind of agree with him and kind of don't. I mean, it sounds fair but I am not sure it is. I mean it makes it pretty easy for Golam. And for Hena. Even Matt. I get my back broken and my legs aching and my arms falling out.

Matt says, 'Look at it this way. If things go wrong or you can't do any more we can take your load. But you can't take my brain or Hena's mind or Golam's smile, can you?' he says.

Smart ass.

It still don't seem fair to me.

I walk on for some time, then stand for I've thought of something else to say.

'Don't stop me from getting tired,' I say. 'Being big don't mean you don't get tired out.'

I look pleased with myself for saying that.

'I get tired thinking, y'know,' he replies.

'And Golam cracks his face smiling I suppose,' I say, wishing he would.

'He does help when you need it, don't he?' Which is true enough so I shut up and move along.

'You can take Kimo's load,' I hear Hena's voice talking to Matt, 'but can you take his strength. Can you? Can you?'

She is the only one who can turn the tables on Matt.

My heart warms to her in spite of her face.

Matt is not to be outdone though.

'No. But I can take your mouth for I won't take your mouth,' he says calmly.

I don't get what he is on about but it shuts her up.

Matt can make anyone shut up. Even Masters. Even Hena.

But not Golam for he never opens his mouth anyway. Except to grin.

The upshot of the argument is that things get divided up.

Matt takes the clock and the radio – there are no batteries in it, though – and the cigarette lighter. Matt hates cigarettes but loves the lighter. He likes watching fire. Golam gets to carry the food. Hena keeps a piece of cloth, a mirror, combs, a lump of soap and a few other useless things. I'm left with shawls and everybody's shoes. I end up heavier.

'Look at it this way,' says Matt, 'soon we'll need our shoes, and soon again shawls, maybe – ' He adds maybe for he hates shawls and shoes – 'and you'll be the best off.'

I say nothing.

'Oh all right,' he goes, 'don't mope. I'll have some of your stuff.'

But I carry on.

It don't surprise him for I am like that when I'm like that.

Golam stops me, puts his hands into the bag, takes out a couple of shawls, wraps them round his shoulders and grins. I grin back.

We've hardly moved ten shadows of a tree away before I hear the screech of Hena's words shoot past my earholes. 'I hope it's worth it. Worth all the walking and haggling. This Spirit Dance.'

The light shines inside my head. I understand.

That's where Matt is leading us to.

To the Spirit Dance held in Gonta this time of the season every year. Chiefs and tribes from the North and South and West and East gather to dance for the Spirits. The Spirits then come over from the North and South and West and East to join in and to bless and make happy all those who dance for them. And their friends and relations. Bless them and make them happy and cure their illnesses for one whole year until the next Spirit Dance.

A grand fair is also held in the village in honour of the Spirits – with slides, roundabouts, picture shows, even a circus – to go with the Dance.

So famous is this Dance that even those who don't believe in the Spirits, the Christians (we have one or two in the village) and the Muslims (Golam is one), also take part in it. Sometimes just to enjoy the dance, often because in their heart they still believe in the Spirits, like their fathers. And their fathers before them. Not the Children of Moses, though. They never join in the Dance. But even they come to the fair.

And so do white men.

Matt has always been set on Spirits and Gods and suchlike. He don't often talk about them, but he feels for them. He wants to know about them. He wants to know about the whole wide world. He is like that. Curious as the black cat. Never satisfied.

'How come Hena knows about it?' I say. I often say that. With good reason. 'How come Hena knows we're going to the Spirit Dance!'

'How does Hena know anything!' says Matt, making his shoulders jump up and down. 'Black magic. She's a witch, she is.'

'Maybe I am and maybe I am not,' says Hena, going quiet and mysterious again.

As long as she didn't find out from Matt I don't care. It would've burnt me up if she had. If not, I don't care.

I am surprised. But I don't care.

Truly I am not surprised either. I wouldn't be surprised if Hena truly was a witch. Or the Spirit of a witch, which is worse.

'It is thirteen seconds and thirty-three minutes after nine o'clock of the night,' says Matt. I don't know why he says it, but he says it. It is earlier than I think. The clouds are making me believe it is later.

Matt says something else but his voice is lost in the thunder of an aeroplane, flying so low it could've been just on top of our heads.

*

We've been walking for full four hours and fourteen minutes. I know for Matt's been shouting the time all the time. He calls it regular intervals. I call it all the time.

Matt says we should be far enough out of the village before we stop for a rest so that if our Dadas come looking for us they get tired and go back.

I am tired. Golam is tired. Matt is tired. Even Hena is tired though she says she is not.

I say it is safe to stop for the night, what's left of it. Matt says it is best if we get to the copse and shelter in the trees. That way we can hide ourselves even if someone does come this far.

I don't think no one will. I don't think no one'll look for us at all. My Dada don't trust me but he trusts Matt so he'll think it's OK. Golam don't have a Dada. Hena's Dada has plenty of land and crops but no sense. Anyway he is drunk most of the time so he's not likely to bother. Besides, like my Dada he trusts Matt.

And it's not like it's the first time. We've been gone before and come back right as sunshine. If one of us was missing on his own, or her own if it was Hena, there'd be great worry. But with all of us gone there will only be rolling of eyes and heaving of sighs and making of remarks but no more.

But Matt likes to play safe. Always does when he wants something, and he wants to get to the Spirit Dance. He don't want to miss it for nothing. He's not taking any chances so we keep limping on till we get to the woods.

Luckily it isn't too far. Not any more.

We are now in front of the copse. We stop to wonder at the size of the trees. And the strength of the trees. And the magic of the trees. My Dada believes our family comes from the Spirits of the trees. That is why we grow tall and are built strong and live long.

Matt sometimes thinks he is the Spirit of the fox: small, cute (he thinks), and clever. But mostly he believes he is the Spirit of the black cat on account of he is always up and about at night and always looking for something not knowing what it is. I'm not sure if that's what the black cat does, but Matt says so.

If Hena is not the Spirit of a witch, which she is, she is the river Spirit: murky deep winding and unreliable. Dry or overflowing. Golam is not allowed to believe in 'all this nonsense' but I'm sure he secretly believes himself to be the Spirit of something or other. I think it is the Spirit of the wolf on account of his teeth.

*

One step inside the woods and it's black as Hell with its fire out. We thought it was black out in the open but we think again now that we are not.

Matt says it is fine. Safe. He's always on about safety, which is strange for he is often out catching lizards and snakes with his bare hands. Our Master says that is not safe at all but Dada says a man must learn such things. Me, I'd rather not. Matt says he does as the fox or the black cat: lives dangerously but plays safe.

The woods don't prove too safe though. Serves him right for being cocky.

Two

The Poor Naked Man

I don't like being shaken up when I'm awake. I hate being shaken up when I'm asleep. I wake up being shaken up after being shaken up while sleeping.

It is Matt (who else!). His bony fingers are digging deep into my arms like the claws of an eagle. I don't wake up early at the best of times. After a long day and a long night and a long walk I wake up slower than death.

'Can you hear something?' I hear Matt saying.

'Wh... wh... what, wh'what?' I drumble – that's what Mam says I do when I mumble in my sleep.

'Can you hear something?' Matt goes again.

'Yes,' I manage to let slip out of my sleep-swollen lips.

'What d'you think you hear?'

'I hear you saying "Can you hear something?"'

'I don't mean that, stupid.'

I always promise I'll scream next time he calls me stupid, but never do. I decide this is as good a time as any to start.

I scream.

He nearly chokes me to death.

'What d'you think you're doing?' he shouts in a whisper.

'What do you think you are doing?' I whisper in a shout. It is not a loud whisper for my throat is still choked up even though his left hand is no longer on my mouth and his right hand no longer round my neck.

Both his hands are back on my arms and I'm being shaken up again. Matt don't understand why it takes me so long to wake up. It's easy for him. The slightest noise or change in the air and he is out of his bed quicker than a fart out of an ass, and as smooth.

Anyway, shaken up like a rattlesnake's tail even I wake up, in a muddled sort of a way.

He puts his hand on my mouth again, just in case, and says, 'Now don't make a sound. Just listen. D'you hear anything?'

I try hard but my ears are still dreaming. Dreaming of nothing. The sweetest dream of all.

But all dreams come to an end, says Grandma Toughtits. So does this one. I hear like a rustling sound. Like leaves moving.

It's not like someone is walking on leaves; just the sound of leaves moving.

'It's like leaves moving,' I say.

'That's how it sounds to me. Leaves moving.'

'Now why would leaves move?' we both say, sort of together.

There isn't a breath of a breeze anywhere. It'd have to be a whacking great wind to get into the thicket and stir the leaves on the ground (it is the sound of leaves moving on the ground, not on the trees).

The leaves around us are lying happily dead, buried in each other's laps. The weird swish swishing follows a fairly regular pattern. Not altogether regular, but fairly regular.

'They're walking the night,' goes Matt in a hushed voice. I've never heard his voice hushed like that before. It shakes my mind like his hands shook my body. I look up at him but it is still black and I can't see his face. Not even his eyes. Not properly.

'That's no man's walk,' I say, 'nor woman's nor child's neither. And if it is an animal's I'll eat my shoes.' I am a little scared as I say this for my Dada will hang me by the toes if I have to eat my shoes. If it turns out to be an animal Matt will make me.

But he takes no notice of what I say.

'They are walking the night,' he goes again.

I get worried for him. I've never seen him like that.

All I do is repeat, 'That's no man's walk, nor woman's nor...'

'I heard you the first time,' he cuts me short and I'm glad for I don't really like saying all that all over again. 'I don't mean man, woman or child – or animal. It is them.'

By now I'm losing my cool. 'Them. Who's them?' I go crossly.

'The Spirits.'

Suddenly I am awake proper.

Suddenly I understand Matt's behaviour.

'Going to the Dance?' I whisper. 'Like us?'

I am not crazy about Spirits like Matt, but I am interested. Who isn't? There's no doubt about that.

The swish swishing seems to become faster and less regular,

then stops. With the noise of leaves gone we expect silence. We hear other sounds. Unclear sounds we cannot put a name to.

We listen. We listen in fear and hope.

Fear of crossing angry Spirits; hope of meeting happy Spirits.

In fear and hope we stand up and without thinking start walking towards the mystery noises. Both Matt and I believe we are aces at tracking signs as well as sounds.

It is different this time.

The trees and bushes hide the sounds one minute and let them through the next. We get nearer and are still far.

It goes on like this forever until we come to this place where the trees are taller than my Dada stood on his head ten times over, and darker – which is unusual for my Dada is darker than the night.

The bushes are as sweet-scented as Mam and I snuggle close to them. All goes completely silent here.

We think we've either moved too far out of range or the Spirits have heard us and gone quiet. We think we best turn round and go back. We think we have lost our way. We think we are in true trouble. In following the sounds we have strayed away from the narrow path smoothed out by years of feet and are now on hard ground with little mounds and tufts of sharp grass here and there.

We are frightened. At least I am, and I am sure Matt is too.

We start scanning the ground to see if we can spot our tracks to make our way back, but it's too black for that. Matt curses the black which shows he is worrying for he loves the black of the night.

As it goes the black is good.

Suddenly we see a faint flicker of a pale light. It is so faint that if it had been less black we'd have missed it. It shines through the dark trees, disappears, then shines again.

'Spirit of Light,' shouts Matt, forgetting the first rule of tracking.

*

Now the Spirit of Light is the best there is. She is the Mother of the Spirit of Life.

No wonder Matt forgets the first rule of tracking in the excitement.

If you meet the Spirit of Light you live for ever and ever.

For some time we completely freeze up; then, very slowly, very carefully – so as not to anger or frighten the Spirits – we edge our way towards the trees through which we saw the light shine.

Thick bushes surround the place. We jump with shock as one bush runs off when our feet kick it by misstate. We learn that it is just put there and not actually growing. Then we find many more like that. It is getting stranger and stranger. Who'd cut away so many thick bushes and then set them in a careful line? Not a straight line, more like a curve.

Not only who, but why.

We are about to find out.

Matt is already moving as if in control of great powers or controlled by them. I am having difficulty keeping up with him. There is a flicker of light again. This time sharper and nearer. Matt streaks through the trees like a hunted deer or a hunting cat and then stops dead.

Is he bitten by a snake? I think to myself and am struck by a new worry. I am a great worrier. Matt always says that. So do Mam and Dada. Even little brother and big sister say that, so I guess I must be. But no, he is not bitten by a snake. He is standing tall and straight and stiff with a gaping mouth. I can see it for there is light here.

Has he really seen the Spirits? I think to myself; and is it the Spirit of Light which makes this dark night brighter? I am now worrying good worries. Matt says there is no such thing as good as worries but I say there is. I should know for I worry with good worries. Matt can't know everything.

I am so busy looking at Matt I don't see what's in front of me. So busy worrying nothing worries that I nearly step into the heart of a real worry. Matt grabs hold of me, puts his hand on my mouth and drags me behind a tree. He does not take his hand off my mouth till he is sure I will be quiet. By now I have seen what there is to see. At least enough to know that it is not Spirits and it is not good either.

Hidden behind those cut bushes and huge trees I see a clearing. A man-made clearing, quite a large one almost the size of two or three houses. It is roughly in the shape of a circle. There are two huts in the circle. One smaller than the other. They are covered with fresh leaves swept from the ground or taken from the trees to make them look like bushes.

'We must've heard them sweeping the leaves to lay some fresh ones on the huts,' goes Matt in a voice so low I can hardly hear him.

Even I've worked that out, but I don't say anything.

We see a man dressed in a sort of spotty green trousers and a spotty green shirt talking softly to another man dressed similar. He's carrying a small light in his hand which is quite dull but he is still covering it with his other hand to try to keep it from showing at all. Soon three more people come out of the larger hut: two men and one lady. One of the men tall with a fat stomach, and the lady tall with a fat ass, are also wearing spotty green clothes. The second man has a dirty white robe on his body and a look of anger on his face which is kind of all puffed up and is different colours and shades all over.

The tall man with the fat stomach and the tall lady with the fat ass are both carrying guns. Same as the two men we saw first.

The man in the dirty white robe is being pushed and shoved by the other two. The tall man with the fat stomach gives him a strong kick between his legs and the tall lady with the fat ass gobs him in the eyes.

The one with the light and his mate go towards them and join in beating up the man in the dirty white robe.

They are also shouting at him. Not loud, but still shouting.

Not the lady though. She isn't shouting. She is hissing and spitting, words as well as gob.

I do not understand what they say for it's not the language my Dada speaks. That is the only one I know except for a little bit of English. Matt can understand most of it. It has words in it of the speech of the north which Matt knows. Also they mix their speech with words of another white man's language which Matt understands a little. Whatever they say scares Matt stiff for his bony fingers grab my arms and drag me into the bushes.

'Don't move,' he says in a tight whisper, 'and don't say a word,' which I find odd for he is the one who is moving me and he is the one who is speaking. Slowly and smoothly he folds himself and crouches beside me, both tense and relaxed, like a cat.

He brings his mouth so close to my ears his lips tickle my lobes. 'They're saying to that man he has some others with him not far from here. They say they know for they've heard about them from very reliable sources. They say when they find them they'll make them wish they'd never left their mother's womb. They're saying if his mother was here they'd force him back into her...'

Matt is talking fast and low and what he says makes me wish I was back in my Mam's arms. I feel like crying but I know any noise and we're as good as dead. I don't know why but that don't matter. All that matters is that I want to get out of here.

Matt knows what I am thinking.

'It's best to wait till they get back into their hut.'

'What if they don't?' I finally bring myself to speak. 'It'll be light soon. They're sure to spot us then.'

'There's that,' agrees Matt. It's not often Matt agrees with me. Or anybody. 'Let's give it a little while. If they're still outside we'll start back,' he says.

I think this is the best time as they are arguing and won't hear us. Matt says nothing which is greatly unusual. I then understand why he isn't back-tracking straight away as any normal person would. He is curious to know what is going on.

One day he'll get us all killed. Or worse, get us into trouble.

Which reminds me of Hena and Golam. I only hope they're still sleeping and not looking around for us. If they do they'll end up making enough noise to get themselves caught. And us too.

Golam I know never wakes. Hena, on the other hand, never sleeps.

Leastways that's what I believe. She can't rest from scheming long enough for sleep. I'm worried what she'll do if she finds us gone. Matt is too busy bending his ears and squinting his eyes to see and hear all he can see and hear.

The four spotty green ones are being really cruel to the poor man in the dirty white robe. Even I forget thinking my troubles and start thinking his troubles.

They tear the robe off his body and kick him in the chest and stomach and between the legs. The lady sits on his face so he can't scream or shout. Every so often she lifts her fat ass off his face as if giving him a chance to tell whatever they want to know. But he don't.

'Why don't he tell them?' I say.

'How can he? He don't know. Leastwise that's what he says.'

'He could be lying,' I say.

'That don't matter,' Matt goes. 'He don't have to tell them just because they're beating him up.'

'He must have done some bad,' I say.

'I don't know if he's done some bad or not,' he goes, 'but I can tell you for nothing they're doing some bad.'

Suddenly they stop their kicking and beating. We are happy for the poor man on the ground who is no longer wearing the dirty white robe. But we also wonder why. We don't wonder for long. There is another man coming towards them. He must've come out of the hut as well for we'd have heard if he'd come through the bushes. The three men who've stopped kicking and beating the poor man who is no longer wearing the dirty white robe stand all respectful waiting for the new man. The lady gets off the poor man's face and joins the men.

'He must be the king,' says Matt.

When Matt says king he does not mean king as the husband or the queen or nothing like that. He means the big boss.

I always say that when Matt says 'king' and everybody goes 'ain't he clever' or 'well I never' and makes faces at me as if I'm a real dumbo jumbo. But I still say it for I never understood when Matt first said 'king', so I think it best to explain for if someone had explained to me I'd have understood right the first time instead of going on thinking wrong as I did. But no matter. I best stop for breath.

Anyway this man comes and the beating stops. I am happy. I think maybe he'll let the poor man off and tell the bad men off. And the bad lady. Maybe then we could start on our way back. But I think wrong.

When this new man comes and the other men stop kicking and beating and the lady stands up; the poor man on the ground also makes a try to raise himself on his elbow as if hoping to stand up too, or at least to sit up. As soon as he moves, the tall man with the fat stomach lifts up high his right boot studded with shiny nails on its sole, brings it straight above the poor man's middle, and stamps down hard between his legs. Direct on the poor man's one and twos. I die with fear. Matt grips my wrist strongly enough and I feel him shake.

The new man is now with the others and they have a quiet talk. They light cigarettes and throw burning matches on the poor man below. All this time the tall man with the fat stomach is crushing the poor man's dooda and things with his big boot.

The lady has put her fat ass back on the poor man's face for a bit of peace and quiet for he started shouting rude words. We can't hear him any more but we can feel his body shouting in pain as it twitches and gasps for air.

Something the new man says makes them all laugh. All except the poor bugger on the ground on account his face is sat on. It is difficult to laugh or be cheerful if your face is sat on though I can't say for sure on account I've never had my face sat on and jolly glad I am of that.

They laugh so much that the tall man with the fat stomach lifts his boot off the poor man's crossroads, raises his leg and slaps his thigh. As he does so the poor bugger decides it's time to do something. He bites the lady's fat ass. She jumps up screaming like she's been bitten in the ass which of course she has. As she jumps up, he aims a double kick with both feet straight up the crotch of the tall man with the fat stomach. He still has boots on even though he is buff naked otherwise. The double attack of these boots does no good to the man's balls. He doubles up over his fat stomach and groans something awful.

The naked man then jumps up on his boots and runs.

We both get excited and cheer him in our hearts.

The lady forgets her bitten ass and shoots after him. After a second to take in what's going on the men do too, except for the one holding his balls.

If the naked man makes it to the dense bushes and thick trees behind the huts there's a good chance he can escape.

He don't see a tree branch that sticks out so a blind man could see it. But fear blind is worse than real blind, Grandma Toughtits says. It catches him in the neck and he is back on his back.

The four jump on him and this time the lady with the fat ass sits on his stomach. Two men hold him down on each end and the third rushes into one of the huts and comes back with sharp wooden pegs. They hammer four of these into the ground. Two men pull off his boots and tie his ankles with a twisted rope to two pegs. They then start to beat the soles of his feet with the hammer while the third man ties his wrists.

He is now lying spread apart on the ground, arms pulled up above his head, legs stretched and wide open.

The lady with the fat ass has now got off his stomach.

The two men have stopped hammering the soles of his feet.

All are standing calmly round him, saying nothing, doing nothing.

Nothing at all.

I think I can hear Matt's bones crackle as his whole body gets harder and harder.

I, on the other hand, am turning to butter.

I say the poor man is now going to get the beating of his life.

'Of his death more like it,' Matt hisses back.

But they do nothing.

Just stand round him calmly, saying nothing, doing nothing.

Nothing at all. I find that more and more scary.

'What d'you think the poor bugger must be feeling?' Matt goes.

The poor bugger don't shout or scream or anything like that. I would have. I would have shouted and screamed the woods down.

The new man now does a strange thing. He makes the lady turn the other way and pulls her trousers down, and her knickers. He bends at the knees and the lady's fat ass is now staring him in the face. He is looking, I think, to see the teeth marks on the lady's fat ass.

He kisses it better.

It must be worse than I think for it takes a lot of kissing to get better. That, I think, is the reason why he takes the lady's trousers down. To kiss her better.

But it is not. There's more to it.

He straightens himself up, lifts the lady up by putting his hands under the back of her thighs which are open. Her knees are almost up to her ears.

He moves her until she is on top of the poor man's face. She sort of giggles in a girlish way, then lets her dirty water spill below on to the poor man's face.

It must have been a long time after her last go for she goes on and on. It sounds like meat frying.

The new man then jerks her up and down to let the last drop fall. I look at Matt's face. I don't know why I look at Matt's face but I look at Matt's face. I feel ashamed of myself for being so interested in what's happening. Matt does not look interested. He looks strange. Strange and angry.

The new man now stands the lady on the ground, her trousers round her ankles. He makes a sign and all men unzip their trousers and pull out their dinguses which are big and strong and hard, except for the tall man with the fat stomach, his is a bit wimpish. They press these down with their hands, down towards the man's body, and let flow their dirty water. They shake their dinguses about to soak him all over.

The poor bugger neither struggles nor swears, just closes his eyes and mouth. The lady with the fat ass kneels down and pinches his nostrils so his mouth is forced open. The tall man with the fat stomach and the smallest dingus aims straight in.

The man chokes.

They all laugh which shakes their jets about and luckily does no good to the aim of the tall man with fat stomach and the smallest dingus. It sort of shoots up and hits the lady's face. She jerks away cursing but soon starts laughing again.

The poor man neither struggles nor swears, just closes his eyes and mouth. Once they have shaken the last drops of their dirty water out, they put their dinguses back in their trousers, but quickly pull them out again. They pull them out again for the lady with the fat ass makes a fist with her left hand and shakes it about, pointing to her naughty parts. With her right hand she pulls her trousers and knickers off her ankles.

Before straightening up – she was bending over while pulling her trousers and knickers off and fist-pointing her parts – she stuffs her knickers into the poor man's mouth, so hard and deep I think his breath'll stop.

The men now start taking all their clothes off till they are naked as the man spread about on the ground, except they keep their boots on.

For some reason the lady kneels to have a closer look at the new man's dingus. The other three men start moving towards them, all grinning, but the new man pushes the lady away and makes a sign to the men to stop. They all look at one another sort of puzzled and wait to see what he does. He makes towards the smaller hut, his dingus beginning to hang its head down, in shame – leastwise I hope that's why. When he comes back his dingus is up and about again, strong and ugly, wobbling greedily in front of him. He has a tin of some sort in his hand and a funny kind of twisted knife.

I get so scared I start to cry. Matt puts his hand firmly on my mouth to stop any sound but tears trickle down my face faster than our local stream and I can hardly see what's going on which is just as well. It must've been real bad for Matt breathes real heavy and takes his hand off my mouth and puts it on his own.

I dry my eyes with the back of my hands and look up. It is coming to dawn now and easier to see.

Strangely the four men and the lady are now pinning each other on the ground. It must be hurting for they are groaning.

The poor man is spread as before except that there is some sort of stuff sitting on all parts of his body. The tin the new man brought and the twisted knife are lying close by along with the poor man's boots.

The others are well away, this side, almost in front of us.

I stare at them with my mouth open. They start playing a game called 'Find the Hole' or 'Make a Hole' or something silly like that. They are opening and closing each other's bodies with each other's bodies – or parts of bodies.

I feel a strong fear enter my blood and pierce my spine and tingle the tips of my fingers and tickle the soles of my feet and burn the tip of my tongue and set fire to my brain. It is a strange fear for I do not want to run away from this fear. I like it. I like it when I feel I shouldn't like it. My tears start again.

I look at Matt again. He is not looking at the four in front of us. His eyes are fixed on the man further away, spread out on his own.

'D'you know what they done to him?' he asks in a choked voice.

I go, 'What!' only half listening to him.

He goes again, 'D'you know what they done to that poor man?'
'Oh that,' I say, taking my eyes away from the four in front to the
one further away. 'Course I know what they done to him.'
I get stirred a bit. What's he think I am, a complete dumbo
jumbo or something!
'Then tell me,' he goes, cocky when he hears my stirred-up voice.
I tell him.
'Not that. Any dumbo jumbo can see that.'
I hate him when he goes like that.
'Then what, smart-ass.' It's not often I call him smart-ass to his
face. For once he don't seem to mind.
'They've killed him, that's what.'
'Go on,' I say, 'he's not dead.' But he will be if they go on like this,
I think to myself.
'They have killed him. Leastwise as far as they are concerned.
And in a real bad way, too.'
I don't understand.
He explains. He explains to me like I am a little child. But I don't
mind for what he says frightens me too much to worry about
putting on the hump.
'The smell of their piss will bring the big red ants out of their
holes. Millions and millions of them.
'More so as their piss gets into his wounds and mixes with the
blood. It'll give out a stinking rotten stench.
'To make sure, in case the piss smell fades away in the dawn air,
they've put meat or some other food from that tin all over him.
'The ants will come for the smell and the blood and the food.
They'll eat the food and then get into his wounds and into his
blood. They'll eat his flesh. Bit by bit. Nibble nibble nibble, with

their sharp bites. Nibble nibble nibble. So fast his flesh will go before you are three hours older. There'll be nothing left of him but bones. Not even eyes.'

Before I can stop myself I am sick. It is a quiet choking sick, not noisy but not altogether silent either.

Matt puts his shawl on my mouth.

He looks up sharpish to see if the four have heard anything but they are too busy groaning to notice.

Very softly he wipes my face. Then he says, 'Let's start moving back. Like the black cat. Like me.'

I try to but I can't.

My feet are stuck to the ground.

My eyes are stuck to the scene.

My heart is stuck in my mouth. Along with little hard chunks of sick.

Matt puts his left hand on my left shoulder and his right hand on my eyes. We remain like that, silent and still, for a long time.

'I'll take my hands away now. Don't open your eyes, just move back.'

I feel that I can move again. It's a great relief for I had begun to believe that I'll never move again and birds will build their nests on me thinking I'm some sort of a tree. After all, we come from the Spirits of trees, our family.

We move back.

When we are gone a few metres Matt tells me to stop moving like a cat and start moving like a crab. Sideways.

I don't understand.

We're in a position to make a run for it and he is telling me to move round the bush circle!

'We've got to get that poor man out of there,' he goes in a harsh whisper. I understand but I'm still not sure.

'Hurry up,' says Matt, 'we don't have much time. It'll be light soon.'

He looks at the clock. It has stopped.

Just like Hena not telling us when to wind it up. Not that we'd have remembered, being in the position we are.

For once I wish I was with her. Right this minute.

'It's light enough already,' I say.

'It's dark enough still,' says he, 'besides, the poor man hasn't much time.'

We now move sideways, round the bushes till we're on the opposite side, close to where the man lies. Near the two huts.

The man hears us as we get closer. He jerks his head our way.

The pain the shame and the fear in his eyes change places with shock and surprise. But just for a little second. The pain the shame and the fear return, the shock is gone, the surprise remains.

The four are still playing 'Hide the Dingus'.

Matt makes signs to the poor man to show that we are friends. That we are here to help.

I think he understands. At least, he understands what, I'm not sure he understands why.

I am not sure I understand why.

Grandma Toughtits says why don't matter. It's what that counts.

And how.

How was the question now.

'I can crawl up on my belly and cut his ropes with that knife thingie over there,' I say, proud of thinking it and scared of doing it.

Matt looks at me sharpish. 'That's smart my boy,' he goes, which pleases me in spite of the 'boy' bit; but then he goes and spoils it all by saying, 'Just what I was thinking. But here, use this. I don't trust that thingie over there.'

Matt always carries this pocket knife. He won't part with it for nothing. He never lends it to no one either. Not even to me. Not normally. But nothing is normal this night.

I take the knife, put my shawl to one side next to Matt, lie flat on my belly and pray to the Spirits of Gods for courage.

I start to move, like the desert lizard.

'Be like the snake, not the lizard,' says Matt.

Smart-ass. Why don't he do it himself? I go to myself.

My hand is hardly inside the clearing before I feel Matt's bony fingers round my ankles. He pulls me back.

I often wonder where he gets such strength in that skin-and-bone frame of his.

'What's the matter?' I whisper as loud as I dare. 'You nearly skinned my knees and elbows off.'

'Look at them, out there,' he goes in my earhole, pointing to the bad men and the bad lady, 'they'll spot you. Sure as eggs they will.'

The lady and two men are still playing but the new man, and the tall man with the fat stomach and the small dingus, are squatting on the ground and smoking. They are pointing to the poor man in front of us and them, and saying something.

Their eyes and parts look fresh and perky as if looking and hoping for some action, but their shoulders droop and their arms and balls hang tired. But no more tired than all of me. I am sure. It seems to me I haven't hardly slept. It seems to me

I haven't slept for months. It seems to me I'll just fold up and fade.

'What will we do?' I say hopelessly.

The poor man spread apart on the ground is looking at us as if he don't like the taste of the lady with the fat ass's knickers at all.

The light of dawn is here now. We can see his bruises and wounds and burn marks.

'Just cool it a while, will you!' Matt practically yells. 'You're such a baby.'

That makes it worse. I pick up my shawl, stuff some of it in my face, cover my head with the rest and start having a good boo hoo on the quiet.

Matt puts his arms round my shoulders and says, 'The ants will be here soon. We've got to do something. Look at them. They're waiting to watch. See their eyes, how they search. Even the eyes of their dinguses are starting to look out of their heads. See how they shine in the new born light.'

I look up to see.

Their balls are bunching up like fists.

The sight sobers me up.

Three

The Big Bangs

'I dunno what to do,' I say, even more hopeless than before.

He says nothing, just sits there thinking.

I can tell he's thinking for I can tell when he's thinking.

When he remains quiet I say, 'What'll they do if they catch us?'

I've been thinking this all along but not daring to say it. It sounds even worse said than thought.

'They won't,' says Matt, 'and they won't watch the big ants eating the spirit out of that poor bugger either. I promise.'

It is not often that Matt says 'I promise'. But when he says it he keeps his promise.

Suddenly I feel strong again.

'Tell me what to do and I'll do it.'

'There's nothing else to do except what you said in the first place. Crawl up and cut him loose. But – ' he stops me as I try to put a word in, ' but – ' he goes on, 'I'll do something to take their mind off you. So they won't see what's going on. By the time they do, you'll have cut him out and we'll all make a run for it.'

'They'll follow us and tear us to shreds.'

'Naked like that! Not for long.'

'He's naked too,' I say, pointing to the poor man.

'We'll give him our shawls.'

'What if there are others?'

'I'm sure there ain't. We'd've seen them by now if there were.'

'But what will you do?'

'I'll thump round that thick head of yours if you don't stop your jabbering on like a fool monkey and let me get on with it.'

He takes the lighter out of his pocket. It is an ugly old one, big and heavy. More fit for the cooking pot than the pocket.

'Gimme your shawl,' he says.

I give it to him.

'Bull's balls. You've wet it with your baby crying.' He throws it back to me. 'Have you got another one?'

As it goes I do have two left in my bag. The two spare ones Hena brought for herself.

I wonder why he don't use his own, for whatever he wants it. I wonder but I don't say.

He almost snatches it from me.

His movements are becoming quick and sharp.

This happens when his body tries to keep up with his brain. Before my worried eyes he holds up the shawl with both hands and tears it in half. That's what Hena is going to do to him when she finds out, I say to myself.

He unscrews the base of the lighter and sprinkles some of the fuel out of it on to both halves.

'I'm going to that little hut to throw fire in it. There are green leaves on the top but it's all dry underneath. They will run to see what's going on at the hut. You cut the man's ropes and come out here. I'll be back here by then and we'll run for it.'

'What's the other half for?'

'We'll light it and chuck it in the bushes behind us. That'll stop them if they run after us. Leastwise for a while.'

'Are you sure it'll work?' I ask, not sure that it will.

'We'll see,' says Matt. 'Now find me two sticks. One thin and dry, the other strong and green.'

We both look as quiet as we can.

It is not difficult to find two sticks among all these trees and cut bushes. Matt tells me to be ready to dash into the clearing and free the poor man as soon as they notice the fire.

I position myself.

*

Matt goes behind a thick tree trunk next to the smaller hut. He puts one half of the shawl at the end of the green stick and sets fire to it with the help of the lighter and the other stick.

With magic speed he flings it on the dry twigs that form the back of the hut.

I see a look of utter terror come into the poor man's eyes.

Are the ants marching in already? I ask myself in panic, but have no time to answer. Little birds of smoke start flying out to the skies from the roof of the hut.

I watch the men and the lady, ready to make my move.

If Matt hopes they will rush to save the hut he is wrong. If Matt thinks they won't run fast and far, naked as they are, he is even more wrong.

The two squatting sniff the air as they smell the smoke, turn their heads and see signs of fire.

They freeze, they jump up, they go down again – crouching this time rather than squatting – jump up once more and start running in the opposite direction. Running like their own private bush between the legs is on fire.

They trip over the three still at it.

The one on top of the lady has his dingus pulled out so roughly it starts jerk-shooting forceful squirts of what looks more like cream of milk than dirty water. He starts to curse then stops as he sees the smoke. Stops with his mouth wide open, his eyes wide open and his dingus working overtime all by itself – though by now it is more coughing and spitting than anything else.

The lady is still lying with her fat ass on top of the other man, smirking to herself.

The three men scramble back up to their feet and run so fast all I see is heaving bum cheeks and dangling balls and tree-trunk legs. I blink and the tree-trunk legs are lost among the tree trunks.

The lady soon cottons on to the reason for all the upset and takes after them, letting out creepy fut farts as she goes. The man underneath her jumps up and follows.

I get so taken up with the goings on I haven't moved a step from my place.

The eyes of the poor man on the ground are getting more and more weird in the way they look. I can't understand what they are saying but I can bet my little brother they are saying something.

By now Matt is back where I am.

'What d'you think you're doing? Gimme that knife.' He's so mad at me he says no more, snatches the knife from my hands and rushes to cut the man loose. I get my legs back and rush with him.

While Matt uses his pocket knife I pick up the funny twisted one from the ground.

As soon as one of the man's arms is free he pulls out the lady's knickers from his mouth and shouts, 'Run. Run for God's sake, run.'

Between us we free him in two flaps of a bat's wings.

Matt picks up his boots and we run.

The man has to hobble something awful, like a rabbit with its legs ripped by a trap, but he's still so fast we wonder at him.

We thought we'd have to half carry him, being in the state he is. It ends up he's half carrying us.

We're not many breaths away when we hear the first bang.

Instantly the man throws us on the ground and himself along with us. As he hits the earth with his belly he lets out wild yells for he's forgotten he's all damaged on his front.

Quickly he turns over, all the while holding us down with one arm each. Only he is holding me down with his left arm now and Matt with his right arm, while a wink ago he was holding me down with his right arm and Matt with his left arm. This is so on account he's turned over and his left arm is where his right arm was and his right arm is where his left arm was. But that don't matter really. Except I don't like the smell of piss and blood and tinned food. Also, I'm not sure if I feel funnier lying down with the naked man when his frontals are facing the sky or when his bum is raised to the winds.

I truly shouldn't be thinking like that but I have a sinful mind.

Of course I don't know it then for I don't know what sin is then. I learn that later from this missionary bloke from Pasadena, California, USA, wherever that may be.

By now there are enough bangs to make many new worlds. Maybe that's what's going on, I say to myself. The Spirits are cracking up the old world to make lots of little new ones which will grow up to be better ones. Grandma Toughtits always says this world is ready for the big night of fire. And the big night of fire it sure is – or day if you're particular about such things.

Things – bits of broken this and broken that, I know not what and suchlike – are flying past and above us in a mad rush to get nowhere.

Flames are rising all round the clearing and the dry cut bush circle is lit up like Hell's front yard.

Suddenly the whole hut is thrown upwards.

The noise kills my ears and I hear no more.

The light kills my eyes and I see no more.

Four

Gonta, At Last

When next I hear, I hear sounds of laughter and bells and drums and creaking wood and clanging metal and gentle snoring.

When next I see I see sunlight and see-saws and slides and colourful tents and bright clothes and Matt sleeping.

When next I feel I feel this heavy weight round my arm so I cannot move it.

Am I dead? I wonder.

If so I must be in the world of the Spirit of Light and her happy friends for what I see is good and what I hear is pleasant. Also my best friend is with me.

So I'm not too worried if I am dead.

Even if I am not dead, I'm sure Matt is.

Matt who wakes up at the fall of a needle or the first smell of light cannot sleep through all this noise and all this brightness.

Leastwise that's what I say to myself.

Loud, so as to find out if the dead can or cannot speak.

They can.

Anyway, I can.

Satisfied, I snap my eyes shut and lean back to relax. I am lying on something soft and cool and it feels good.

I like being dead.

'So you are awake at last,' I hear a heavy voice growl, 'or still talking in your sleep?'

I snap my eyes open.

There is this big ugly face with this big ugly nose and these big ugly eyes set in a big ugly head sitting on a tiny ugly body staring down at me.

If I was standing up I'd be staring down at him.

Of course I'm big, but I am still a child – not that I like to own up to it. This man must be shorter than Matt. And Matt is short – not that Matt likes to own up to it.

Do dead men grow down instead of up? I wonder.

Now that part of being dead I don't like.

I want to grow up tall and big and strong – whether dead or alive. In fact I'd rather be alive without the laughter and the colours and the happy Spirits if I am to grow down dead.

The man holds me by the shoulders and shakes me.

Now you know I don't like being shaken up. I don't like being shaken up asleep or awake.

I don't like being shaken up dead, either.

'You've been sleeping for a day and a night. I think you'd better wake up or you'll miss all the fun.'

He is short and he is ugly and he growls at me and he shakes me and there is love in his hands and care in his bloated eyes.

'Are you God?' I ask.

But I can tell by the surprised look in his bloated eyes that he ain't so I add, 'Or just a Spirit?'

'I am Kofi,' he says. 'I'm with the circus. I'm the midget. I found you sleeping in my tent yesterday afternoon when I came back from the second show.'

'My friend, my friend Matt,' I say sounding stupid, 'he is lying over there. Is he sleeping or dead? I am not sure.'

'No one is dead,' he says. So that is settled.

He looks at me for a look, then goes, 'You must be hungry. Have something to eat first. I'll explain later.'

The thought of food puts life back into my dead body which wasn't dead in the first place. I try to sit up to feed the face but have problems on account I can't move my right arm.

'I'm not sure I can eat,' I say near to tears. 'My right arm has died, even if the rest of me hasn't.'

He looks at my right arm with a look of worry, then smiles, 'It's just heavy. Your parents must have tied this bag to your arm so that you don't lose it or forget it somewhere. Your friend,' he says pointing to Matt, 'has got one as well.'

I know my parents did no such thing but I say nothing.

I look at Matt. Tied to his wrist is this big brown cloth bag, like a small rucksack.

I look at my own arm. I'd been frightened to look before on account I did not want to see my arm lying dead without me. Tied to my wrist is a similar bag.

I untie the bag and look inside. I find two thick white shawls, one embroidered red and a yellow silken robe, a large box full of food and a brown paper bag which has in it more money than I've ever seen in my life!

I'm still lost in wonder, not knowing what to say or how to ask him some more questions, when he puts all this food in front of me. My favourite flat bread and honey syrup and chunks of dried meat that smell freshly-cooked on an open fire, and fruit. I forget about everything else.

'Thank you very much,' I say to show I know my manners, 'I am starving.'

'No, you're not,' he suddenly shouts so it frightens me away from my food. 'It's people down east who...' he stops as suddenly as he began. 'I'm sorry. Don't mind me. I forget you are only a child. You don't know what is going on. I am sorry. Eat your food. Go on.' He puts his arms round me like he is my mother, only I hardly fit in both his arms. My Mam can hug me with only one of hers.

As I start eating I look at Matt.

'Don't worry,' he says, 'there's enough for him when he wakes up.'

I feed my face, gobble gobble gobble, while trying hard not to seem greedy. If only I could eat like Hena – sort of like a queen with tiny bits of food taken slowly to the half-open mouth, eyes far away hardly looking at the food – I would cut a fine figure. Enough to make Grandma Toughtits proud.

But I can't.

I can never have Hena's ways, witch that she is.

I don't feel guilty eating for I know Hena and Golam have food so they can't be hungry.

I am thinking of Hena and Golam without thinking of Hena and Golam when suddenly I think of Hena and Golam.

Where are they?

I start worrying for them full speed.

And they must be worrying for us.

The thought of their worry gets put on to my worry and I worry even more.

I nearly lose my hunger but in the meantime I've eaten seven meals in one go.

Matt's ears have not noticed the noise in his unnatural sleep and his skin has got used to the new air but his nostrils can't fight the smell of food.

He wakes up, takes in the scene like me, but unlike me he don't wonder where we are. He knows it.

'We're in Gonta,' he says.

He don't stop to wonder if we're dead, but I'm happy to see that at least he is surprised.

I can tell he's surprised for I can tell when he is surprised.

'Are we!' I say before I can stop myself. I should have been able to tell: the roundabout, the drums, the circus – everything.

'How did we get here?' says Matt to me to Kofi and to no one, 'and what's this bag doing round my arm?' He don't even wonder if his arm is dead. Smart-ass.

'Kofi says,' I say pointing to Kofi, 'that he found us sleeping in his tent yesterday afternoon after he came back from the second show. The circus show.'

I'm enjoying this. It's not often that I get the chance to explain things to Matt. It don't matter that I don't understand it at all myself.

'Kofi is the circus small man,' I add, not wishing to say midget on account of it might hurt him even though that's what he calls himself.

Matt opens his mouth to say some more as he looks in the bag but is so amazed, like me, at what he finds that, like me, he can't say nothing. At least something shuts him up.

Caught in the bottom of the bag is what looks like a dirty rag. It is the second half of the shawl we didn't get to use the other night. So that was real.

I had nearly forgotten about it. Well, not truly forgotten, but remembered more like a dream than a true fact. A nightmare I reckon is the proper word for what I thought it was.

And where are Hena and Golam! I can't believe I'm so worried about Hena.

But I am.

And of course Golam, which is only right.

I look at Matt. His eyes are like glass pebbles. There is a look in them the like of which I saw in a half-cut lizard last summer which was being attacked by buzzards in the school ground.

I think he is seeing last night all over again.

I also think he is trying to make up his mind about something.

When Kofi brings him his food he eats slowly, forgetting to chew every so often and staring in front of him, mouth half open full with food.

'What's the problem, young man?' says Kofi looking at Matt. 'If you are worried about your homes and families, just tell me and I'll see that you get to them safely. And comfortably.' He smiles a dancing smile. 'That's the least we can do after what you've...' He suddenly stops talking, his smile suddenly stops dancing.

Matt jerks his head up, his sharp look returns and he waits for Kofi to finish his sentence.

'...after what you've... you must have been through,' Kofi manages to say.

'How do you know what we have been through?' says Matt, his voice going a little hard and a little 'posh' as it always does when he is on his guard and careful, not fully trusting who he is talking to.

'I... I don't. It's just that you were alone and looked tired out – you've slept nearly fifteen hours – so I naturally thought you must have... might have had some difficulties.'

Matt don't argue.

Matt can argue for seven days and seven nights when he wants. But he don't argue sometimes when I think he ought to.

'Have you seen our other friends?' Matt at last asks what I know he has been thinking all along. 'A boy and a girl.'

For once Kofi looks truly surprised. 'You mean there were two more with you!'

He looks more than surprised. He looks frightened.

'Yes. We lost them... We forgot about... We couldn't help what... We lost them,' I end helplessly with what I began. I wish I hadn't started and let Matt carry on. But I am so worried about Hena and Golam I can't help myself. 'Please help us find them.'

'Just tell me where you last left them,' Kofi goes in quick short gasps, moving his podgy little hands all round my face in quick short movements, 'and I'll see that somebody goes over there as soon as possible.'

He looks at me.

I look at Matt.

Matt gives me the look and is about to say something when two more little people enter the little open tent. One is a man and one a lady. They are a little taller than Kofi, about my height. But I'm nine so it isn't too tall for grown-ups.

'It is time for our act, Kofi,' the two new midgets say together, in one voice which sounds sharp and crackly.

Kofi lingers a bit then says, 'You go out and enjoy yourselves. I'll be back in a short while – won't be long, promise. We'll sort out about your friends when I'm back. Promise.'

'Don't worry.

'Oh, and leave your bags with me. No point in carting them around. Must be heavy. You can take some money from them of course. You might need it.'

Of course we'll need it, I say to myself. All ours is with Hena. Not that it was much, but she always takes charge of the money.

'These bags are not ours,' Matt goes.

'Oh yes they are. Believe me, they are. I don't lie. That's one thing I don't do. I may not tell the truth,' he smiles his dancing smile, 'but I do not lie.'

'Where is the Spirit Dance?' asks Matt.

'They danced all last night,' Kofi replies, then he sees Matt's very disappointed face and adds, 'but they will dance again tonight. We'll take you there ourselves. I'll even introduce you to some of the dancers. They are my friends.'

'Come on, hurry up. We're getting late,' say the two new midgets – again together, in one voice.

Kofi hurries out taking the bags with him and making us take some money before going.

Before I go enjoy the fair I must enjoy a quiet sit down behind the bushes. Matt feels the same. We haven't been for four and twenty hours and all this food we've had is pushing matters down something awful hard.

We get out of the tent, put our hands in front of our eyes and peeping from between fingers make our way through the fair. The reason we cover our eyes is that we don't want to see any of the fair till we are really seeing it so as not kill the surprise of seeing it. Of course we've seen bits of it from the tent but that's not the same thing as walking through it with naked eyes.

Also we want no one to see us, yet; and Matt says if you don't take notice of others they don't take notice of you.

We are dying to go and therefore want to be out of the crowds soon, but we don't want to be out of the crowds soon for we want the fair ground to be truly large so there is more to see when we do see it with our eyes open.

We are out of it but still not out as we are in the cattle and sheep market.

We have our hands off our eyes now.

I hope we don't end up in the town next, which we would if we are going in the wrong direction. But Matt says no, cattle markets are always on the other side of the town.

We're soon out of the market and into the open plains with plenty of bushes, even trees.

We both run like the Spirit of Shit is behind us, which in a way she is. We both get behind the third set of bushes we come to. The first of everything is for greedy guts; the second is for fallow fools; the third and fourth are too far away, so we settle for the third as good people should.

We settle down in not many winks. Matt first, for he has floppy shorts on which are round his ankles in no time. I take longer with my trousers. By the time I'm ready Matt is flying pheasants all over the place. With a true sigh of happiness I sit and hear this sharp voice say, 'You took your time, didn't you.'

Spirit of Shit.

I nearly jump up the bush.

It is Hena.

What is the world coming to if a man can't even shit in peace without having a woman poke her nose into his private business.

Luckily Golam takes her to one side and makes her wait.

On our way back to the fair Golam tells us how they were sleeping peacefully when they hear the world coming to its end and see the fires of Hell overtaking it. Just then three naked men in big boots go running past them followed by a naked lady in big boots, followed closely by another naked man.

Hena and Golam climb up the tree and hide till all is quiet.

When they come down and don't see us, Golam wants to turn round and go back home but Hana says if we – meaning Matt and me – are not dead or taken away we'd go to Gonta. She insists on going forward.

Luckily they meet a party of people walking to Gonta for the Spirit Dance. Hena and Golam walk along with them.

They have a search for us at the fair and then come and wait here, for it is easier to spot us on the way to the fair than at the fair in the crowds, Hena thinks.

Golam asks Matt what happened with us but Matt don't want to talk, which is surprising for Matt likes talking about things that happen.

I am not sure I like talking about it either but I do, though I'm not sure I ought to. Not in front of Hena for I don't think it is nice, and even though Hena is a witch she's still nice.

I tell them. I tell them what I understand or remember or know. I know nothing of what happened after my eyes and ears were killed – though they weren't really. As you know by now.

Matt says he don't know much after that either, except being carried on the shoulder by the poor man while he carried me in his arms.

We've been in the fairground hardly long enough for the shadows to change any when Kofi and his friends catch up with us.

'You needn't trouble about our friends,' goes Matt to Kofi, 'we've found them.'

Kofi looks very happy to hear it. Like a great fear has gone from his eyes.

'And what are the names of your charming friends?' go the midget and the lady midget, together again. I am beginning to find their speaking the same words at the same time in the same voice a little scary.

'This is Hena,' says Matt, 'she is probably a witch. She can always find us. She found us today as well.'

Golam smiles when he hears this and the midget couple take their round little hands up to their round little cheeks and sigh and say together, 'What a lovely smile this boy has, like a star from Dallas. He should be on television.'

We don't know what they're talking about but Kofi later tells us they have travelled to rich countries in the West and have seen many wonderful things, like Dallas, which people in poor countries know nothing of.

We all want to see Dallas after that but doubt if we ever will.

Anyway Matt tells them Golam's name and they smile at him and kiss him on both cheeks. I'm not quite sure whether I'd like them to kiss me on both my cheeks, but that's not a nice thought to think so I try not to think it but still do.

'And this,' says Matt, pointing to me, 'is Kimo. He's our best friend.'

'He's big, isn't he!' they go, together again, feeling my arms and standing shoulder to shoulder with me and measuring my height against theirs.

'You still haven't told us your name now, have you?' they go to Matt. 'But we haven't told you ours either. That is naughty of us, don't you think?'

They ask these questions but don't wait for an answer. I wonder more and more at them talking the same words at the same time in the same voice.

'Well,' they carry on, and I say to myself now they'll have to say a few words separate to give their separate names, but they go together, 'we're Jon and Donna.' As they speak they point to each other to make clear which one is Jon and which Donna. I'm glad they do so otherwise I'd not have known. I've never heard these names and couldn't've said which is a girl's name and which a boy's. As it happens the man midget is Donna and the lady midget Jon.

'Now's your turn.' They look at Matt all excited like it's a big game.

'My name is Jomo,' says Matt.

You may well wonder why Matt says his name is Jomo.

But to tell the truth, he tells the truth.

Matt's real name isn't Matt at all. Well it is now, short for Matthew. But he was born Jomo and was called Jomo till this missionary bloke from Pasadena, California, USA (wherever that may be) and his miserable wife brought Jesus home to us darkies, and saved his soul. And other souls. Not all mind you, for some souls are just not good enough, but quite a few. Not mine, I'm sorry to say, though I truly did so want to have my soul saved, honest. But Grandma Toughtits would have none of it and shut the door on his smiling face.

It makes me sad for Matt says, the missionary bloke says, she'll never know Heaven now, whatever that may be. He says, the missionary bloke says, her soul will be lost for ever in Eternal Darkness, wherever that may be. Might even be Pasadena, California, USA from the way the missionary bloke speaks of carnal sin and mortal evil, whatever that may be, which is rife there, whatever that may mean.

Matt says the missionary bloke first taught him how to be a Christian, and then how not to be a Christian. I never understood none of it. But all this is later and you'll soon find out when it happens.

Anyway, now that we are all properly met we have a great time at the fair. I've never enjoyed myself so much before or after.

I truly begin to like my new friends though they are not very pretty to look at and talk funny and work in a circus.

But when they're not talking to us, John, Donna and Kofi don't look much happy. From where I stand they've got the hump over something so that even good things seem to worry them. Like the price of cows and sheep and goats and camels. It appears they are going real cheap this year. I think they ought to be happy over it. Mam is always pleased when things are cheap. But Jon, Donna and Kofi worry over it.

There is also something more to their worry. I can tell for I can tell. I've seen a lot of worry in grown-up people to know.

I reckon little grown-up people are no different from big grown-up people.

Five

The Spirit Dance

Grandma Toughtits says there are two sorts of people.

Those who believe that when the Spirits dance the world dances with them; and those who believe when the world dances the Spirits dance with it.

I myself don't see no difference but Grandma Toughtits says there is all the difference.

She says always be the first to dance.

She also says never stop dancing, though I can't see how that's possible.

Anyhow, I jump up, tall silent and strong like a boy tree would if it could, and start to dance.

The flames are all swaying and flickering on top of tall black poles held by little boys and girls in black robes. In the dark of the night you can hardly see the black poles or the children in black which makes it look like the flames are dancing on their own in the black air.

The white and yellow and red robes of most dancers also take the eye. They jump and whirl and jerk and sway like the flames themselves. They pretend to be the Spirit of Light and dance in the hope that the real Spirit of Light will join them.

There are other people dancing as other Spirits: the Spirit of Crops, the Spirit of the Rain, the Spirit of Mountains, the Spirit of the Earth and many other Spirits, including the Spirits of different animals.

Golam gets up and joins the dance though he knows his Mam won't like it. He won't normally do what his Mam don't like but I think he is not thinking.

I am wearing my beautiful new robe and I wish Golam had one as well. I think of giving him one of my new shawls so he can also look smart but forget in the mood of the dance.

Matt stays sitting. The flames of the night dance in his eyes and I can see his Spirit dancing outside in the eyes of the fire. Jon, Donna and Kofi are soon dancing as well.

New dancers join in wearing masks over their faces. Long ribbons of all colours are flying all round their bodies covering their robes.

This gives the real Spirits a chance to join in the dance without being found out; for no one can now tell the difference between the people dancers and the Spirit dancers. The colours and masks of the Spirits will get lost in the colours and masks of the people. The Spirits don't like to be found out. If someone unmasks or uncovers any of the dancers in order to truly see a Spirit he is forever cursed. There is the sound of a slow drum beat in the air. One beat at a time, soft and muffled with long uneven gaps in between.

There are many pipe players all around the dancers at different places. They play the same notes but at different times so the music shifts from place to place making the whole scene appear to go further away, then come near again and then move away again – all the time. The moving light of the flames adds to this trick of change. You not only see dancing within the dancing space but feel the dancing space itself dance from place to place. There is a soft buzz buzzing noise far away in the skies, like millions of butterflies dancing in the night air. Matt notices it first for he is sitting down while I am lost in dance. I notice because he notices. I chance to look at him and see his eyes are not on the flames or the dance but on the dark and on nothing; above our heads.

Slowly, as the buzzing gets louder, others begin to look up.

'The Spirits...' one voice cries above the bells of the dancers.

'The Spirits...' goes a hushed whisper beyond the footfalls of the dancers.

'The Spirits... the Spirits...'

'The Spirits are coming...'

'The Spirits are here...'

'The Spirits are flying down to our dance...'

'The Spirits... The Spirits... The Spirits...' sing many voices to the music of the pipes.

Excited hearts beat louder and faster than drums.

This is what everybody hopes will happen one day. This is what everybody knows happened in the old days. In the old days, when men were good and lived and worked with the Spirits and not against them, as nowadays. Then the Spirits came flying down from the Heavens to sing and dance with people.

When it happens again the world will again be a place of happiness for all and for all times.

Everybody always says this, not many believe. Not because they don't have no faith in Spirits, but because they don't have no faith in men.

But it is happening. It is happening at last.

The Spirits are now almost upon us.

Kofi screams his ugly midget scream and runs. Runs then stops, grabs my hand and drags me down to the ground.

My face hits the earth for the second time in two days. I don't know what's going on. I think I hear Matt's voice but I'm not sure. I think I hear Hena's voice but I'm not sure. I think I hear Golam's voice and I'm sure. You don't often hear Golam's voice but when you hear it you hear it. It's like his smile. You can't miss it.

The drum beat gets sharper higher quicker, faster higher faster faster so it don't sound like a drum beat at all.

'Guns.' I hear a voice.

'Helicopter...'

'Take cover...'

'Hide...'

'Bullets...'

I hear screams I hear names I hear shouts I hear cries I hear names I hear guns I hear bullets I hear myself.

I am crying.

I hope Matt don't see me crying.

I look towards him but can't see him. All I see is streaks of fire in the sky. Sharp spitting fires, nothing like the gentle torches of the Spirit of Light.

Suddenly all is darkness and silence. Silence except for the buzz buzzing which also starts to grow gentler and softer, like Matt's lullaby, and then fades out altogether.

My eyes are living and my ears are living and my arms and legs are living and I am sitting up straight right as sunshine. But my brain is sure feeling poorly. It's not top of the world at its best, but at this time it is right down at the bottom.

I see things and I hear things but I don't understand half of it. Some people carrying flame poles are moving around looking for friends or relatives.

Someone shouts, 'Put those bloody fires out. They'll only bloody come back and finish the rest of us.' But nobody takes notice.

People are thrown all over the place like so much litter. Some are lying stark still some are moving in jerky movements. Some are sitting down shaking some trying to get up some doing nothing at all. Some are silent some talking to others or to themselves some crying. Some have bullet wounds some are cut by metal some burnt by falling flame poles.

Two men sitting in front of me are having a quiet argument like they are by their food fire.

'So it's started. Really started. I always knew it would.'

'Probably wouldn't have if some damn fool hadn't blown up a whole hutful of their guns and ammo the other night.'

'They'd have started anyway. They were just building up supplies and hiring more killers.'

'It's their revenge for some smart asshole being too clever for anybody's good.'

'It was coming, no matter what you say. At least some of their murder weapons are gone. I say all praise to the one who did it.'

'It's we who have to pay with our lives and homes...'

My hand feels wet. I look at it. It is red with blood. I just look at it. There is no pain. It is not my blood. It is the blood of Jon who lies next to me with her flesh a mess. Next to her Donna is lying very still, with no wound that I can see. Kofi is sitting between them, quietly, saying nothing, doing nothing. I wish he wouldn't just sit there, but he just sits there, quietly; saying nothing, doing nothing, seeing nothing.

Matt, Golam, Hena and me carry the bodies of Jon and Donna and bring them back to the tent. Kofi follows us like he's walking in his sleep. When we remove Jon's blouse to clean her and make her look nice for the Spirits to take her away we see that she has no breasts like a woman. We wonder but we say nothing. We also wonder how Donna died as there is not a mark on his body; but again we say nothing.

Kofi suddenly starts explaining, more as if he is talking to himself than to us.

'They were brothers, twins. Always thought and spoke alike. Did everything together. Got paid good money at circuses and freak shows. Not much, but enough for food and a bit left over.

'One day they were both getting ready for a show. For a change they decided to dress up as women. As it happened the man organising the show got talking to Don. Donna he called himself later, just for the fun of it. When it was time for their act only Jon was ready to come as a woman. The show went down really well. People didn't think too much of twin brothers talking alike,

but they were very surprised to see a man midget and his wife midget – that's what they pretended to be – thinking and talking together. It worked so well they kept the same act ever since.
'I guess the Spirits did come to the Dance tonight. The twin Spirits of Death. Death that parts and Death that unites.'

Part II

GOLAM'S COW

(two years later)

One

The Missionary's Balls and Aunt Tima

Two years have gone by since our trip to Gonta to see the Spirit Dance.

We've had many worries on our minds all this while.

One of the big new ones is how to find out if white men have three balls.

Matt says they have. Matt says that's why they rule the world on account three balls give you more power than two. He says it's a known fact.

At first we think he's joking and having us on, as he sometimes does. Like the day he said, all serious, 'If you wanna learn to fly you oughta take a prickly lizard up your bum.'

Now that's an easy one. Anybody'd fly up in the air if a prickly lizard went up their bum. It's only natural.

But sometimes he comes up with truly tricky ones that leave you wondering. Like this thing about white men and three balls. It don't sound natural to me.

But he has this picture with him. No one knows how he got it and he's not saying. Of course it's an old picture and has been through the hands of thousands of people thousands of times so it's all smudgy and cracked and not very clear. But it's the picture of a naked man. A naked white man, of that there's no mistaking. You can see him standing, slightly bent forward, all pink – smudgy pink – and naked. There is another white man behind him, more straight. You can hardly see his body but you can see his face quite clear. It's the clearest part of the picture on account no one looks at it much, but I do. He has his arms round the shoulders of the man in front and a truly happy grin on his mouth. He's looking up a little, chin forward, eyes half closed half open – seeing and not seeing. Like his mind is on higher things.

The man in front has his rude part all swollen and red and hard. Hanging below are his balls, as you'd expect and nothing unnatural in that. Only next to the pair is what looks for all the world like an extra ball.

'Maybe he's a freak,' says Golam.

Like those people in the circus, I think. I think but I don't say it. We don't like talking about that.

'Yes, maybe he is,' I say. 'Maybe they took his rude picture to show him off.'

'And maybe he don't like to be shown off,' Golam goes, 'that's why they have this other man holding him down.'

But Matt says, 'Then why is white men kings? There's got to be something extra. Stands to reason.'

'How'd you know white men is kings?' says Golam.

We all look at him, pleased for we are thinking the same.

'Why *everybody* knows that!' goes Matt, throwing his hands up in the air. 'Surely,' he adds looking at each of us in turn.

We can't fault that. We're still not sure though. Leastwise not about the extra ball.

The trouble is how to find out, one way or the other. The only white man in the village is the missionary bloke. He's been here for seven months helping with the school, and has saved Matt's soul. He has this jeep and travels to many villages but stays in our village on account there are more trees in our village and better fields and more food. Of course Gonta and towns to the west of us are even better off, but they have their own missionary bloke, only he is black like the rest of us. Not white like our own special one.

Now we can't very well go to this missionary bloke of ours and say, 'Sir, may we have a look at your balls, Sir?'

Especially as he don't like being called Sir.

He wants us to call him Tom which is his name. But my Dada says you shouldn't call older people by their names on account it is disrespectful, so I get truly confused. But no matter, Sir or Tom, I can't go and ask to see his balls.

Matt says you don't have to ask to really 'see' them. Just ask to tell you if he has two or three. 'He is not going to lie, is he?' asks Matt. 'After all, he is a man of God.'

But I'm not sure he can't tell a lie just because he happens to be a missionary bloke. Anyone can lie, especially over something as important and personal as this. Besides, Grandma Toughtits don't believe what he says!

What's more I can't very well ask him that either. 'Sir, Tom, have you got three balls? You don't have to show me them, just say yes or no and I'll believe you.'

I can't do that, and although Matt says there is no harm in it he won't do it himself.

'Why don't you ask him?' I say. 'You've had your soul saved by him and your name changed and your head drowned in water. You know him best.' Sounds fair to me.

He says he don't doubt it, so there's no cause for him to ask. We doubt it so we should ask. This sounds fair as well so it makes it worse for us to argue.

'Don't say "balls, Sir", say "testicles, Tom",' goes Matt, then stops as if to think and goes again, 'On the other hand "balls" is friendly like and so is "Tom", while "Sir" and "testicles" are both proper; so perhaps it should be "testicles, Sir" or "balls, Tom".'

But I won't say any of it. Neither will Golam. Nor any of our other friends. Hena might for she's not afraid of anything or anyone. But we can't ask her to ask, being 'a delicate issue, strictly among us men', as Matt says, going all posh.

This makes us all the more determined to find out.

We make a promise by our little tree on our little hill that we'll know before the season changes.

In the meantime there are other worries.

My Dada is more worried about the rains. So is Golam. He don't have a Dada so he has to do his worrying for him.

Water in the river don't move fast any more and water in the water-holes is going down.

We're lucky being in a sort of a flat valley which helps to store water. Also we're near the woods which helps some more. But everybody looks worried. Even Hena's Dada don't tell his stupid jokes to everyone all the time like he used to.

The stories we hear of other villages are not good stories.

*

But we hear good news as well.

My cousin Joti's coming from the big city to see his Mam, and the rest of the village. He's coming to see his Mam for she's not feeling well. She is really but she wrote him saying she isn't so he will come to see her. He's been home only once in the last four years and that was before our walk to Gonta for the Spirit Dance.

He ran away from home to go to Bader when he was thirteen. He was a big good-looking lad, like most in our family. He was also plucky and much too sharp, not like most in our family. Life in our little village was never for him. There's no future here, he'd always say: always restless; always wanting this or that; always falling out with folk – his own or other people's; always getting into trouble. He'd hear stories about the big city from the travelling people who'd pass through our village with their animals looking for water and food and grass and rest. They don't come around much any more. Anyway, one evening in late autumn when leaves were dying and the travelling people were pulling out their tents and moving west to the big city for their winter supplies, Joti goes and hides in one of their donkey packs. That's the last we see of him.

One year and seven months later we get this huge box from Bader brought to our house by the head of the village himself.

The Master closes the school so that everybody can come to our house to see what's in it and who it's from. The Master uses the special school scissors – which he normally guards with his life on account they were a special gift to the school from the Government along with ten packets of paper and one dozen pencils and one dozen biro pens – to cut open the flaps of the big box.

In it are shawls for Uncle Jam and Aunt Tima, Joti's Mam and Dada. And shoes and coloured beads for the neck and arms and the ears and best of all chocolate.

That is the first time I ever have chocolate.

Also in the box are beautiful scarves for the entire village and hundreds of other things I don't remember any more. Strangest of all was this hat for Grandma Toughtits. It was in a special box of its own within the big box and we kept it to the last not daring to open it in case there was some magic in it which might escape if we did. This hat, made of some pink cloth we've never seen before, is covered with flowers which look and even smell real but are not.

Grandma Toughtits (who'd kill me if she knew I called her Grandma Toughtits – her true name is Grandma Pearl) keeps this hat on the wall next to her bath oils which she uses on her body when she dances for the Spirits. She never wears the hat as she says it is much too good for her old head, but she'd rather part with her life than give it to anyone who'd be only too happy to put it on, like my Mam for one.

Also in the big box is a letter from Joti saying how well he is doing working in a big hotel. He don't say doing what but no one stops to think, at least not long enough to ask. There ain't no one to ask anyway.

What truly leaves us with our mouths open and nothing to say are these photos of Joti.

Lovely shiny photos in full colour.

Joti is in a black white man's suit by a piano – it says 'piano' on the back of the photo.

Joti in a white man's suit sitting in a grand chair covered with leather and buttons.

Joti in a vest and shorts outside this house I don't believe is real, by this car I don't believe is real.

Five months later comes Joti himself. I don't believe he is real. He is dressed up grander than his photos.

He comes in this car. But the car is not grand. In fact it is somewhat falling apart. Joti says he can't bring a fancy car on our dust roads on account it'd be killed off by the bumps and the rocks. So he brings one that's sort of dead already and we all agree and praise him for his wisdom.

That's two years ago.

We hear nothing from him after that except a short letter on the back of a picture which is the picture of a house which could be the palace of the king of paradise.

Aunt Tima then starts writing to him saying she is poorly but he takes no notice. He don't believe her, I'm sure. Neither would I, for Aunt Tima don't like truth much and everyone in the village knows that so it's not surprising her son does.

Then she makes his Dada write saying to him she's dying. Now Uncle Jam don't normally lie but he does on account he too is lonely for his son. Also he feels he isn't really lying for in a sense Aunt Tima is dying, same as everyone else. No one lives for ever and ever, nor will Aunt Tima – though there are those who think so – so it is truly not a lie.

It works, for Joti writes back he is coming this twenty-seventh day of the seventh month.

Today is that day.

Uncle Jam and Aunt Tima have still not sorted out between them whether to tell Joti the truth when he gets there or not. The truth about Aunt Tima not being quite ready for death. The rest of the village will go along with what they say only they can't make up their minds what to say. Or rather they have made up their minds what to say but their minds are different to one another and so of no use to either.

Uncle Jam, as you might've guessed already, wants to tell the truth. But Aunt Tima says: first, it'll hurt him to know that we've lied to him; and second, he'll go away and not come ever again, leastwise not for a long time. This way, if he believes his Mam to be dying, he may decide to stay back, or at least keep more in touch if he goes. Uncle Jam is pleased with this last thought but he says it's not fair to Joti to keep him back if he's doing so well for himself in the big city, nor is it fair to keep him worried if he does go regardless. As to not hurting him, he can't see how it can be right to tell him a lie because it's wrong to have told him a lie. If it was hurtful lying to him once, it'll be more hurtful lying to him again, he says. But Aunt Tima says that was all for a good reason and so is this.

The rest of the village listens to this and waits for them to decide so it can think of the right words to back them up when the time comes.

In the end, as you might've guessed again, Aunt Tima wins.

I don't think Joti will be fooled for longer than a breath, being sharper than a shrew's tongue, but Matt says you can't tell. Matt says Joti loves his Mam, like every man does – some women too – and love, being stronger than the mind, wins.

I say, 'I'll take a bet Joti don't believe his Mam. That'll prove you wrong.'

'If Uncle Jam truly says Aunt Tima is dying and Joti don't believe it, it won't prove me wrong,' Matt says back to me, 'it'll only prove he's in the power of something stronger than love.'

That's an easy way out, I think.

'And what,' I ask in my cleverest voice, 'is stronger than love?'

'Lack of love,' says Matt.

I give up.

*

The day comes and the day goes, but no Joti.

We line up by the big sand and stone road into the village, first altogether, then in small groups. But no Joti.

The sun sets and hopes fade. We feel Aunt Tima is really going to die she's so upset. Uncle Jam is worse though he don't let on so much.

Grandma Toughtits rubs oil over her body, wraps her clean shawl about her head, bows to the Spirits and starts dancing. She dances out of the house, into the front yard and then dances her way to the village centre. She raises her long eyes and her long arms and her long hands with their long fingers up to the skies as her tall thin body moves with and against the gently rising winds.

The big bright moon shines on her happily, making her look young and beautiful instead of old and beautiful. I get a bit worried, but the look in her eyes is still old and gentle and wise. I quickly say my thank you to the Spirits for not making her truly young again.

Her feet make the sand restless. The winds make the sand restless. The sand moves and moans not knowing what to do or where to go.

The winds lift her up and play with her and they mix into one another till both sand and wind dance round my dancing Grandma.

The whole village stops everything and gathers round to watch the sand and Grandma dancing with the winds. Even the missionary bloke is there standing with the school Master. He has on a vest and flappy shorts, but there'd be no point in crawling under and peering up to see his balls. We've tried that before. Many times. He always has knickers on underneath. Besides at this time it'll be too dark up his legs, even for pink goolies to show up proper.

Soon the sand gets her own back at Grandma and makes her restless by thickening and twisting and turning and dancing faster and more furious round and round Grandma herself, daring her to do better.

We wonder for Grandma's feet are quick but they are light; not heavy enough to raise all that dust and sand. Neither are the winds so strong this time of the year and this time of the night.

But the wind and the sand do get more active and it's puzzling. It gets more puzzling as the sound of the wind turns to a strange roar that gets louder by the breath.

Suddenly someone shouts, then all shout. They are all looking towards me. I am worried at first but then find out what's going on. No one's looking at me, they're looking behind me. I jump and turn at the same time.

I see the reason of the dust and the sand and the wind and the roar. It's a car. In it is Joti, waving his arms about and shouting like he used to when I was a little boy and he mucked about with us lot.

Soon half the people in the village are up and dancing round Grandma Toughtits and the other half up and dancing round Joti.

Joti is smiling all over, moving from one place to the other, from one person to the other. 'Hello Uncle' here and 'Hello Grandma' there. Kissing this one and shaking the arm of another out of his shoulder socket. 'You've grown up, haven't you!' to this little mite and, 'Won't you ever grow up?' to that big lad.

This goes on for ever and ever, while all the time I'm tagging along trying to hold his hand and even actually holding it now and then. Uncle Jam now appears on the scene. Joti and him are hugging and kissing and laughing and crying all over each other; wiping their eyes and noses all the time – Joti with his silk handkerchief that sticks out of the back pocket of his tight jeans and Uncle Jam with the end of his shawl.

My Mam and Dada now join in the crying and laughing. Even Grandma Toughtits has got over her dance, said her thanks to the Spirits, and come over to be with the family.

The rest of the village decide to let the family be alone together and slowly drift away, inviting Joti over for the big village feast to be held the next day in his honour.

But where is Aunt Tima?

Everyone's been so busy showing joy over Joti they've forgotten Aunt Tima. Where is she?

We find her sitting by herself, legs stretched out in front of her, back resting against the broken stone wall which runs through the east of the village; no one knows why, no one knows since when. Her eyes are open looking far out searching for Joti. But they do not see him when he comes.

Aunt Tima is dead.

Aunt Tima, big and bouncy and strong Aunt Tima, sits dead by the old stone wall.

Whether her heart burst with sorrow on account she thought Joti isn't coming or whether it burst with joy when she heard shouts saying he's here, we'll never know.

*

The feast next day was the biggest ever held in the village. Old Muslims, new Christians, even the Children of Moses – all came, and brought food and fruit and music and dance and love and memories to honour Joti as Aunt Tima would've done; as if Joti was everyone's son come back home.

Anyone who could move and breathe danced all night to keep company with the Spirit of Aunt Tima as it waited for the Spirits of trees and mountains and rivers and the Earth to take her away till she was ready to come back again as one of them.

Joti's gone back to the big city and the season's changed sooner than we thought; but there's still no rain and we've not yet seen the missionary bloke's balls. Nor heard him speak of them either, in polite talk or in his sermons.

Not that we truly expect him to speak of his balls when he's teaching religion – in school for all the children or in the centre of the village for the grown-ups – but he does speak of such strange and wonderful happenings that we won't truly be surprised either if he does mention them. Especially when he speaks of this great power in us. He says it comes from the Holy Ghost, which is like a Spirit.

Now that I understand. Holy Spirit is the best Spirit of all, I think, but I daren't say it in front of Grandma Toughtits. She says there isn't one Holy Spirit on account all Spirits are holy. But I believe there can be one Spirit holier than the rest, just as the missionary bloke is holier than the rest of us people. It is this which makes me want to have my soul saved, but as I've said I daren't.

Not like Matt who just goes and believes in this Holy Spirit and gets his name changed and his head drowned in water and no matter about his family. In fact so great is his faith, says the missionary bloke, that soon his sister and Dada and aunts and uncles follow his example. The missionary bloke says he's never seen anything like this before where a little boy changes the mind of grown-up folks where he's failed. And he's not the only one thinking that, for more people listen to Matt when he talks of God and Jesus and love than listen to the missionary bloke talk of sin and redemption and resurrection – whatever they mean. Maybe he speaks the language better, maybe it's more than that. Maybe he has some power in him. Even with just two ordinary balls.

Power, that this missionary bloke says comes from the Holy Spirit and from our Father the great God and from his son the great Lord Jesus. But he don't speak of no power that comes from having three balls.

He does speak once or twice of the Trinity, which I don't understand at all but which Matt says means three. Now we don't reckon he's talking of his balls or anyone else's either. But it does make us believe that three is stronger than two and maybe that's why white men are kings, as Matt says, on account that they have three instead of two. Balls, that is.

Anyway, the fact remains we've failed to find out.

We go back to our little tree on our little hill and ask for more time to keep our promise.

But Golam's heart is not much in it any more. His Mam is having difficulties feeding the cow which gives them their milk. Milk they change for food with Leku's family – the Children of Moses.

To tell the truth we're all a bit down these days on account our grown-ups are a bit down these days.

Evenings are getting colder and up on our little hill we wrap our shawls tight round us as we sit thinking our own thoughts, looking down at the village for no particular reason that I can tell you. All except Matt who's looking the opposite way.

Even Leku is with us today, looking down at the village.

Suddenly Matt's back gets all tensed up. I can tell for his back is resting against mine.

'What's the matter now?' I say in my what's-the-matter-now voice which I keep for Matt when he's being difficult.

Not that he's being difficult today, only not looking where we're all supposed to be looking, but still, I like to talk to him in that sort of a voice once in a while.

Matt don't reply which is unusual so I look up at his face to see where his mind is. His eyes are so sharp they could see through my head if it were in the way.

'What's the matter now?' I say in a different voice this time, all eager and really wanting to know.

'There are people coming to the village,' he goes, so soft I hardly hear him.

I take a quick look that way.

'I don't see anything,' I say.

By now the others have smelled that something is going on and are gathered round us, looking in turn at Matt and towards where he is looking.

'I see nothing,' goes Golam.

Leku says he can see the dust rising far away to the left of the Dry Hill. The Dry Hill is to our east about as far off as the woods are to the west.

'Can it be the travelling people?' I ask.

'Silly,' goes Hena, 'they go back at this time of the year, not come!'

'Well they've been neither coming nor going for many years now, so maybe they've started doing things different.' I say one of my longer sentences. I think she needs it.

'Not for many years, only two,' she corrects me. 'Besides, the travelling people never change their ways.'

'Then how come they've stopped coming? That's changing their way, isn't it? Tell me now, isn't it?' I'm really chuffed at catching her out, for once.

She spoils it all by saying, 'I suppose you are right, for once.'

'The travelling people don't come any more,' says Leku, 'as they have either eaten or sold their animals. In these dry days they would rather be finding food for themselves than wandering around looking for grass and water for donkeys and camels. My father told me most travelling people are camping outside cities these days, for whatever they can get. He came from Bandugu only the other day. He saw some there as well.'

Bandugu is an old city to the south.

Leku's Dada goes to the city often. There is a broken-down old bus which runs on the broken-down old dust road between Gonta and our village once a week, most weeks. When you get to Gonta you can catch a bus to Bader and from there you can go almost anywhere.

Leku's Dada often makes the journey on the bus to Gonta. Where he goes from there, I don't know.

It's something to do with his work which has something to do with buying and selling things for the village: things like matchboxes, and sacks for storing grain, and stone slates and chalks for writing in school, and some cooking spices and lumps of soap and goodness knows what. You have to be quite rich to be able to buy some of the things Leku's Dada brings.

'I don't know who they are,' says Matt, 'but they sure are heading our way. And by the look of things there seem to be many of them.'

'You don't think they can be soldiers?' says Golam in a squeaky voice. Ever since our trip to Gonta he is shit scared at the very thought of soldiers.

I am too but I try not to show it.

'Soldiers won't be coming on foot openly like that for all to see. Not with the freedom fighters that hide in the mountain caves on one side and the woods on the other. It's thanks to these woods and caves that we don't ever have soldiers coming here. Not even on their jeeps.'

'It's funny,' I say, 'for earlier on it's the soldiers who were using the woods to hide in.'

'There is nothing funny about it,' says Hena in her hardest voice.

'I agree,' says Golam.

'So do I,' says Matt.

'Me too,' says Leku.

I'm sorry I opened my mouth.

I didn't even mean funny as in 'funny'.

'One of these days we'll get it from the air,' I say.

Am I sorry I opened my mouth!

Everyone gangs up on me so, it's a wonder I live to talk about it.

'I think I best go,' says Leku after they've finished with me, 'my family will be waiting for me.'

Leku can be a good friend, only he spends most of his time with his family doing strange things like always eating together and saying mumbo jumbo prayers three times a day while making funny faces and gestures.

Golam is supposed to do things like that as well, only he don't. His mother prays five times a day. Five times a day! Can you imagine that?

When Leku gets up to go I can see in Golam's eyes that he too would like to go to his Mam but can't bring himself to say it.

Golam has these huge eyes that are truly sad one moment and truly happy the next. They speak all that's in his heart more clear than words. That and his large white teeth and his thick wavy hair make me want to put my arms round him and give him a kiss and go to sleep next to his body; but I don't reckon that's how it should be, and it makes me angry with myself. Anger which I take out on Golam by shouting at him.

'What're you looking at him like that for with your buffalo eyes? You can go home to your little mama if it's getting too late for you.'

Golam nearly bursts into tears.

'There's no need for that!' says Hena, putting her arms round Golam – which makes me angrier still – and throwing knives at me with her eyes.

'You can go with him and baby him. That'll suit you better than being out here with the boys,' I carry on in my worst voice.

'What's come over you?' says Matt, looking at me with that look which stops me doing what I'm doing. Which stops everyone doing what they're doing.

The upshot is that Leku, Hena and Golam all go leaving Matt and me alone up our hill.

I'm so angry with myself and with everyone I cannot say nothing.

Matt puts his arms around me.

He can do that so easy. I can never bring myself to do it. Not even if I want to real bad. To tell the truth, the more I want to do it the less I can.

Matt puts his arms round me and sits. Just sits with his arms round me.

All my anger goes, and a strange quiet takes hold of me. It feels so good I smile in my heart and put my arms round Matt without thinking.

'I think we'd better go too,' says Matt, which surprises me.

'Ain't you going to stay and find out who's coming our way?'

'They're still miles away, and walking as they are it'll be morning light by the time they get here. I think we best go.'

We get up, walk slow for three or four steps, then break into our fastest run till we catch up with Leku and Hena and Golam.

Two

The Outsiders

When I wake up the next morning the floor is so cold I can feel it through the straw in my matting.

To tell the truth the matting isn't much to write about. It's got these big holes in it. Holes that are getting bigger every night. I've had it for as long as I can remember, and before that big sister had it.

She's got a new one now, lucky girl.

Still, I'd rather have my torn one than share with little brother, even though his has fewer holes in it.

Matt says if I put my matting over little brother's matting and then we sleep together we'll both be much warmer, but I'd rather not.

Matt says I'm a selfish hyena.

Matt often speaks like a mother. Probably because he's never had one. His Mum died giving birth to him. He's never forgotten it. I mean, it's not as if he just knows it, which he would of course. He talks like he truly remembers it. It scares me sometimes.

Anyway, back to today. I roll over on my stomach, buckle my knees under me, raise my bum and wonder if I've something to wonder about for the day.

As it goes I can't think of anything, though at the back of my head, just above the neck, I have this feeling there is something very important I ought to be wondering about. I wonder what it can be, but it just don't come to me, though I get more certain by the breath that there is something.

The morning's wind and yesterday's food and water force their weight on my thoughts and my bowels. I make a sudden leap to the standing position and run out the back door to find a quiet place.

I even forget to take my little bucket with me for bringing back water from the hole so as to wash up a bit before rushing to school.

If I'm lucky I may have chores to do for Mam and Dada. The school Master can't be angry with me for being late if I've work to do for Mam and Dada.

On my way out I'm in too much of a hurry to notice anything.

When returning, at peace with my stomach, as I enter the outer circle of the village I feel something different.

I see something different. I see nothing. I see no one.

Now that's pretty strange for at this time there are quite a few people about: going out to the fields or putting their donkeys out or milking their cows or mending their ploughs or something.

Suddenly I remember. Remember what I should've been wondering this morning but wasn't on account I couldn't remember.

The people we saw coming towards our village last night!

I run into the house through the back door and then out from the front towards the village centre. On my way out I can see there is no one in the house. Not even little brother or Grandma Toughtits, both of whom stay home till the sun is well up in the skies.

I'm hardly two metres out when who do I see but Grandma Toughtits on her way back, little brother on one hip, a big basket on the other, shawl off the shoulders, leather tits hanging lower than last I saw them.

So is her face, now that I look at it close.

It's more than just hanging low. It's got this look like she's seen the twin Spirits of Death.

Even little brother's mug shows some feeling, which makes a change on account it normally looks like about as alive as last year's elephant dung.

Grandma pushes the little brat into my crossed arms and says, 'Stay with Limu in the house while I gather some food.'

She practically drags me back into the house, goes into the cooking corner and starts putting whatever she can find to eat in the basket.

'That's not fair,' I shout, tears in my voice – it's not often I dare to shout at Grandma – 'that's not fair. There's something going on and you're all having fun...'

'Fun,' says Grandma stopping me half way, 'fun...' she repeats, and then suddenly bursts into tears.

Now I've never seen Grandma Toughtits burst into tears.

I have seen tears flow down her cheeks, like the night Aunt Tima died, but I've never seen her burst into tears.

Soon her whole body starts to tremble, her hands and fingers turn to rubber sap and the food she's holding falls on the floor, the gasket slides down her hips, the bag of grain tips and the grain rolls out, spreading all round her feet.

She freezes with a look of horror on her face, stops crying, stops shaking, just turns to stone.

I've never seen that look on anyone's face before.

I have seen it since.

The people Matt saw last night and who came to our village by the morning light come from two or three villages about twenty kilometres to our east. They are aiming for Gonta but make a stop at our village before carrying on.

They're going to Gonta for they've heard white men have set up a camp there, a camp where the white men give medicine and food to anyone who is sick or wounded or without food. As most of these people are wounded or sick, and none of them has any food, they're all headed for Gonta.

Their villages were attacked by soldiers last week. Some people were wounded, some killed and some taken away – mostly men but a few women and children as well. The soldiers also set fire to the crops. They were poor crops of a dry season but would've kept life going in many bodies.

They were fifty-two grown-ups and more than twice as many

children when they started. Now they are less. Some turned back, some sat down and never got up to move forward or backward, some died.

The spotted green soldiers led by General Tako have now taken over our country. They keep raiding villages and sometimes take people away. I don't know why for they've got what they wanted. General Tako says it's because some people don't like them so it's natural they don't like them back in return; and I suppose there is reason in it.

He also says these people are 'enemies of real people'. He says they are no good for the country and will 'tear it apart unless stopped'. I don't understand the difference between people and real people, but then I've other things on my mind, what with school work and Grandma Toughtits being poorly and the question of white men's balls.

While on the subject of white men, my school Master says white men are behind General Tako and the spotted green soldiers, paying them money and giving them guns and planes and bombs. But then again, white men are helping the villagers attacked by the soldiers. I don't understand this either.

I do understand why Grandma Toughtits was acting so peculiar this morning. I understand this when I see the people who've come to our village.

None of the children have gone to school today and the Master's running about trying to round them up and take them with him. He keeps saying it is 'not polite to stand around staring'.

Most of our grown-ups are collecting food and milk and water and shawls for everybody. My Dada and Mam are trying to sort out the sick and the wounded from the tired and the hungry.

We can't take our eyes off them nor can we look properly at them. I know it's not a nice thing to say, but they are not nice to look at. Some of them look real sick, some look like they've never eaten in their entire life.

One mother is carrying her dead child in a sort of a hammock thingie made out of a shawl, on her back, on account she's heard white men have a machine which brings the dead back to life.

One of their men, who's been around and seen television and such magic, swears he has seen dead people shook by this machine till they live again.

I don't believe it but Matt says it is possible.

Matt says everything is possible.

Some elders are saying they'll have to steal the child's body in the new night and put it away in peace.

By the afternoon all the people are settled in the schoolhouse to rest for a day or two before starting for Gonta. All except the very sick who are kept by some families to look after.

One very sick mother with two very sick children – one a baby – come to stay with us.

Talk of old Grandma Toughtits' leather tits... You should've seen this woman's. Like rats that've been dead for days and shrivelled under the sun. Her funny shaped baby is biting at them with its toothless gums and then making real ugly faces when it gets nothing out.

Too tired from crying to cry it looks at its mother with eyes larger than the world.

Like me, he don't seem to know what's truly going on.

All he can tell is that things are not quite what they ought to be.

Leastwise, that's what I think.

Seven sunsets have gone, the outsiders are still there.

All our people are doing their best for them. But there are some – Hena's Dada for one – who are beginning to worry about our own food. They are beginning to wish the outsiders would go away now. This is making the others angry.

All this is making the air around a bit thick to walk through and you've to breathe quiet. Someone is likely to snap at you if you're not careful.

The missionary bloke is going around spreading the good word to all the outsiders, telling them their suffering will end if they give their Spirit to Jesus. He says they'll never die and will live forever in the kingdom of Heaven. The trouble is most of them are quite happy to live on where they were born. The missionary bloke tells them they will be born again but I'm not sure they like the idea. At least not much so far.

Even his miserable wife is bringing food and water for the children. She don't speak the language and she don't know how to smile and her eyes don't say much, but she does her best.

One good thing is we haven't had school for the last seven days. Not properly. We just have some lessons under the tree and some work to do at home but it's much better than being inside for half the day, regular.

One strange thing has happened. The dead child has come to life. Of course their elders say he wasn't really dead, just fainted from pain and hunger.

It happened when these elders went to steal its body after the mother at last goes to sleep. She's been sitting the whole evening telling Matt about her husband who's been taken away by the soldiers. When she sleeps Matt just sits there looking at nothing at all. I know for I keep going to him every little while asking for help as I run around doing little jobs for everybody: carrying water to this one and food for that one and holding this one's baby and wiping that one's face. Matt just sits there having a chat with this woman with the dead child and the stolen husband.

Anyway, when these elders come to steal the body away to bury it in a little hole they've dug by the river, Matt tells them not to bother for the child lives.

They don't believe it till they see it; but they believe it when they see it.

Those who hear of it don't believe it even when they see it.

Matt finally gets up and brings some food and water for this child, who don't look too happy at being alive. Its mother don't know yet but she will when she wakes up.

When she does, she is not in the least surprised.

The tired and hungry are now well rested and feeling good. Some of the sick and wounded are getting better too. But some of the sick and wounded are worse.

Leku's older brother, Deku, usually has a stock of white man's medicines and pills which he gives to us when we are poorly. Then there is Rona who helps babies to be born. She also cures other 'women's troubles'. John the village barber cuts off bits of boys' thingies – if the boys are Muslims or Children of Moses. He looks after our wounds and sets broken bones. He treats snake bites and helps men with their special problems – whatever they may be. We also have some elders who give out folk medicine, but Grandma Toughtits says she can do better than them.

All these people have seen to the outsiders but some of them aren't getting any better.

We feel it'll be best for them if they go to Gonta but don't say it in case they think we want to get shot of them.

Out in the open, before the day's work, by the fire cooking the community pot, wrapped in their clean shawls, our grown-ups meet to make up their minds what to do.

They think of sending two of our wiser people to go and have a talk with their wiser people.

Leku's Dada, my Mam, Grandma Toughtits, the school Master, the missionary bloke and John our barber are named. Hena's Dada wants to go along but everyone thinks he'll make things difficult, not having enough kindness in his heart.

The missionary bloke don't want to go as he don't want to get mixed up in something that can cause trouble or bad feeling.

The barber don't want to be the one for he is treating the wounded and he thinks it don't seem right for him to send them away. But he is willing to go along and say it's difficult for him to do the best for them on account he hasn't the proper facilities.

At long last Leku's Dada and my Mam are both chosen.

Having decided who is going they start thinking what they'll say. They think they can ask the people who're well to stay as long as they like but the others must go in search of better medicine. In their hearts they know it's not possible for the sick will not be able to make it on their own.

Leku's Dada being an experienced traveller thinks of suggesting the bus, but there are two problems with that. First: the bus went two days ago. This means it's five days more to come, if it's regular, which it often isn't. It could be another twelve days wait – much too long for the wounded. If it breaks down on the way, which it often does, it can be worse than careful walking. Second, and more important, the bus is run by the Government and people attacked by soldiers fear to travel on it.

They end up by deciding they'll simply go and tell them what everyone here feels and let them make up their own mind.

While the grown-ups are busy with all this the younger folk are hanging about listening or talking in their own little groups. Hena and I are by ourselves for Golam is doing something for his Mam, Leku's home reading his holy books or similar and Matt is not to be seen. We've looked for him at all our places, starting with our little hill, but not a sign.

Leku's Dada and my Mam get up to go and Hena tells me to tag along and see what goes on.

'After all, your Mam is going,' says she.

Sounds reasonable but not right.

Luckily I don't have to make up my mind. Before Leku's Dada and my Mam have finished collecting everyone's best wishes and thank yous, we see two of the outsiders coming towards us from the schoolhouse.

Everybody waits to hear what they've to say.

They say they've decided to start walking to Gonta by noon today. They thank us greatly for our food and medicine and kindness and say they would've been happy to stay here forever but it wouldn't be fair on our food. Also their wounded need attention by the doctor in Gonta.

We're all pleased they've been thinking what we've been thinking and everyone's happy, though sad as well.

We all decide to put something extra in the cooking pot and to hold a dance.

Some of us go to bring over the outsiders to join in the dance or to settle round the fire and the food. The others go to their own houses to bring mattings and shawls to make the sick and the wounded as comfortable as possible.

While everyone is being settled we hear this big shouting and screaming and running. The outsiders get all worried but I roll my eyes and sigh and so does Hena and so do all children and most grown-ups of our village. For we know what it's about.

One of the children has pulled Grandma Toughtits' tits. She is running after him full speed and in full voice.

Just shows that after the last few days' worry, things are getting easy again, and back to normal.

Soon we hear more shouting and running. This time the outsiders don't bother, thinking it's more of our silliness. But we do. It is Matt running towards us, shouting and waving his arms about.

Now Matt is cool as a cat's nose. Especially in front of other people. For him to be shouting and running before a village full of outsiders means something is not quite what it ought to be.

He comes over, all gasping for air, and says, 'There's jeeps looking for the village.'

We wait for more but he's silent.

I think he's realised he was over the top and is trying to get his cool back.

'Go on,' says Matt's Dada, a bit angry.

But Matt just looks at him.

I then see Matt's not trying to be cool or difficult; he's just scared.

Three

White Folk and Farts

We finally find out what Matt has to tell which isn't much, but enough to give us a dream of the twin Spirits.

He's up at dawn and not able to sleep – as often happens with him. He goes out for a long walk towards the woods – as he often does when he can't get to sleep.

While still going forward he hears this funny roar. He quickly moves out of the way of the bushes so as to see what it is.

It's two jeeps followed by a van coming on the road from Gonta.

They're still far enough away but Matt hides himself behind a bush. The jeeps and the van move on past the turning to the village – which is not a proper road like but just a dirt track. There are three or four such tracks though only one leads to the village, the others get lost in open space or among the bushes.

Matt comes out of hiding and is walking back when he sees the jeeps and the van returning. He hides again. They go past very slowly this time and although they miss the turning again Matt is certain they are looking for it to come to the village.

Matt thinks maybe it is the Government come for the outsiders. Maybe even seeking to punish our village for keeping them. Maybe they've hunted down and caught or killed the guerrilla fighters who hide in these parts. Maybe that's why they come so openly and boldly.

The outsiders look very worried and very sad. More for us than for themselves. They feel they've brought us pain and suffering in payment for our food and care.

Leku's Dada says we have two options: one – we gather whatever weapons we can, like stones and sticks, and fight what we can; or two – we run and hide where we can.

He says we should stand up and fight.

The missionary bloke turns all white. He says he must 'inform my wife of the situation' and walks home fast.

Grandma Toughtits pushes everyone aside, moves into the middle of the circle where people are gathered, close to the fire where the food is cooking; and starts to dance.

This is the first time I see Grandma Toughtits dancing without first oiling her body or arranging her shawl properly across her shoulders.

Everybody stops talking and watches as Grandma Toughtits dances round and round the food and the fire, arms flirting with the wind, eyes daring the skies, feet playing with the sand.

Some others join in. Before long many are dancing, the rest are watching in silence.

All are swaying, gently and softly, like trees come to life; their roots more high above the earth than in it.

Some children start playing the flute, some start beating the drums.

Nobody's said anything but it's decided without words. We won't hide and we won't fight. If they are going to kill us or take us away, we want them to find us dancing like Spirits – not hiding like cowards or fighting like fools.

Even Matt dances. Matt who's always shy of dancing and only does so when pushed on account he's not very good at it. Even Matt dances, his fear all gone.

The roar of jeeps draws near.

No one pays any attention to it. Or if they do they don't show it.

I pay attention to it and I show it. I look up. I stop dancing.

The jeeps roll into the village, slow down and stop.

White men come out of the jeeps. White men come out of the van. Two white ladies as well.

They are all holding strange looking guns and bombs in their hands. I've never seen the likes of them.

So the school Master was right: white men are behind the Government, I say to myself foolishly. Foolishly for it don't truly make no difference. Not to me, not to Matt, not to Grandma Toughtits – not to any of us. Leastwise that's how I see it. Whether I'm killed by a white man holding a white man's gun or by a black man holding a white man's gun, I'm still dead.

'Start shooting,' says one of them, 'we're damn lucky to come across so many like this.'

I close my eyes.

But I hear no guns. No one cries. No one dies.

I just hear this strange whirring and clicking noise.

It turns out it's a television crew.

Leku's Dada knows about it.

I've never heard of such a thing and am still not sure what it's all about. I certainly don't know how it works.

It seems these white folk make these pictures and send them back home to their country to show them what's going on in our country. It's strange for I don't know what's going on in their country. They can see us, our sick and hungry hiding their pain and shame in dance, but we don't see what they do and why.

But no matter, we all see what we can see.

They have with them a nurse, a reporter and another missionary bloke.

When I see the cameras and machines of these white men working away and instant pictures coming in this little box they're carrying, I'm hit with wonder.

They all look so careful about what they're doing. They organise everything and everybody. They ask questions holding this little metal carrot full of holes and you can hear the sound of your voice again and then all over again as many times as you like.

The same with our pictures, made so they tell the story of our lives. Our bodies speak our pains and joys, our eyes speak our hopes and fears – for all to see in their homes. Moving pictures. My eyes and my Spirit are caught, to live long after my grandchildren are dead.

When I see all this I truly believe, for the first time, that white men have three balls. And if they haven't they ought to – or else there's no justice in the world.

But what about the white ladies, I wonder, for they are doing these great and wonderful things as well. Katuna, one of the older boys, says they have all the fun for they get to play with three balls and a bat which makes a better game than two balls and a bat.

We all grin over it, but I'm not sure I understand it completely.

After our dance they tell us about themselves.

It seems they hear of this new attack by the soldiers of the Government on the villages to our east. They travel there on their jeeps and van but don't see many people. As they're coming from the south they don't meet the people on the way who are going west to Gonta.

They make pictures of burnt fields and broken houses and dead bodies, then travel to Gonta.

When the white men get to Gonta the people aren't there either. Someone says they might've stopped over at one of the villages in between, so they come looking to our village and find them here with us.

Matt is having a great time translating all round, even though he's not the only one who understands English. But he speaks it best. Better than Leku's Dada even.

Also he speaks the language of this other missionary bloke, which is not English. Matt don't know it too well but he does a little, which impresses this new missionary bloke. He is different, this one, from our one. He don't talk much of saving souls. He is running around trying to see what he can do to help. Our missionary bloke don't think too good of him on account he is not what he calls a 'proper Christian'. But Matt has taken a great shine to him, and the other way round. To tell the truth all the white folk seem to have taken a great shine to Matt. Smart-ass.

After a lot of quiet argument among the white folk, the very ill and the wounded are packed off to Gonta in the van and one of the jeeps.

The rest of the outsiders say their thank yous to all and start their walk to Gonta.

This leaves more white folks than even fit into one jeep. A camera man, a lady reporter and two others get on it and follow on hoping to make more pictures and news on the way.

Alberto – the new missionary bloke – and five other white folk, including one white lady, stay behind with us until the jeeps come back to fetch them.

That is what the plan is but it don't work out that way.

By the time all arrangements are completed and everybody who's to go is gone, it's nearly night time.

The schoolhouse is cleaned and tidied up to sleep the white folk for the night.

We have put a new pot on the fire for the white folk but our missionary bloke has asked his miserable wife to prepare white man's food for them.

Alberto says he'll stay and eat with us which makes the other white folk look at one another wondering who to offend. But our grown-ups tell them we don't mind if they eat with the missionary bloke and his miserable wife.

This makes them breathe easy. They relax their shoulders, they spread their legs by the dying fire, they cup their heads in the palms of their hands and they lie down for a little rest after the tiring day.

The white lady takes out this little box she's been carrying and opens it. I've been wondering all along what's in it. I try not to break my neck as I stretch it giraffe-like to see what's there. It's another box. A box that flattens itself to make waves of music.

One of the white men starts singing. He has a sad voice that rises in the night like an old bird flying for the last time.

There aren't many people left outside by now. Most have gone to their homes and their lives till the day breaks.

Matt stops talking to Alberto and listens to the music box and the song with wonder in his eyes.

I have a hard fart coming. I hold on to it with all my strength not wanting to put unwanted wind into the air but can't stop it. I can tell it's going to be a loud one. I try to squeeze it out gently so it won't make much of a sound. Luckily it don't; but it smells something awful. All that extra food we've had today after days of going very careful with grain – eating no more than a handful, and that with water rather than milk – has turned the stomach a bit rude.

Grandma Toughtits always says, 'Too much food makes a body rude.'

There is no way I can control the smell once it starts. Everyone is too polite to notice, but when it reaches Matt's nose the wonder in his eyes at the song turns to hunger in his heart for my blood. How he knows it's mine I can't say, but he knows it.

He looks at me without looking which is worse than looking for I can tell he is looking when he isn't. Leastwise, not with his eyes into my eyes but with his whole being into my being.

I pretend not to care though I'm dying of shame. Matt senses it and lets go his unseen hold.

Such a big fuss over such a little thing. Matt can be like that sometimes. I hate him.

All of a sudden I'm hit by a thought which cheers me up. With so many white folk about we might be able to solve the mystery of their balls if we make sure one of us is following them about all the time. Carefully, of course, at a good distance or from behind the bushes.

Our missionary bloke has this special closet with a deep hole in it which some of us got good gifts for digging. He even baths in the house. But these white folk may not be so particular. No one can be so particular as our missionary bloke.

They might even take their clothes off and have a dip in the river like the rest of the world.

I have another fart coming.

I think I best run out of here for a while.

I stand up to run at the same time as I think of running.

This makes me careless and out goes the fart with a loud bang.

Followed by a tiny squeak. Just as I stand up.

The white man singing misses a note.

I am so ashamed of myself I run and run and run till I'm on the other side of the village.

I feel I can never ever go back there again.

If I hadn't had the clever idea of running I could've squeezed it out quiet as the first one. Or even, if it escaped noisily, pretended it wasn't me. But now there's no hope. My fate is sealed. Pity it wasn't my lower windpipe.

I'm in real tears. The cold wind hurts my stinging eyes and I shut them tight. I stand on the edge of the high fields, breathing in and out very slowly, trying to think of something different.

I stand there for so long I nearly fall asleep standing up.

I hear these strange voices: strange but familiar, far off but near. I hear but don't listen on account I'm not sure if it's real or a dream.

I feel my knees giving way. I let my body knuckle and buckle till I am half sitting up, half bent on the cool sand.

I think I really fall asleep.

Soon I'm being shaken up.

I don't like being shaken up when I'm awake. I hate being shaken up when I'm asleep. But what I hate most is being shaken up asleep to wake up and find myself being shaken up awake. But I expect you know that by now.

I expect you also know who's doing the shaking up. Matt!

'Starving hyenas. Just let me be,' I go.

'Just wake up. Wake up you farty fool,' he screams in my ear.

It was the worst thing he could've said this time.

I jump up and grab him by the neck. In the space of a breath I have him on the ground and I'm hitting out at him in white madness.

He just lies there and takes it.

Arms by his side, eyes looking up at me with... with... gentleness. I don't know what to do.

My arms and hands stop half way and stay there.

I'm more frightened than if he'd turned the strongest of guns on me instead of eyes full of gentleness.

But it is a good fear. It brings with it peace and a feeling of being free. Free from anger and hate. Free from fear.

It all happens in a moment. The moment passes.

I see Matt with a worried look in his eyes saying, 'They've taken them. They've taken them away.'

At first I don't get what he's on about.

'Who's taken who away?'

Then my brain works.

'The soldiers have taken our people away!' I say, my throat drying up. My whole body drying up.

My Dada... my Mam... Grandma Pearl...

I can't speak any more. I think more than ever before, but I can't speak.

'I knew we shouldn't have kept those outsiders. I knew it. I knew it. I knew it...'

I think I'm saying it, but I don't think I'm truly saying it because my mouth though open isn't moving, and my voice though I can hear it is not coming out of it.

'It's not the soldiers who've taken our people away,' says Matt, 'it's the guerrilla fighters who've taken the white folk away.'

Just when I had hoped to see their balls!

Things never turn out the way you plan them. Leastwise not the way I plan them.

Four

Murder in the Mountains

Matt has this plan to get the white folk back.

It's so simple you won't believe it.

Leku don't believe it.

'I don't believe it,' says Leku.

'Why, what's wrong with it?' asks Matt.

'It's... it's... it's more like a little baby's dream than a grown person's scheme,' says Leku after some thought.

'Do you really think so?' says Matt.

'Of course I do,' Leku goes, acting more sure of himself now.

'Thank you,' says Matt. 'Nice of you to say so.'

Before I say any more I think you ought to know what the plan is. Matt says we should follow the guerrilla fighters, find out where they are, walk up to them and ask them to let the white folk go on account they are our friends.

'You know for a smart-ass you can be really simple,' says Leku.

'Naïve,' says Hena.

We all look at her surprised for we do not understand the word. Leastwise I do not.

Matt says to look at it this way. The guerrillas want to help our people. The white folk are helping our people. So there's no problem.

'Not all white folk are helping our people. The school Master says...' Leku is saying this when Matt cuts him short.

'We're not talking of all white folk. We're talking of these white folk. Besides, no matter who they are or what they are it still don't make it right taking them away like that.'

'You try telling them!' Leku goes.

'That's what I am trying to do, but you say it's foolish. First you tell me not to do it, then you tell me to do it. Make up your mind.'

I think Matt has him there but Leku goes, 'I was only being sarcastic.'

'And anyone can be mad.'

'Not anyone. It takes a very special kind of person to be called mad. In a madhouse you have to be truly sane to be thought mad. In an upside-down place you have to be the right way up to be thought mad. In a...'

'Oh all right, all right. Don't go on.' This time Leku cuts him short.

'Have it your own way, but don't blame me if you are hung by your toes and have your asshole removed. Good luck to you and your plan. I don't want any part of it.' Leku goes home.

We are on our little hill when all this is going on. Matt and me have gathered our friends for a meeting.

'How're we going to find out where they are, even if we do try to do your plan?' says Golam.

'Easy,' says Matt. 'I give Alberto a whole bagful of food that was left over. The one we put in the pot extra for the white folk. He is going to drop bits of it here and there all along the way for us to follow. Like in the story our Master read to us in school.'

I am truly shocked. For the first time in a long while I am truly shocked.

'You mean you gave all that food to be thrown away on the sand!'

I remember the look of pain on Grandma Toughtits' face when she spilled the grain for the hungry on the floor.

'You shouldn't have done that Matt, you shouldn't have.'

'It would have lasted my mam a whole month,' says Golam, in that voice of his which makes everyone look at him when he speaks.

Everyone who don't known him, that is. We who do know him are used to it by now. Like we are used to his flashing eyes and smiling teeth and dancing hair.

'It would have lasted the whole village for a whole month,' I say, which is not quite true. But it would have lasted the whole village for a whole day.

'Don't look at me like that,' says Matt. 'We're not that short of food, yet.'

'Tell that to my Mam,' says Golam, who's usually never angry with anyone, much less Matt.

'I only used it to try to save people's lives. Food is for saving people's lives, isn't it?'

Matt always has an answer you find difficult to argue with. But we're still not happy about it.

'How do you know it will save their lives? How do you know the birds or animals won't eat it before anyone can find them? How do you know their lives are in any danger? The guerrilla fighters are good people, they won't kill them.' Now Hena's on the warpath against Matt.

'It's still not nice to be taken away like that and kept hidden away if you don't want to. Would you like that?'

'That's not the point,' Hena carries on. 'Besides, you still haven't answered me about the food being eaten up by the birds or animals.' She looks at him real angry. 'Like in the story,' she adds.

'They'll only eat it if we let it be till the morning. The creatures that come out at night don't like grain.'

'I think I best be going,' says Hena to our great surprise.

What's more she actually trots off without even waiting for our reaction. Golam sits there trying not to look at us.

'You best go as well,' says Matt. 'Your Mam'll be waiting.'

Last time we went to Gonta Golam's Mam nearly died of worry. Having lost his Dada she is always worrying about losing him too.

'You sure you don't mind?' says Golam. It's difficult for him. He truly wants to please his Mam and he truly wants to be with us.

'We're sure,' says Matt.

'Yes, sure,' say I.

Matt and me are left on our own.

'You won't fall asleep on the way, will you?' says Matt.

Just because he never goes to sleep he thinks I'm always going to sleep.

Well, there's some truth in it. That's why it angers me when he says it, but I say nothing back.

*

We start following the food. It is going away from the woods. That's what we'd expected. The woods are a good place for hiding when you are running to or from something. For a short while.

To have a proper hiding place, a regular one, the caves are best.

Matt keeps putting the food in a bag as we go along.

'You're not going to eat it now?' I say.

'I might,' he says. 'Also we don't want anyone else to follow us, do we?' I expect he's right.

We keep walking till I feel my legs can't carry me any more. I'm tired and worried and no longer sure if we're doing the right thing. It is weird how Matt never seems to tire. And he's only half my size.

All of a sudden the trail stops.

Up to now it hasn't been too difficult. The moon is bright and makes the sand shine. It is easy enough to see lumps of food on it. Our main worry is snakes which start coming out at night this time of the season as the foods gets less and less. We are careful not to go too near the bushes.

We are by the mountain walls and don't know where to look except close to the bushes. Behind us are the plains and certainly no sign of food there. Ahead the rocks rise steeply. The only chance is they've gone along the bushes to our right.

I'm more afraid of hyenas than snakes, but Matt says hyenas won't attack two of us, but if we get near a snake it might hit first and hiss later. It's good that we're looking for our trail which means if there is a snake about we're likely to see it before it hears us.

Scorpions are different. Both of us haven't got shoes on. Mine have holes in them big enough for a scorpion to bite through anyway.

Matt's Dada hasn't been able to buy him another pair after his feet got too big for his last one.

We're going backward and forward but no joy. Even Matt is ready to give up hope.

My eye catches something shiny on a craggy bit of rock. Matt sees it too. We both go to it. It's part of a shawl, white with a funny little pattern on it. I pull it up for a closer look. Seems familiar.

While we are wondering about it we see a big crack in the rock walls. It is at such an angle you'd never know it was there. We'd never have seen it if it hadn't been for that bit of shawl.

Just by the opening to the crack is a little lump of food.

We've found our trail.

We get into the crack and keep going. We don't find any more food.

Even if it was there we couldn't've seen it, it's so dark in there. I'm almost too scared to go on, but Matt holds my wrist in that iron grip of his and pulls me along.

I lose my feel for time and distance. To save Grandma Toughtits' life I couldn't tell you how long we've been in that crack or how far in we've gone.

Both my arms are held by two strong hands. Even Matt can't have that kind of strength. Besides he'd need three hands for that as one of his hands is still on my wrist.

But not for long.

I am pulled to one side as if by wild camels. My wrist is wrenched away from Matt's hand.

This frightens me more than anything else.

'Here are two more,' I hear a voice say, sounding as surprised as I am. Luckily I don't have time to think. Thinking always makes things worse. Leastwise for me.

I'm in this room with walls of rock. A cave really, but set up like a room.

It is brightly lit. So bright that after being blinded by the dark outside I'm blinded by the light inside. But I can see that Matt is there, next to me. I feel safe again.

'You took your time coming, didn't you?' goes a sharp voice through my ears, like a needle of cold wind.

It is Hena.

Matt and I look at each other. Our shoulders jump up and down. The men who bring Matt and me in are wearing dirty blue jeans and dirty blue shirts. There is another man in the room. He is sitting on a sort of stone stool, wearing a long white robe. His head and face are covered in a white shawl, with just a little round opening through which he can see without being seen.

I can see his body jerk strangely as he sees us.

He remains sitting for a short while, then makes a sign to one of the men. The man walks up to him all respectful. The hooded man bends, on account he is much taller, and whispers through his shawl in the man's ear.

The man looks a bit upset.

He turns round and asks us how we got there and if there is someone else following us.

We give a quick glance at Hena. His eyes follow our eyes and his mind follows our mind.

'No, she didn't tell us anything,' he says.

If Hena don't want to say nothing Hena don't say nothing. We all know that.

'We followed bits of food. We picked it up as we came along so there isn't any trail left,' says Matt, which is true enough as the wind keeps blowing the footprints off the sand as soon as they're made.

The man looks a little less upset now.

The hooded man whispers something else in his ears and they both walk out of the room through another crack in the rock wall, to the right of the one which we came through.

One man remains in the room with the three of us.

There is no sign of the white folk.

'How did you get here, Spirit of a witch?' I say, trying to look angry though I am really full of wonder at what Hena can do and know.

'Same way as you, I hope,' says Hena. 'I nearly missed the crack in the rock. I tore up a piece of my shawl and stuck it there to help you. I see that you found it.'

Now I'm really angry at Hena. I should truly be thankful to her.

One of the men in jeans comes back.

He is looking at us with a new look in his eyes.

'Why have you followed us here?'

'To meet you,' says Matt.

'And why do you want to meet us?'

'We want to ask you a favour.'

'And what is the favour you would like to ask us?'

This is getting us nowhere, I say to myself.

'We want you to give the white folk back to us.'

'How do you know the white folk are with us?'

'Because you took them from us only a short while ago.'

'How do you know we took them? You couldn't have seen our faces as they were covered.'

Matt says nothing to that.

The man understands his mistake, but it's too late.

'And why do you want us to give the white folk back to you?' he says at last.

'Because they are our friends. And we think you are our friends. Friends shouldn't take away their friends' friends.'

It's getting worser by the breath.

The man seems to think this over.

'Are you hungry?' he asks after a while.

I am, after all that walk. But Matt says, 'No thank you.'

I hate him.

'No thank you,' says Hena.

I hate her.

'No thank you,' I say.

The man looks at us with a smile, then turns round and disappears into the rock. He is gone for a long time.

The man with us in the room says nothing at all.

I start getting more and more worried.

At last the other man returns.

When he comes back he has this huge paper bag in his hand. I think maybe he's got some food for us. My mouth waters like the river in the rains.

But he don't give us anything.

He just stands there all quiet for some time.

'Don't you ever sleep?' he asks, looking from one to the other.

'He don't,' I say, pointing to Matt.

The mention of sleep brings back with power my sleep which had been chased away by fear and worry.

'I'll tell you what we'll do. We'll let you go back home now as your family will be worried. They might think you've been taken as well. Then come and see us in the morning and we'll talk it over. That fair enough?' he says, again looking our way from one to the other.

Sounds fair maybe, but the thought of walking the long walk back in the night, maybe losing our way without the trail, and then walking the long walk back here again, it nearly kills me with its weight.

The man seems to think what I think. He must have a cruel mind for he seems to enjoy it. He cuts his face in two with this big grin and says, 'All ready to walk back then? I'll see you out.'

I can tell by Matt's face even he don't think it is funny. Nor does Hena.

'Can't we settle the matter now?' Matt says. 'We are in no hurry to go.'

'I am afraid that's not possible. There are a lot of things to be talked over. It's not quite as simple a matter as you might think. You'll have to come in the light of the day when we've all had time to rest and time to think. I'm tired even if you aren't.'

Like hell we aren't! I think. But I say nothing.

I think he'll have pity on us and ask us to sit down for a while or bring us some water to drink or something, but he don't.

'Let's go,' he says, and walks past us making a sign for us to follow. We go back into the narrow passage, but instead of turning left – the side we came from – we turn right.

We keep walking through the unlit craggy break in the rock till we come out into the moonlit plain. There are many trees and high bushes this side of the mountains.

The man takes us towards one of the larger trees. Underneath is a green jeep. With a happy smile he pushes us up in it. He gets in himself in the driver's seat.

'Have you ever ridden in a jeep before?'

'Only once,' says Matt.

That was the time we were brought home from Gonta by a friend of Kofi, after the air attack.

The man is a bit disappointed to hear that. He'd wanted to thrill us by what he thought would be our first ever jeep ride.

We're thrilled plenty anyway and he can see that. He soon forgets his disappointment.

He gives us the bag he holds in his hand. 'Here, something for you to eat while I get you home.'

He takes us to the outer edge of the village, close to our little tree by our little hill. We pile out one by one.

'I will come here to pick you up tomorrow when the shadows are no shorter than up to that stone over there. Wait for me if I'm late. But don't be late yourselves. I can't afford to hang out here for long.

'We'll talk about your white folk when we get back to our place.

In the meantime they'll be well looked after. Don't worry. Take care, and don't get into any trouble.'

So saying he drives away, waving cheerfully as he goes.

Early next morning Matt's Dada takes him to the fields to help him clear the furrows. My Mam wants me to sift grain out of dirt and sand she and big sister have been gathering from the old fields over the last many days.

We do what we can as quickly as we can and as best we can; and then we rush to our little tree by our little hill. We were hoping to take Golam with us but as we're getting late we make a run for it.

Hena is sitting there.

'If you say "You took your time coming, didn't you?" once more, I'll jump into the river and not come up,' I say to Hena.

'You took your time coming, didn't you?' says Hena to me.

That cuts me up.

'See you at the bottom of the river when it dries,' says Matt.

I don't think that's a nice thing to say.

Even Hena don't think it's a nice thing to say.

'I don't think that's a nice thing to say,' says Hena.

'You started it,' I turn on Hena. I'm still cut up with her sharpness.

'I started it! I?' goes Hena. 'You asked for it.'

Maybe I did, but I'm not about to say I did. Nor can I say I didn't.

So I keep my mouth shut, though I'm not happy about it.

The shadows are getting shorter. Much shorter than what the man had said. But he still don't turn up.

We're getting worried. We're getting worried why he don't come.

We're also getting worried the school Master don't send anyone looking for us – everybody knows where we hang about.

We start wishing we'd gone to look for Golam.

Somehow it's not best without him. He don't say much bit it's good to have him around.

'If the man's going to be long I think I might as well go and get Golam,' I say.

Matt don't look too sure one way or the other. He wants Golam to be here but he also wants us to wait in case the man comes and wants to go back at once.

Just then we see him coming. Not raising sand from the east but crunching earthy soil from the west.

He's looking much more thoughtful than last night.

He don't say much, just helps us into the jeep and drives along with a frown on his face. Maybe it's because the sun's in his eyes. But we can tell there's some difference. And not a happy one.

In the light of the day and on the jeep we get to the hiding place in no time at all.

We don't notice the hollow plain where the jeep was kept until we are upon it. It is hidden away so well by rocks and trees and shrubs that even the man has to slow and look carefully about before finding his way in.

We are truly surprised to see the place now that we can see it properly. There is almost a little village in there, with a few straw huts and even two small stone buildings – all flat and low and hidden under trees and behind tall bushes and in the belly of the mountains.

We get off the jeep and the man tells us to follow him.

We seem to be going towards the opening in the rocks leading to the cave room we were in last night.

The shadows are still long but shortening fast. The chill of the morning is still in the air though the heat of the noon is not too far off.

All is still and silent.

Suddenly Matt stops. He stretches out his hand, grips my wrist and holds me back as well.

I can see his whole mind is leaning towards one side of the ground. I can't tell what it is but I can tell his whole mind is taken up with it.

'Come on, let's go. We're already late,' says the man.

By the nervous way he looks around I think he knows what Matt has seen or heard. He wants to hurry us out of there.

By now even I can tell there is something in the air. Strange soft sounds. I can't tell if they're human or animal – or just wind in the bushes.

Hena is listening, a funny look on her face, eyes turned to glass.

Matt's whole body which was stone a breath ago turns to wind.

He rushes past us all in the opposite direction, practically pulling my arm out of its socket on account he is holding my wrist. I'm left with no choice but to follow.

Hena runs with us as well.

The man tries to catch hold of us one by one but we slip out of his hold.

By now we are in front of a large stone room the size of a medium house.

Matt runs in followed by me. The man has managed to grab Hena and carries her with one arm trying to stop her from screaming and shouting with the other hand. He don't know whether to come in after us with Hena struggling or just take her away. He settles on taking her away.

Inside the stone room three men are hanging by their arms from the ceiling. They are not wearing much. There are spotted green clothes lying about on the floor.

Also on the floor, beneath each man, is a big box with high sides and an open top. In every box there are three snakes. If the men let go their hold they will fall into the box with the snakes. Not just that. They have to keep pulling themselves up, for fear if their feet dangle too low the snakes will rear up and bite.

The men are gagged but they are still making muffled sounds: half squeaky and sharp, half rough and gruff. Sounds that stopped Matt on our way to the caves.

Standing in front of the dangling men, holding a big ugly gun, is the man in the white robe, the man we saw last night. He still has his shawl round his head and face, but he turns sharply when he hears us enter and it slips, showing his face.

'Not you again,' he says.

The voice and the face look familiar, but I cannot be sure who they belong to.

'I think you were expecting us,' says Matt.

'Not in here I wasn't,' replies the man.

I remember. It is the poor man we saved from the green soldiers more than two years ago.

'You shouldn't be doing that,' says Matt.

The man looks partly embarrassed, partly annoyed; mainly just taken aback.

'You shouldn't be here,' he says.

'Do you know who they are?'

'You still shouldn't be doing that.'

'Do you know what they have done? They have taken men, women and children from Nedika only last night. They have killed at least sixty people and thrown their bodies in the only water-hole in the village! Can you understand that?'

Matt's eyes are filled with pain and anger and sorrow.

'You still shouldn't be doing that,' he says.

'I'm trying to find out where they have taken the people they have taken, strong men who were providing food for their families, mothers with children left behind, children with their mothers left weeping. Can you understand that?'

Matt is silent for a long time. He is having difficulty breathing. He moves back to the stone wall and leans against it.

'You still shouldn't be doing that,' he says.

They both stand silent, looking into one another's eyes, bodies turned to stone.

Neither bats an eyelid or moves a finger.

I hear the snakes hissing louder than the wind flying through the cracks in the stones.

The eyes of the three soldiers dangling from the ceiling with their hands bulge so I fear they'll fall out of their sockets into the snake boxes. I'm not sure they are breathing any more.

The man and Matt keep looking into one another.

Gradually the man's body relaxes, his arms hang lower, his head looks up at the three soldiers.

He pulls the shawl from round his head and chucks it on the floor. He moves forward and puts back the lids on the snake boxes and kicks them to one side.

'Their biting teeth were removed anyway,' is all he says.

The soldiers keep hanging for a while, then let go and steady themselves on the floor.

The man kicks their uniforms towards them.

In slow, jerky movements they start getting dressed.

Matt walks up to them.

'Where have you taken the people of Nedika?' he asks.

One of the men takes a paper and pencil out of his pocket and draws a map showing where those and some other kidnapped people are kept. He also tells when it will be best to try and save them. The time when most of the soldiers are either resting or out on raids with only a few left to guard. But he says we may not find all the captives living.

The man slides down on the floor in one corner and holds his head in his hands.

Matt goes and sits down beside him. He puts his arm round him and runs his fingers through his hair.

'What are you going to do with us now?' says one of the soldiers.

'We are no use to them any more,' says the second.

The third says nothing.

I think they are going to make a run for it but they don't. I expect they haven't the nerve left after their fight.

The man gets up from the floor and leads us out of the room, locking it up after him.

'We'll take them out tonight and leave them in the middle of somewhere to get back to wherever,' he says. 'If some villagers

get them before they can get to their friends it's their bad luck.
I can do no more.'

On our way to the caves Matt stops again.

'What now?' I say in my moaniest voice.

'Can I go and let the snakes out, please?' says Matt to the man.

The man don't know whether to be angry or amused.

'Oh all right,' he says, 'but don't go on your own.'

He makes a sound like a dove and suddenly from behind the
bushes or from inside the caves – I'm not sure which, it happens
so fast – four or five men come out and walk towards us. They
are wearing blue shirts and blue jeans.

To our left I hear a scuffle and many shouts.

It is Hena running towards us, followed by two men. They slow
down when they see us and let her join us.

'She's quite a fighter, that little girl of yours,' one of the men says
when they get near us.

It seems they've all been kicked good and hard and bitten deep
and sharp by our Hena.

The man who brought us in the jeep has actually gone to put
some sticky plaster on one of his bites. She drew blood from
round his neck and he don't want it to get all over his shirt.

The man in the white robe says to two of the men, 'Take these
kids to the... that shack. Let them in. Here are the keys. Let
them take the snake boxes out, but see the prisoners don't
escape. OK?'

He winks at us sadly.

We start walking with the two men to the stone room. Hena
comes along with us.

We've just reached the door of the stone room when we hear this roar, getting louder by the breath.

Before we know it, it swoops down on us. There is one bang, then two more. Then fire and smoke and dust.

Hena, Matt and I fall on the ground, but the men remain standing; stunned.

Our eyes see the dust and the sand stretching out in front of us. Some of it is red. It is red where we left the man in the white robe and some of his friends standing. The man's white robe is red too.

We want to get back to our feet but can't and then can.

One of the men has rushed to his friends. The other is still standing there muttering something about the white man's radio, over and over again.

The blast has blown away the door of the stone room. The soldiers are crouching in one corner, looking up in panic.

I don't truly remember paying attention to any of it, but still I remember it. I don't know how or why.

The soldiers have by now realised what has happened. Their shock turns to joy. They run out shouting happily. I remember seeing their wobbling bottoms.

Both the men who came with us are now kneeling by the bodies of their friends and their leader. The man we helped to live once; and now helped to die.

His name was... is Kabir. We never knew it when he lived.

The bombs have brought the stone wall of another building down. Out of it come the white folk. They take one look about the place, then run out, straight towards the jeep.

They get into it and drive away. All except Alberto who has seen us and walks towards us, waving to the others to go on without him.

By now some other people have come out of the buildings or the caves, but no one does anything to stop the white folk nor says anything to us.

Matt goes into the stone room, picks up the boxes one by one, brings them out and lets the snakes go. He thanks them for saving his life, and saving my life, and saving the life of the two men who came with us.

Five

Golam's Cow

Alberto and Hena and Matt and I walk back to the village. I don't know how we find the way back, but we do. It takes a long time on account we don't walk too fast and we wander a bit.

By the time we get back the shadows are long again and getting longer.

The white folk are already there and waiting for Alberto. Another white man has come from Gonta in the van to take the white folk back. He knows nothing of what has happened and is listening with great interest. We listen too.

It seems the guerrillas wanted to hold the white folk hostages – whatever that means – to make the Government of the white folk speak to the guerrillas about giving them some help instead of helping our Government, which is a bad Government.

I don't think I understand all of it, but I understand quite a lot.

But all that is past now.

At least for the time being.

The white folk think other guerrillas here and elsewhere might try even harder now to hit at the Government and its friends on account some of their friends are dead, and so is one of their leaders. A good leader, from what we hear. Even the white folk know of Kabir and are sorry that he is dead. They think it'll only make matters worse.

All our people have heard the planes and the bombs and are crowding round us for information. We tell our story to one and then have to start all over again for another. Sometimes even if he – or she – has heard it already.

While we are in this confusion Golam's Mam comes over, all anxious, and asks where Golam is and where we have hidden Kato. Kato is their cow.

Now we have no idea where Golam is, much less Kato. In actual fact we were thinking of going over to Golam's Mam to ask her where Golam is. For usually when we are out somewhere and Golam is not with us, he sits and waits for us by our little tree by our little hill. And today we don't see him there.

If it wasn't for the mad rush of white folk coming from the guerrillas and white folk coming from Gonta and all wanting to know what's been going on and we in the middle of it all, we'd have been looking for Golam ourselves by now.

When we tell this to Golam's Mam she at first looks at us like she don't believe us. Then she looks at us like she believes us. Then she falls in a faint on the sand.

Alberto says it is hunger, but my Dada says it must be worry for he took her a bowl of grain only this morning. Grandma

Toughtits asks if he saw her eat it as she saves every bit she can for Golam and the cow and don't eat herself.

We're still not sure what it's all about when Leku explains.

'Mino,' he says – Mino is the name of Golam's Mam – 'Mino agreed to sell Kato to Fakeer for a bag of grain. It is not a good bargain for the cow is worth more but she agreed as it will save her feeding Kato. She don't like it but she feels she has no choice. When Golam hears of it his heart breaks.'

You can imagine that for Golam loves Kato like his own sister.

Leku carries on: 'He nearly dies when he finds out Fakeer plans to kill the cow and sell it as meat in Gonta. He is doubly angry that Fakeer should take advantage of his Mam when he too is a Muslim like them and should be kinder. At least offer more grain and look after the cow rather than buy it for less and kill it for meat.

'So Golam has a big row with his Mam and also shouts at Fakeer.

'His Mam leaves him to cool off. When she looks for him later she cannot find him. Nor can she find the cow. So she comes looking for Matt and you and me. I tell her you're not in the village. This calms her down for she trusts Matt, and even you, and thinks you will stop Golam from doing anything silly.

'Naturally when she hears you're back she comes running round to get news of Golam and Kato. She thinks you have gone to hide Kato somewhere safe.

'She's decided not to sell Kato after all and has been telling me and other children in the village so they pass the message on to Golam and you lot so Golam comes back and brings Kato with him.'

Now we're as worried as Mino. Perhaps not as much as Mino,

but very worried and no doubt about it.

The white folk say they'll take us in their jeep to look for Golam, which is very kind of them, while Grandma and Mam take care of Mino.

Matt thinks Golam must have gone towards the woods, for that's where he can hide Kato as well as have some grass and shrubs to feed her with.

It don't take us long to get to the woods on the jeep, but once there we have to be on foot. The jeep can't go any further even though the woods have thinned out a lot, what with no rain and the people cutting more wood than ever before. The trees nearby are not heavy with branches in the dry season anyway, but these days are worse than usual on account they've been cut right down.

Once in the woods it's not easy finding anyone.

We don't tell the white folk that there may be guerrillas hiding in the woods as well. I don't think they'll like being taken again – though our worry for the moment is about Golam and our sorrow for Kabir and his friends. We're not thinking much of the white folk even if we are happy for their help.

We look as deep into the woods as we can but no sign of Golam. Both Matt and me keep shouting for Golam, but no sound from him.

As the light goes we decide it'll be useless to carry on.

Too worried to think properly we come out of the woods and start driving round and round in the open plains.

It is beginning to get bright again as the moon's come up, but we see nothing of Golam.

The white folk think it's time we went back. They think maybe Golan's come back home by now.

Matt says maybe he didn't come this way at all but went towards the mountains thinking we went there looking for the white folk. We all say that's what must've happened. It seems obvious now but didn't even cross our minds at first. I am really angry at myself for not having thought of it before and Matt feels the same. We were only thinking of the woods being the best place to hide the cow. We didn't think of Golam wanting our help. That's the first thing we ought to have thought of!

We're driving fast now to get to the village, find out if Golam's back, and if not to try the other side.

We're really thankful to the white folk for agreeing to take all this trouble.

We're in such a hurry to get back that we're not even looking for Golam when we see in front of us what looks like any other bush.

Only it moves. We turn towards it and stop. It's Golam.

He's hurt so bad he can hardly move or speak.

As he was taking Kato to the woods this morning he was attacked by some people – he don't know who they are. They take Kato away from him. When he tries to get her back they beat him up and leave, taking Kato with them.

Golam don't want to go back home. He just wants to lie down and die.

The white folk make some pictures of him with their magic light on the cameras. Then they put him on the jeep and we start back.

Matt holds Golam in his arms.

We thank the Spirits of the Night for the dark that hides the shame and sorrow of our faces.

We pray the white folk don't make pictures of us.

When we get home the white folk make some more pictures. Matt and I try to hide our faces but they are too quick for us.

As it turns out Golam is not badly hurt at all.

A few days later Alberto comes to see us. He brings with him some of the pictures they made the other day.

In the pictures of Golam made where we found him he has deep cuts and wounds, while in those made a short while later in the village there are just small cuts and bruises.

Part III

HENA THE WHORE

(one year later)

One

The Last Dance

The missionary bloke packed up and left soon after the air attack on the guerrillas and the taking away of Golam's cow, without ever showing us his balls or even so much as mentioning them in passing.

He's taken his miserable wife with him which is good for us but may not be so good for him. It's best for her though. Matt says she must've hated it here, poor thing, though she never said it. There was no one she could really talk to and nothing she could do that she wanted.

But that's in the past. Maybe a year ago.

Many things have changed since then, but I reckon you'll find them out as we go along.

Our little tree by our little hill is now a little black stump; but I don't think that bit of information is of much use to anyone.

Some of the villagers are happy today and some are sad. I think it's the same ones who get happy who get sad. The others don't seem to feel much these days, one way or another.

Except perhaps today, when I've seen a look in some eyes where I hadn't seen a look for a long time.

A look which shows they know what's going on. A look which shows they may even care what's going on.

Grandma Toughtits is dancing her last dance today.

She has been poorly for the last many months. She don't eat hardly at all these days. She says she isn't hungry but I think she don't eat so big sister and I can eat a bit more. She's been like that since little brother went.

She is so poorly she can hardly walk, but she is dancing tonight. Dancing for the Spirits and hoping they will take her away while she's dancing.

Grandma says it's because we've stopped singing and dancing for the Spirits that our troubles have started.

I reckon she's right.

We don't talk much to the Spirits since Matt turned to Jesus.

Leku never believed in them and Golam's not supposed to.

Hena don't talk much unless she is spoken to, Spirits or no Spirits.

Ever since her Dada died, after his fields turned to dust and his things sold or gone, Hena don't talk much at all.

She's still proud and would rather go bare-headed and cold than put on a torn shawl, but it don't help her any when it comes to food. She's got to eat, like the rest of us; and when she hasn't got any to eat, like the rest of us, she feels hunger, like the rest of us – pride or no pride.

She still don't talk much to the Spirits. Neither do many other villagers who have already left the Spirits for Jesus or Mohammed – and that's what's brought on the troubles, says Grandma Toughtits. So she's dancing tonight and laying down her body for the Spirits to take away in return for some rain for the people.

Grandma Toughtits looks beautiful as the winter night. The beads in her hair shine as the stars.

She wears this black silk scarf round her hips. The black silk scarf that was a present from Grandpa Biglumps. A present she's guarded all these years in his memory.

He was swallowed by a crocodile ten days after their marriage when he fell off a tree into the river. At the time he was quietly watching the young girls bathe by the bank, doing no harm to anyone. Least of all the crocodiles. But what's to be is to be.

There is hardly any water in the river now, no crocodiles and no trees.

*

The wrinkles in the fine silk are pretty, but not half as pretty as the wrinkles in Grandma's skin. They are the finest of lines drawn through to her very bones, as there's no flesh in between. Lines drawn by the Great Spirit of Time, the truest picture-maker of all picture-makers.

Her large eyes are larger than ever, her magic hands are more magical than ever. She puts on her head this wonderful hat that

Joti brought her and throws away her shawl.

The fresh oil shines on her body like the light of love in a cow's eyes when she's just given birth.

She starts to dance and we wonder in silence and sorrow and pride how she can dance now when she could hardly walk last night.

All the village is out but no one is dancing. They are not even moving much. Just gathered round in silence watching Grandma Pearl dance.

The school Master's father, who's as old as Grandma Pearl herself, sits cross-legged on the sand and stares at Grandma Pearl without so much as blinking.

He has the best voice in the village but he hasn't sung since his son left for Bader taking his wife and children with him.

The old man left all on his own sits cross-legged on the sand and stares at Grandma Pearl. He's loved her all his life, but she won't have him for she's living with the Spirit of Grandpa in her heart. The old man sits cross-legged on the sand and stares at Grandma Pearl without so much as blinking.

His eyes are as glazed cooking pots that've stood without food or fare since they were made, stood in the shop without a buyer. But his body is the cooking pot that has been stepped upon by an angry horse.

He starts to sing.

His voice is still the voice of a young lover. But his singing has the sorrow of many deaths and many births.

Between him and Grandma Pearl they've seen enough children born to fill many villages; and enough children die to fill many villages. And grown-ups too. But the hurt of those who stop loving you is worse than the hurt of those who leave you – in death or in life. The hurt of those who never love you is the worst of all.

The old man sings of all these things in his songs. I understand some of it. I don't understand some of it. But I like all of it.

No one plays the drums. No one plays the flute. No one dances. Everyone watches and listens as Grandma Pearl dances and the old man sings.

The old man everyone calls the old man for he's been like an old man since Grandma Pearl married Grandpa all those seasons ago. All those seasons ago when the inside of the river was full of water and crocodiles; and its outside covered with trees and young girls bathing. Young girls who lived and died as young girls; or grew up to be old and beautiful, like Grandma Pearl.

The sun hides its face in the shawl of the evening, but Grandma Pearl still dances and the old man still sings.

The evening takes the sun with her to sleep with for the night, but Grandma Pearl still dances and the old man still sings.

Morning, the first born sister of the evening, brings the sun back out with her to dance with the day, but Grandma Pearl continues with her own dance while the old man sings.

Grandma Pearl stops dancing and the old man stops singing at the same time. Their bodies lie in the centre of the village.

Grandma Pearl wishes to lie there till the rains come. She wishes her last bath to be a rain bath.

No one knows what the old man wants but they let him lie next to Grandma.

There is always someone nearby to keep the animals and the birds away.

Two

The First Rain

All day there are groups of people making a circle round Grandma Pearl and the old man. They are letting out their grief in weeping or singing or dancing, or just by talking.

The people keep changing but the groups remain.

It is the third day since Grandma Pearl and the old man lay down in the centre of the village, tired of dancing and singing and living.

Everyone is sure their Spirits are now ready to be with the Spirits of their old and young gone before them.

It is decided that all will go to their homes and find a little gift to bring and lay down by their side, so the Spirits of the gifts go along with them. For them as well as for those they go to meet.

It don't matter if the things are old or broken. When their Spirits rise they will be whole and new again with the love of the givers, and make truly wonderful gifts.

Some bring their shawls. Mam brings Grandma Pearl's own bread plate and puts a pearl of grain on it. Others bring little toys of clay, beads, scarves, even an old shoe.

Matt leaves his big round clock that Hena gave him and which he never parts with. Hena gives her battery radio. It don't work but it's still a battery radio.

I draw my best picture of a tree on my school slate and leave it next to Grandma Pearl on account she's the Spirit of a tree, like all our family.

But the best gift is of the old man for he's laid himself down by her side.

Everyone takes care to bring something special for him.

We make sure that his son's picture which the white folk made is there beside him, under his grain bowl.

It's mine and Matt's turn to stay by Grandma and the old man.

When we get there we find Hena and Leku parked on a big stone they've dragged from the nearby rocks.

Hena don't say, 'You took your time coming, didn't you?'

It used to get on my nerves so, but now she don't say it I wish she did.

Leku is telling her his family has been asked by some folks they never knew or heard of to go and live with them in the country to the south of us. A rich country full of green fields and big cities. He says those people will make all the arrangements to get them there. We all feel very jealous of him but we all tell them we are very happy for him which is not a lie either.

He says they are doing so on account they share the same faith.

Matt says that's how it should be. Hena nods her head and I agree with them though the reason don't mean much to me.

But the talk of faith makes me remember the missionary bloke. I wonder if he is right that the Spirit of Grandma will be lost in 'eternal darkness', or go to 'hell', or worst of all, to Pasadena, California, USA. That's where the missionary bloke had run out from, and where he said was 'rife with carnal sin and mortal evil'. Whatever that means, I don't like the sound of it at all. Especially the way the missionary bloke spoke of it made me truly scared. My heart is heavy and my eyes are heavy and I can hardly see Grandma lying there so helpless.

I can't say it's right and I can't say it's wrong. I know that's what she wants but I also know she won't let anyone else lie around like that.

There's hardly nothing left of her tough tits but a little mark like a cigarette burn on a crumpled dead leaf.

Perhaps that's how a tree dies.

She was the most alive person I knew. The only thing alive about her now is the black silk scarf that dances in the wind and the beads in her hair that shine in the sun.

I want to speak my thoughts to Leku but I can't on account he'll tell me to be practical and sensible and to pull myself together.

I want to speak my thoughts to Hena but I can't on account she'll look at me with sad eyes or angry eyes or strange eyes.

I want to speak my thoughts to Matt but I can't on account he'll hold my heart in his hands and squeeze gently till all the pain goes – and I'm not ready for it yet.

I want to speak my thoughts to Golam but I can't on account he's not here. Ever since his cow was lost and his Mam's mind began to wander he has to stay home most of the time looking after her and to stop her body from wandering away with her mind.

Not many days ago we spent a whole day searching before we found her hiding in the big hole in the ground, the big hole that was once the oven in which we used to bake flat bread for village festivals. In fact *we* didn't find her. It was the village dogs that did.

They are all bony and mean and angry these days, barking at the least little thing. Even at people they loved before.

It is late in the night. A moonless night. We are all tired from looking all over the place the whole day long. Up to the woods on one side and to the Dry Hill on the other. But no sign of Golam's Mam.

Then we hear all this barking.

It goes on in an untidy chorus, so loud and on and on that we pay attention to it even though we've stopped paying attention to it. We wonder if something is the matter with the dogs, more than just hunger, for we know when their hunger gets worse they stop barking – except now and then in a tired sort of way – till it's time for them to go when they whine and cough a bit.

With the wind going round in mad circles it takes us a while to find where all the noise is coming from.

Then we see all these dogs. Hundreds it seems but truly no more than twenty. Maybe twenty-five.

They are gathered round this oven which is more or less all caved in now it's no longer needed.

Our first thought is maybe there's still some old bread in it and we wish we'd got there before the dogs. But then we're ashamed for thinking so for the dogs have to find some food too.

*

When they see us coming the dogs start moving back, baring their teeth and growling. They're no longer our friends now that we don't feed them any more.

It is only when their barking turns to a sort of low snarling that we hear another shrill barking noise coming out from inside the hole.

We think maybe one of the dogs has fallen in and that's why they're all gathered round making all this rumpus.

Our elders tell us to pick up a few sticks and stones just in case the dogs attack us. Matt don't but the rest of us do. Those who can find anything, that is.

The dogs move back though not away. They keep going forward in ones and twos, and then going back again.

By now we've moved close to the edge of the hole.

Before anyone can be sure what or who it is, Matt puts his hand over Golam's eyes and pushes him backwards.

This makes me even more curious. I rush up and see that it's Golam's Mam.

She's on all fours, dog-like, barking away, baring her teeth and snarling. She is all naked; her hands and feet cut and bloody – as is the rest of her body – hair covered in sand and dirt, eyes flashing like on fire.

She don't listen to no one when called. She can hear – we can tell by the way she jerks her head and ears to one side – but she don't answer. When one or two try to get her out she bites and claws with power known only to the unknown Spirit of the unknown beast.

Everyone stands around wondering what to do.

We're quiet and silent, not moving much, only thinking. This makes the dogs bolder.

They start barking louder and snarling uglier and begin to close in on us.

Suddenly they are all around us.

One of us throws a stone. Another rushes waving a stick shouting in a screaming cracked voice. A battle starts between folk and dogs. One younger one kicks out at one of the big dogs who snaps at his leg and holds on to it, sinking its teeth in. He screams to scare the night away but the night don't go that easy. The dog neither. Other dogs want their share of the young man's body. They fall on him, but cannot get their teeth properly into him like the big dog. Folk start pulling the young man which only makes the dog's teeth cut deeper into his leg. He screams louder. The dogs bark louder. Everyone is talking and shouting and pulling and kicking. Most people have lost their sticks in the night after throwing them at the dogs. In some cases the dogs have snatched the sticks away from the people.

There aren't many more sticks or stones in the dry sand and people are getting sort of scared.

The barking and snarling of Golam's Mam in the hole is becoming more human, more like a hiccuppy laugh. This makes it worse. This also makes Golam know, for the first time, that it's his Mam down there.

He cries, struggles and shoots out of Matt's arms, who's already having difficulty keeping him back.

I've been standing in one place without moving. I've been thinking I can't move if I try.

But I move like the Spirit of the Wind and put my arms round Golam and hold him down. I haven't grown as big and strong as Mam said. In fact my arms and legs are thinner than they were a year ago when the outsiders came and Kabir was killed. But I'm still bigger than Golam on account he's shrivelled more than me. And he weren't as big as me to start off, as you well know. So I am able to hold Golam down.

As I do so Matt pulls off his shawl and with the lighter he got off Hena he sets it on fire. Using a stick he waves it about.

The dog who has got his teeth into the young man's leg lets go and runs back. So do the other dogs.

The men and women try to chase them but Matt stands in front of them. They sort of calm down and stay back.

Now Matt turns towards the dogs and starts talking to them.

He tells them we are sorry we can't feed them on account we have no food for ourselves. He asks them to forgive us and tells them how truly grateful we are to them for having looked after our fields when we had fields to look after.

He tells them our Spirit shares the pain of their Spirit as our body shares the hunger of their body.

The dogs stop barking and they stop growling and they stop snarling. They whimper a little but that's the only sound they make. They sit on their backsides with their front legs straight and listen to Matt.

All the village folk also listen to Matt even though he is talking to the dogs.

Now the only barking we hear is Golam's Mam barking away in the hole.

Her throat is sore now and the cold has got to her naked body so her bark is gruff and sniffly. It's not much human any more.

Matt stops his talk to the dogs and looks round straight at Hena. He stands silent for a while, then says, 'Go to Golam's Mam and bring her up. She'll be all right.'

Hena looks back at him, saying nothing doing nothing. She's not used to being told what to do. By Matt or no one.

Matt says, 'Please.'

Quietly Hena moves out of the crowd and goes to the mouth of the hole and jumps in.

Matt turns to the dogs again and starts talking again.

People forget about him and turn to see what happens to Hena. They think Golam's Mam will tear her to bits.

But when they get to the hole they see Hena holding Mino in her arms like she is a little baby.

Hena is running her fingers through Mino's gritty bloody hair and singing a baby song.

I let go of Golam. He falls on the ground, sobbing, without bothering to hide his face.

I am happy the white folk aren't here to make a picture of us.

Matt is so long talking to the dogs and they seem so interested in what he's saying we don't want to disturb any of them. We all decide to take Golam's Mam home. She is all shivering and helpless. I take Golam's hand in mine. Hena and her Mam carry Mino. The rest of the folk follow.

I turn to look back at Matt. He's still talking to the dogs. I hear a strange voice in his voice.

The wind is stronger and madder. We hear it scream and feel it whirl. Round and round in angry tightening circles, coiling upwards but going nowhere, like the spreading desert and scatters it in our eyes and down our throats. We choke on our way home, half blind half dead.

Mino's mind is better since. We'd expected her to lose it. Her wounds are healed. But Golam don't leave her alone any more and stays home all the time. Except when we go round so he can go out, like for a shit, or to look for some grain or grass or water. So we sit by Grandma Pearl and the old man on our own, without Golam.

We don't see the dogs in the village any more.

The air don't seem as clear or as bright any more.

The sun don't seem as sharp.

We think it's just the heat haze.

But it keeps getting less bright till it is downright dull.

It is then we look up and see the soft silvery clouds.

The wind starts dropping.

Soon it is still as a dead man's heart.

It gets darker and darker. Now it is night during the day. A strange shiny sort of night.

Everyone has stopped doing what they are doing and left their homes or wherever and are coming out to look up at the sky in fear and wonder and hope.

Suddenly the silver-black sky splits in a zig-zaggy crack of sharp light. Splits, cracks, and falls with the loudest rolls that living ears ever heard.

Falls in solid drops of mucky white ice.

Lightning and thunder and hail.

And after that, rain.

It rains for three days and three nights.

When it is over every little bit of crop or grain in our fields is washed away.

Even the good earth is gone, leaving rocks or sand underneath.

Golam's Mam is missing and big sister is showing signs such as little brother showed before he went.

We bury Grandma Pearl by the bank of the river near the spot where Grandpa was eaten by a crocodile.

We don't know whether to put the old man by her side or not, on account we're not sure what is right.

In the end we make a half-way arrangement. We bury the old man near Grandma, but not too close.

We can't find Mino this time.

We think she's fallen into the river and got carried away by the fast shallow waters.

We've enough water now.

*

We're lying in our homes. It is the middle of the day but we're in our homes trying to sleep on account we haven't slept much during the last four days.

We hear this roar above our heads.

Mam and Dada wonder what it is. I know at once what it is.

It is planes coming our way.

I tell Mam and Dada.

We go outside.

The rest of the village is out too.

The planes draw nearer.

They swoop low to drop their bombs.

Some of us run, some lie down.

Some hold on to their children, some crouch over them.

Some stay standing, silent. So do their children.

The planes slow down.

We see bombs falling out.

They are bigger than I ever imagined. And slower.

They float through the air.

They dangle above our heads.

There are many of them.

I wonder why there are so many of them.

They dropped only three for the guerrillas.

Why should they waste so many for a group of useless people?

One of the bombs falls not far from where we stand. It don't go boom. It don't go red. It don't turn to fire. It don't kill.

It just lies there like a large hessian sack.

It is a large hessian sack.

Another one falls with a dull heavy thud. Then another.

They are all large hessian sacks.

They are followed by two men falling out of the skies with a little sky of their own.

Leku tells us it is a parachute.

The men explain to us they know the rains have washed away the crops of many villages. They have some food and some medicines and some blankets given by some helping agencies. As the roads are flooded they are throwing 'supplies' from the air to as many villages as they can.

They also send one nurse down to see if there are any sick. They also send a reporter from the white world. Although he is from the white world he is black, which confuses us.

*

We all gather in the schoolhouse to store the food and to share some of it out. More important, we gather to make some plan for the future.

We are very happy now but we also wonder what will happen when the food runs out.

'If we don't have enough coming out of the land through the Spirit of the Earth, what falls on land through flesh and steel cannot last for ever,' says Ebono in his sad slow voice.

Ebono is the village poet. He sings songs and tells stories. He has taken over the running of the school now that our Master has gone. Everyone don't often agree with him on account everyone don't often understand what he says. But everyone agrees with him this time.

It is decided to put some grain away for seeds and to look for places near the river bed, or by the old graveyard, or some low areas where the good soil might've gathered, to make new fields.

It is also said that we might let some of the younger ones go to the city to look for food or work. Like Joti and the school Master did.

Most people are sad at this new idea but they also agree it is better that some of us leave now than for all to be forced out later in search of camps where the hungry gather.

Golam says he'll go on account there's no one to worry for him. My Dada tells him we all worry for him, and he's too young anyway.

I say I'll go on account Joti's my cousin and he promised he'll help me out if ever I get to Bader.
Some people say it makes sense, some say I am too young.
'But I'm only a little younger than Joti when he went; and look how well he did for himself,' I say.
Matt says Golam, me and him should all go together as we've been out before and know how to look after ourselves. Which is true enough and everyone knows it.
Leku don't want to go as he and his family have other plans.
Oteng wants to go.
Mustapha wants to go.
Tony wants to go.
There are others who want time to think.
Many more don't want to leave their homes and their families.
Mam cries and Dada sighs but they decide to let me go and look for Joti. They tell me only to look for Joti and then do as he tells me to.
And to come straight back if I can't find him.
Golam is allowed to come with me.
Matt says he will come too and very glad I am of that. Matt's Dada lets him do what he wants.

Since we are going to Bader to look for Joti some others decide to go south to Bandugo. They say it's best not to depend too much on one place or to put too much burden on Joti.

The black reporter from the white man's world says as soon as the roads are dry he'll radio for a jeep to come and pick them up. Him and the black nurse from Gonta. He says some of us can go up to Gonta with them, and then travel to wherever we want to go, however we can manage.

Just as we are about to leave, taking our share of food with us, Hena stands up and says she too will go to the big city. She says she is going to make up for all her Dada lost. She says she wants to make enough not just for herself and her Mam but for all the folk in the village.

She looks at Matt and me and Golam. She says she's happy to go along with us, but if we don't want to take her she'll go on her own.

She looks so thin and brittle that no one dares to argue with her. It is difficult to argue with bones.

She looks so strong and intense that no one dares to argue with her. It is difficult to argue with eyes.

Matt says we'll be pleased to have her come with us if her Mam don't object.

Her Mam says nothing, just hides her face in her shawl.

The black reporter from the white world makes another picture.

Three

Stealing the City

Our farewells are still in our hearts, our village is still in our eyes, our little food bags are under our arms.

Joti's photo and address is in my pocket.

Our dreams are in our minds. Our fears are all around us.

We stand in Gonta.

It is strange. It is like we've never been here before.

It is no longer like a big village; it is more like a big town.

The village centre – where the fair was held – is now full of little brick buildings, like shoe boxes. This is where the sick are kept and given medicine. The outside of the village – where the Spirit Dance was danced – is full of tent-like huts. This is where the hungry live. When they are not spread out in the open like mouldy logs of wood.

This is where the hungry lie. To die.

Little and not so little children are sitting or standing or limping about everywhere. Their arms and legs are made of bent and dried twigs of dead trees. Their hands and feet are crow claws. Their chest and bellies are not quite joined together. Their faces are the faces of old men and women long dead. Their lips hang loose, their eyes bulge.

*

They make very good pictures. The black reporter from the white world shows me my first ever white people's newspapers and magazines. The pictures of the children we see in front of us are the pictures of the children we see in front of us.

We're told these people are from the north-east where the food and war situation is the worst in the country.

Till it's time for us to start for Bader, Matt spends all his time with the little children. Hena spends her time with her parents. Golam and I run errands and do little jobs for the doctors and nurses and reporters and anybody else who wants anything done.

The two white doctors in Gonta don't think we should be going to Bader on our own. They say it is a big city and we will get into trouble and end up worse than at home.

We tell them we have a cousin there who's doing very well for himself and who will look after us.

The black reporter from the white man's world backs us up saying he's met our parents and knows we tell the truth.

We show them Joti's picture next to the big car in front of the big house. And we show them his name and address.

They say we should not try to walk it or 'do anything silly like that'. They say they'll buy us a ticket each and put us on the next bus to Bader whenever it comes.

The white folk say it is a broken-down rotten old bus, filthy and unsafe; but I'm truly thrilled at the thought of travelling on it. So much so that I nearly forget my worries and my sadness and my fears and think of my hopes.

Golam comes running across the open stretch between the tents and the brick buildings, nearly tripping on the bodies rolled up log-like in dirty white sheets.

A bald boy, with sores on his head where you and I have hair, looks up in true surprise at Golam as he jumps over him. The boy, who is as long as I am tall, lies on the same spot since the day we came.

Only his eyes move.

The white doctor and her golden assistant tell me he is hoping to join the rest of his family soon.

'The bus is coming,' shouts Golam, running and flashing a smile. I haven't seen him smile like that in a long time.

His teeth are not as glinty white as I remember them in my mind's eye.

As he runs his hair don't bounce much either.

I suppose that's what happens when you get old. Not true old, like Grandma Toughtits. You grow a new kind of beauty then. But sort of in-between old, like thirteen.

'The bus is coming. The bus is coming,' shouts Golam.

'Are you sure?' I say.

Golam is never sure of anything. He was always like that, even as a child. He's been much worse recently. I'm sure he'd get confused if you asked his name twice and then added, 'Are you sure?'

Of course I didn't mean to do that.

I only said 'Are you sure?' like one says 'Are you sure?' without thinking too much about it.

His chest is going up and down and he's not breathing regular. I don't think he's run for some time and his body's having problems dealing with it. His stomach is jumping up and down like a chicken with its throat cut.

I feel a strange sick feeling in my own stomach when I see him like this.

I see him lying down like the bald boy with the sore-covered head waiting to join his family.

I shake the sight out of my eyes.

'What's the matter with you?' says Golam, forgetting about the bus and looking at me with worried eyes.

'Nothing,' I say, 'I'm all right.'

'Are you sure?' asks Golam.

It makes me smile. 'Sure I am sure. Where is the bus?'

'Can you see that dust over there?' Matt says, pointing far away towards our village. 'That's the bus.'

'Let's get our things sorted out,' says Hena, practical as ever.

I begin to feel easy again. I'd started to think Hena and Matt might want to stay on in Gonta, the way they were busy with the folk in the camps.

Our things are a bag of food each, a leather bottle of water each, an extra shawl each, and a box of pills each.

The white doctor gave us the pills the very first day we got here.

She also gave us two injections per person, one on each buttock.

My backside hurts when I think of the jabs.

The golden assistant is by our side now.

'What are you all so excited about?' he says.

'The bus is coming,' says Golam.

He's flashing his teeth again. They're still not quite right. But his breathing is better.

The golden assistant behaves in a very peculiar manner.

He starts shouting and hollering and waving his arm about and calling, 'Boota, Karo, Omu – Boota, Omu Karo...'

Two of our countrymen come running towards us, one from inside the buildings and the other from the camp-site.

'The bus is coming,' shouts the golden assistant, looking urgently at them.

They look at him kind of strange.

We look at him kind of strange.

'The bus is coming,' says the golden assistant again. Then adds, 'These kids have to be on it.'

The moment he says this the others start behaving in the same excited manner.

'OK boss,' they say, 'we'll get on our way and you bring them along.'

They run towards the rising dust of the approaching bus, faster than they'd come.

By now the white doctor is here.

'What on earth is going on?' says she.

'The bus is coming,' says the golden assistant.

It is the doctor's turn to look at him strange. Then she sees us.

Now it's her turn to get excited. Only not so much as the others. Even so, it makes me wonder.

'Have the children got their vitamins?' she asks.
'Yes, Madam Doctor, thank you,' says Hena.
'Food. Have they got enough food?' says the doctor, now looking into our bags.
She feels the food and sniffs it like a cat. Then she throws some powder into our water bottles and gives them a good shake.
She stands with her hands on her hips and thinks.
'Here,' she says at last, 'here is some money.' She holds out some money.
We don't know what to do with it.
'Take it,' she says. 'You will need it when you get to Bader. It isn't much but it will do you till you can find your cousin.' Hena takes the money, looks at it for a long time, then folds it and tucks it into her blouse.
The golden assistant takes Hena's hand in one hand and Golam's hand in his other hand and says to all of us, 'Come on, I'll take you to the bus.' Matt and I walk behind him.
On our way we pass the bald boy. His eyes are more open than before but they don't move any more. Nor blink when flies bite into them.

We soon find out why the grown-ups are so excited about the bus when we get to the other side of the camp, outside the little wooden shack where canisters of petrol and water are kept. This is where the bus stops. There is a whole crowd of people waiting there. The bus finally appears, making its way with some difficulty through its own dust.

It is full with people inside. There are people sitting on the roof. The doorless entrance at the back is blocked with people. There are people clinging to the side of the bus.

Before the bus can come to a stop everybody runs towards it like a herd of thirsty cattle towards the water-hole.

A sort of battle starts between people wanting to get off and people wanting to get on.

No one is actually trying to hurt another, but then no one is actually thinking of another.

Many of those struggling to get off are in trouble as they are sick or bringing their sick children to Gonta in the hope of white man's cure.

A tall man forcing his way out of the bus gets his head caught in the robe of another man trying to climb over everyone else to get on the bus. The tall man don't enjoy his face being rubbed against the other man's doodas and flails his arms about to free himself. As he does so the other's robe is ripped apart showing one surprised ass sitting on one surprised head. The face hanging under the head is being tickled by the parts hanging under the ass.

There is a scream of pain from the man with the robe torn from the crack of his ass down. He claims he has been bitten by the other, who screams back calling him a liar. By now they are face to face instead of face to dingus, the one on top having slid down the other's head. He reaches for the throat of the tall man. There is a great hoo ha and soon they are grappling with one another, rolling on the sand as they fall. They are shouting and swearing something awful. The one with his ass framed in the ripped robe is on top getting an extra tan where he don't need it even less than anywhere else.

As some gather round to watch the display, the other get a chance to get on the bus somewhat easier.

The men on the roof are looking down with no particular look on their faces.

The two men sent by the golden assistant have got on the bus through the door by the driver's seat. He lets them in, then quickly locks the door after them.

Once in, one of them looks around for an empty seat, finds one and stands guard by it. The other leans out of an open window and yells out to us. We rush to him and he yanks us up, one by one, and pulls us in through the window.

The four of us are made to sit on this seat meant for two, which is not easy with our bags even though there isn't much meat on any of us. One of the men gives us our tickets.

We say our thank yous to the two men and they leave the same way they came.

When everyone who can get in, gets in, the driver and his helper get out of the bus, stretch their legs, look at the engine, get petrol and water for the bus, and some tea for themselves.

There is a bad smell inside which is not just people smell, but sick and shit smell.

We can also see sick and shit.

As a matter of fact we are sitting on some. And there is some under our feet.

By now we're all so packed in we cannot get out or even stand up properly without being crushed down by other people.

Hena looks so upset that I think that she's going to add her sick to what's already there.

I almost begin to cry. I wish I was home.

Golam looks like he's about to faint.

Matt tears off part of his shawl and tries to clean the place up a bit.

Hena seems to take control of her feelings and helps him.

I think we might have been better off walking, but Hena – back to her practical self again – says it's too far and through deserts and dry rocks that burn during the day and freeze at night and that we are lucky to be going on the bus.

I still wish I was out of there and maybe back home.

I say my thoughts.

Matt says nothing.

Matt hasn't said much at all during the last few days. That is strange for Matt. He also looks strange.

I'm beginning to worry for him.

It seems like hours before the driver and his helper get back on the bus.

We think the bus is going to start after all, but it don't.

Then it does. Then it don't. Then it does. Splurts and coughs and jumps and dances and moves and stops again. Hiccups and moves again. Hiccups and moves again. Moves until it's on its way at long last.

Hena is sitting by the window so she's better off, but the sun is coming through that side and soon she'll be boiling. Matt and Golam are in the middle and badly squashed. I am on the inside edge of the seat and half falling off. My ear's stuck firmly in someone's bum.

Then I turn to see who it is, my nose goes up him. I'd rather it was my ear so I turn my head towards Golam again, who's next to me. His body next to mine don't bother me any more.

There's an old man sitting in front of us. He'd been turning round to look at us when we were cleaning up the floor, throwing the mess out of the window on Hena's side.

When the bus is safely out of Gonta the old man turns round again.

Only this time he don't just look, he speaks.

He speaks in a strong voice. It is not the voice of an old man.

'Count yourselves fortunate,' he says in his strong voice, 'you sit on the shit of the blessed.'

'What does he mean "blessed"?' says Golam softly in my ear.

'Perhaps he means the poor,' I say, remembering our missionary bloke who used to say something about 'blessed are the poor'.

'Why should the shit of the poor be any better than anybody else's shit?' asks Golam.

'Perhaps because their everything else is worse than everybody else's everything else,' says Hena. 'Anyway, everyone here is poor, near enough.'

'Perhaps he means the Christians.' I make another try: 'The ones who've had their souls saved. Like Matt here.'

'I don't see Matt shitting any different now he's a Christian than when he wasn't,' says Hena.

'When did you last see Matt shit?' I ask, half angry, half curious.

'Come to think of it, when did you first see Matt shit?'

Hena says nothing. Just glowers at me like I'm a fool or something. I decide to ignore her and think about the unsaved soul of Grandma Toughtits and a great heaviness takes hold of my spirit. I don't want her soul to go to Pasadena, California, USA.

'I mean the dead,' says the old man with the strong voice, or the young man with the old face. 'I mean where the living are cursed, blessed are the dead.

'They died here, the ones who sat here where now you sit.

'This was their last shit on this earth. You have now removed the final trace of their existence from this planet.'

Golam is more confused than ever.

So am I, truly speaking.

'No we haven't,' Matt speaks for the first time. 'Man does not live by shit alone.'

The man looks at him in surprise.

'What do you know of people? Or life? Or death? You're just a kid,' he says.

'I have seen many years of suffering in many years of life,' says Matt.

The man goes very pale.

'Who are you?' he says, his voice not so strong, 'You are not...'

'Who are you?' Matt interrupts.

'I used to be a lecturer at the Mission College in Bader, now I ride the bus.'

'Ride the bus!' Even Matt is puzzled at this.

He says he has nowhere to go and no one to go to. So he keeps going back and forth on the bus.

He has given all his wife's silver and gold to the bus people, and in return they let him be on it.

Also he helps clean the bus now and then.

He remembers the time when the bus was new and clean.

When few people travelled on it. Only those who went to the
big village to buy or sell; or to change grain for goods; or to the
cattle fair or the Spirit Dance.

'Now the bus is dying. And so are the people.

'But neither the bus nor the people are dying as they should – in
peace and quiet. The bus is running around when it hardly can.
The people are running around when they really shouldn't.'

'And why not?' says Hena, quietly angry.

'Because it is best to avoid the futile pain of false hope,' says the
man.

'Sounds clever,' says Hena, all cold and proper, 'doesn't make it
right.'

'Sorry,' replies the man. 'I didn't mean to be clever. I was just
trying to be... be... fair.'

'Makes it even less right,' Matt goes.

The man looks annoyed for the first time. 'All right then, you
tell me what is right,' he says, 'and why.'

Matt looks straight into him.

'I don't need to tell you what is right. Or to anyone else.

'Everyone knows what is right. Even the clever and the fair, only
they make it difficult.

'Nor can I tell you why what is right, is right. It just is. It is its
own reason.'

Matt's voice is not the voice of a smart-ass, but the voice of an
old man.

The man is amazed.

'Why do you say what you say about the clever and the fair?' he
asks.

Matt replies:

'We all know what people need.

'The clever give reasons why they can't have it, which is bad.

'The fair give opinions on what they deserve, which is worse.'

The man says, 'I think you are the one I dream of and wake up sweating.'

Matt says nothing.

The stones are hot as burning coal. The sand is like the inside of a roaring bread-baking oven, without the life-giving smell.

But at least there isn't the stink of shit and sick and sweat. So we'd rather be outside than inside.

It is three o'clock in the afternoon. The bus left Gonta at about midday. It was meant to be at Bader by the early hours of the evening, after first going south to Mozapu. On the way down and then on the way up it stops every half-hour or so for rest and for cooling the engine.

This is not one of those stops.

The bus has broken down.

Everybody is looking worried and wondering what will happen and when and how we'll get to Bader. The sick are looking sicker than ever.

The lecturer man is not bothered. The bus is his home, wherever it is. He's sitting in its shade, smoking a funny-smelling mix of tobacco and something black I've seen Hena's Dada smoke in the last months of his life.

The driver and his mate aren't bothered either. After opening the bonnet of the bus to have a quick look at the engine, and doing a bit of tapping and patting here and there, they too have lit their cigarettes and are sprawling in their seats. They have opened the doors on either side, so it is cool and airy for them in their little section, which is separated from the rest of the bus with a barrier as high as my chest.

We slide ourselves next to the bus-riding lecturer man. His name is Bill but he likes to be called Mobu.

'Mobu,' I say, 'how long are we going to be here?'

'Why isn't anybody *doing* anything?' says Hena.

'We can't just sit here for the rest of our lives,' Golam goes.

Mobu sighs, opens his mouth to say something but stops when he sees Matt. He shuts his mouth. He opens it again to say something but stops when he sees Matt. He shuts his mouth. He opens it again with a different face.

He says, 'The bus company runs a jeep, for more important people, between Bader and Mozapu via Gonta. When we break down we wait for it. It has our best mechanic on it as the driver's mate. He can usually help us start. If not, he lets our office at Bader know that we're stuck. They send a relief bus with any spare parts or equipment needed. It also takes away the passengers while this bus is repaired.

'Soon it will be beyond help.'

'How long does all this take?'

'Can't say. If all is well, the jeep should be here tomorrow. If it can't help, then we'll have to wait till it gets back to Bader to inform the bus company.'

'And then they'll send this other bus,' say I.

'When they are good and ready,' says Mobu.

'This could take days,' says Golam.

'At least,' says the man with a smile and a wink.

'We don't find it funny,' says Hena.

'I was only trying to cheer you up.'

Hena don't say nothing, but I can tell she's not cheered up.

'If that other bus works better why don't they use it in the first place?' says Matt.

'Because it's older than this one. It's all right for occasional use. On a regular basis it would be less reliable than this.'

'How far d'you think we're from Bader?' asks Hena.

'About the same distance as from Gonta, I should think,' answers Mobu.

'That's helped us a lot,' I say.

'But,' says Mobu with some feeling, 'the route is pleasanter.'

I look round us at the burning sand and the fiery stones, and then look up at Mobu.

Golam loves the sand and the stones. I don't.

'There is only a few kilometres of desert. After that you come to green hills with trees and water, even flowers.' There is a sudden happiness in his eyes and voice as Mobu speaks of flowers.

'My wife loves flowers,' says Mobu softly. I look at him strange. He carries on as before. 'You could even see the hills from here if it weren't for the haze.

'Bader is in the centre of this green belt. That is why it is such a prosperous city. Even in these hard times. That and the fact that the Government spends all its money there instead of on the land where it is really needed, and where it would be much more useful in the long run.'

'What is prosperous?' asks Golam.

'Prosperous means – sort of doing well, you know. Business, factories, hotels... that sort of thing, you know.'

'Not really,' I say.

'It means there is work and food for people,' says Hena.

'Well, it's not quite so simple,' answers Mobu. 'There is work and there is food. Plenty of it. Only not for all. A lot for some, not much for others. For some hardly any.'

'Will there be some for us?' asks Golam.

Mobu says nothing.

'Joti will help us,' I say.

'We'll help ourselves,' says Hena.

*

We decide to walk to Bader. Like we'd planned from the start.

In one way we're upset on account we've had the bus journey for nothing and the white doctor has wasted her money. In another way we're happy as we'll be going along a better route.

We ask Mobu if he'd like to come with us.

We can tell by the way he looks he truly wants to, but he can't.

Leastwise that's what he says.

He says he can't leave the bus. He says if he's so much as away from its shadow, a strange fear takes hold of his heart.

He says it's 'psychological', and explains it all in big useless words.

He says he can't fight it even though he knows it is 'irrational'.

He says when he first started riding the bus he could walk away from it, though he always came back. Gradually he stopped walking away from it, but believed he could if he wanted to. Now he knows he can't, no matter how much he wants it or how hard he tries.

'What is psychological?' I ask, looking down, not wanting to appear foolish.

'It's... it's what's in the mind,' says Mobu, thinking hard.

'Isn't everything?' I say, also thinking hard.

'Well, yes and no. I mean only in the mind...'

'You mean like seeing a cow when there isn't a cow?'

'Exactly. But sometimes it is more... more complex. More difficult...' He tries to think even harder than before.

So do I.

'You mean,' I say slowly, 'if you haven't had food and you feel hungry it is all right; but if you have had food and you feel hungry it is psychological?'

'Yes, yes. That's it.'

'That is not psychological,' says Hena, 'that is greedy.'

'That too, I suppose,' says Mobu, looking at Hena more careful than before.

'And what is irr... irr...' begins Golam.

'Irrational?' says Mobu.

'Yes. Irr... irr... the same.'

'Irrational? Let me see. It is something which does not conform to facts; or deviates from or contradicts the validity of external verifiable data; or is inconsistent in itself. But I don't think that helps you.'

'No sir,' says Golam, looking very confused and very sad.

'He means cuckoo,' says Hena.

Golam's face lights up. 'Why don't he say so in the first place.' He flashes his teeth. 'That's easy. I was beginning to think I can't understand or nothing.'

Matt looks like he's still thinking hard. It also looks like he isn't listening and doesn't know what's going on around him.

But he's listening and he knows.

'You say you act irrational,' he speaks at last, looking straight at Mobu.

'Yes,' says Mobu, wondering what Matt has in his mind, same as we are wondering what Matt has in his mind.

'But you are not,' says Matt.

We all wait for him to explain, but he don't.

'How do you mean?' Mobu asks, when he knows Matt isn't about to say no more without being asked.

'You believe you can't leave the bus, true?' says Matt.

'Yes,' says Mobu.

'And do you leave the bus?'

'No.'

'That is rational. You are acting as you believe.'

The man thinks this over.

Matt carries on, 'If you were to get up, dust your clothes and walk away with us, in spite of what you believe, that would be irrational.'

'But my belief itself is irrational.'

'Why?'

'Because it is irrational to say that I cannot walk away from the bus. I *can* get up, as you say, dust my clothes and walk away – if I choose.'

'Most rational,' says Matt. 'If you know this, you can't be irrational.'

'I know it but I can't do it. That's what's irrational.'

'Not particularly. Same as most. No more no less. Most people act on what they believe and not on what they know.'

The man remains quiet for some time, then stands up, dusts his

clothes and says, 'Let's go.'
He hasn't walked away from the bus for the last three years.

We start our walk to Bader, all set to steal the city. Like Joti. To steal it, make it our own, and bring it back for our families.

*

We get to Bader. It takes us two days and two nights to get there.

We could've made it in half the time, but there were so many soldiers all around the base of the hills and everywhere else that we hid ourselves during the day and walked carefully at night. Of course the soldiers might not've said anything to us but we didn't want to take any chances.

Mobu was right, it was a pleasant route. The hilly part of it. We were sorry to see signs of drying up there as well, but it was green enough and there was water in many holes.
The river that later goes through our village runs from here and it has plenty of water, but it is taken up for use in the big city. There is a 'dam' and a 'reservoir' in the valley to keep it in. We tried to go up for a closer look but the place was crawling with soldiers. So we moved down to hide. We found a cool leafy spot beside some wild flowers. I got drunk on the scent and went to sleep. My mind danced in dreams. It was like being in the Palace of the Spirits. I wouldn't be surprised if it was.

When we reach the big city we're feeling fresh and rested and all looking forward to meeting Joti and finding work and doing well for ourselves and our families.

Mobu says he'll take us to an old university friend of his called Peter. He says Peter will put us up for a few days in his 'flat' till we find Joti and sort ourselves out.

'Flat what?' I say.

Mobu looks at me like I look at him – not understanding.

He understands first.

'Flat... house,' he says.

'Flat house?' I repeat, understanding even less. Flat bread I love, flat land I know, flat heads I've seen and flat faces too. But flat houses...

I don't think I'd fancy living in a flat house. I'd be flattened or something.

I tell Mobu that.

'It's not a flat house,' he says, 'just a house. On top of a building. It's called a flat. An apartment.'

'Oh,' I say, still wondering why anyone would put a house on top of a building, but not saying it.

*

By now we are all in shock and amazement at the sights of the big city and I forget about the flat.

Mobu takes us to a bus stop. He says the bus from here will carry us near to the place where Peter lives.

I can't believe the bus when it comes. I can't believe I'm sitting in it when I'm sitting in it.

My heart still hasn't settled down. It fell to my knees when the glass door split in half as we neared it, all by itself. I couldn't hardly bring myself to pass through it in case it closed in on me and swallowed me while I was only half in.

This place we got off at is not as classy as some of the places we've been through.

The road here don't have the face of a smooth slate. It is cracked and holey. The buildings are neither too high nor too low, nor separate, but joined together in a broken sort of a way. There are more people here than I've seen before but they aren't dressed up special smart or anything like that.

They look tired and thin, but nowhere near as bad as the starving and the sick in the camp. Some are even fat.

I ask Mobu why the hungry don't come here to look for food.

He tells me they're not allowed. He tells me if they do they are only sent to special camps. He tells me they even check the outside bus for 'undesirables'.

I think it's just as well we didn't come by the bus. Who knows. I mean, I think I'm quite desirable, but who knows. I mean.

Mobu says he's going to Peter's flat for the first time after more than three years. Peter's often been to the bus to see him, though not for some time now.

We come to a few shops with their windows boarded up. Parts of the wood and brick work are black and charred. There are big tin drums standing about the place. They are full of all sorts of paper and bottles and tins. One drum is rolling on its side. Most of its rubbish is spread on the footpath. It don't smell too good.

We go to a doorway half hidden by piles of empty and not so empty boxes.

There are stairs going up. They are dark. The steps are high and chipped. There is a cold wind blowing here which isn't blowing outside.

We climb three sets of stairs and turn right after the third. We walk along a dark cold way with shaky fence on the right side of it and three doors on the left. There is a fourth door at the end of it.

Mobu stops in front of the third door and knocks.

There is no answer.

He knocks again.

The door opens very slowly.

Mobu walks in. We follow. We see a broken floor, three chairs and a table with two legs. One side of the table is held up by a pile of books. We don't see Peter. Or anybody else.

The door bangs shut. There is a man behind the door. He is holding a gun. The gun is pointing towards us.

Two other men appear from behind another door in the room. They too are holding guns. The guns are pointing towards us.

All three men are in uniform. It is not the uniform of the soldiers.

The man behind the outside door says to Mobu, 'You are William John Adelo, also known as Mobu?'

Mobu's eyes are wide open, but they are not seeing the man with the gun. They are seeing the black star of death.

The man repeats the question. As he speaks he starts walking towards Mobu. So do the other men.

Mobu makes a rush for the door.

The man in front fires. Many times.

The men behind fire. Many times.

Mobu falls on the floor. He is full of holes. Holes in the face. Holes in the body.

The holes are a lovely shade of red. My favourite colour.

The colour moves, comes to life, and spreads itself all over Mobu. He begins to look like a painting. A painting with the form of a human being. The black of his skin, the white of his eyes, the grey of his robe, the red of his life.

The men move closer. One kicks him. Mobu quietly turns over on his face. Another kicks him. Mobu quietly rolls back on his back.

The third man nods.

They are satisfied. They smile for the first time. The worry on their faces is no more.

They are looking happy. Like I do when I've done what I've been told. I know I won't be told off. Might even get a pat on the back for being a good boy. Maybe a piece of bread. If I'm real lucky.

They go out of the flat.

*

Hena kneels beside Mobu and closes his eyes. She is having difficulty bending her fingers.

She says we should go to the other room to see if there's a sheet there to cover Mobu's body.

I hold Golam's hand and pull hard before he can move.

We leave Matt folded up on the floor, arms around his knees, rocking himself.

The other room has a bed in it. The bed has a sheet on it. But it is not a clean sheet. It is covered with the blood of another man who lies on it.

I feel like someone's slapped my heart. I see Mobu dying all over again. The man's eyes move. He looks at us like he don't know who we are, for of course he don't know who we are. It is not Mobu.

His lips move. He speaks in a broken whisper.

'Are you angels of death?' he says.

'No we're not,' says Golam.

'You look like death,' says the man.

'Perhaps we are,' says Hena. 'Who are you?'

'I am Peter.'

'We came with Mobu. He said you might put us up till we find Joti,' I say.

'Mobu shouldn't have come here,' says the man in panic, 'the police are after him.'

'They've got him,' says Hena. 'Didn't you hear the guns?'

The man looks blank for a moment, then looks away. He curls his lips in a cracked sort of a smile and tries to laugh a cracked sort of laugh, but chokes in his blood. He coughs and splutters, then seems to settle down.

'What about you?' I ask him.

He don't speak for such a long time that I begin to get worried for him.

'They thought I was hiding Mobu,' he says at last.

He don't look too good.

'You don't look too good,' says Hena. 'What can we do for you?'

'Just help me up,' he says. 'I'll see if I can clean up a little.'

I hold by the right arm, Hena takes his left arm, Golam supports his waist.

We go to a corner of the room which has a little basin. There is a little metal thing on top of the basin which he calls a tap. When he turns this little metal thing round, water flows out.

I think it's a miracle.

We help Peter wash himself.

He tells us that as long as Mobu was on the bus they didn't mind. More than that. They actually enjoyed having him there. Someone they could laugh at. A pathetic 'ex-revolutionary', whatever that means. That morning when the bus came and they found out he had left the bus they didn't like that at all.

They don't want that.

'But why should they want to kill Mobu?' I ask.

'I'm not sure they wanted to kill him. Just hold him for enquiries. I don't know. No one can really tell what they will do or why.'

I still don't understand.

Peter carries on, 'Mobu used to speak against these people. These people who now rule us. At that time they were only trying to take over.

'When Mobu spoke, we all listened. They didn't like that.

'Also, Mobu had written a book. A book they didn't want written. He hid the draft somewhere.

'The soldiers abducted Mobu's wife and raped her. They kept her for days. When they let her go, she killed herself.

'Mobu was in Bandugu at the time. A day South of Mozapu.

'He often went there as exchange lecturer in the Bandugu branch of the Mission College.

'When he came back and heard about his wife, he just went to pieces.

'One day he went out, took the bus to Mozapu – and never got off.

'That was more than three years ago.

'Mobu was twenty-eight that day. Same age as me. Same date of birth even. That's why I remember the exact day.

'I had bought a pink tie for him. And a pair of socks. I don't remember the colour.'

When Peter's washed up Hena wants to clean up the bed. She also wants to borrow a sheet, if there is one to spare, to cover up Mobu with.

Peter says to look in the cupboard. His body hurts much and he's not sure if his right arm is not broken and he's not too happy with his condition from the stomach down either. He says he'll rest for a while before helping us.

He says he'll be grateful if we make him a cup of tea.

He tells us where his things are and what to do.

I can't stop marvelling. First the magic of the tap. Now the magic of the fire burner. Mobu said how poor Peter is. I think he's rich. The thought of Mobu takes my excitement away.

Peter asks what we are doing in the big city, all alone by ourselves.

'We're not alone by ourselves,' says Golam, 'we're with Matt.'

'Is Matt your brother, father or uncle?' asks Peter.

We nearly laugh.

'Oh no, he's hardly a year older than I am,' I say. 'But he knows everything,' I add, to make him understand better.

I don't think he does, but he don't argue.

'Where is this Matt of yours?' he asks.

'He's in the other room,' says Hena, 'saying his farewell to Mobu.'

'I think I'd better go and meet him,' says Peter, 'this Matt who knows everything. Maybe he can teach me something. I've never met anyone before who knows everything.'

'Well, it's not like he knows *everything*,' I say, 'it's just that...' I don't know how to carry on.

'It's just that he learns everything if he don't know it,' says Hena.

'Ah,' says Peter, 'now that I can understand a little better.'

'It's more than that,' says Golam. 'He knows all that is useless and don't bother with it.'

Peter is looking more and more interested.

'And what is useless?' he asks.

'Well...' says Golam, his unlikely sureness cracking a bit.

'Well... sort of everything really.'

Peter smiles a sad smile. 'So that's what he knows about everything, that it is useless. He may be right, you know.'

'It's not like that. Not quite like that. He knows what's useful too,' I say, trying to defend him. To make him sound important.

'And what is useful, er, according to Matt?'

'Food,' says Golam, before I can say anything.

Peter waits but Golam says nothing more. I wait but Golam says nothing more.

'You mean all he thinks important is food?' Peter says, in such

surprise and so loud that his lips crack and his head throbs and
he winces in pain and holds his head in his hands.

'All kinds of food,' says Golam. 'Some for eating, some not.'

'I see,' says Peter slowly, as if seeing. 'And who taught Matt
that?'

'The missionary bloke, I think,' say I.

'Not him,' says Hena.

Golam's arms are down by his side. His shoulders hang low.
'Why are you all looking at me like that?' he says. 'Have I said
something stupid?'

Peter says, 'I must go meet Matt.'

He makes a strong effort to get up, stretching his arms out to
support himself against the wall and setting his face hard to
guard against showing too much pain.

To his surprise he can get up quite easily and his face shows no
pain.

We all go to the first room. Something we'd all been trying to
put off with our minds.

We are now in the room.

There is no Matt there. And no Mobu.

Only blood on the floor.

Peter cries in pain and falls on the floor. His blood mixes with
Mobu's blood.

'The police must have come and taken them away,' says Hena.

'Maybe they took Mobu away, to hide their killing. But why
would they take Matt?' I feel truly alone for the first time.

Golam says nothing. It looks like he can't, even though he's
trying.

By now Peter's managed to raise himself on his elbow and is half sitting up.

'Go out and see if Matt has gone out for some reason. Maybe he's following the police to see where they take the body. Don't go too far or you may get lost. Come back soon if you can't find him. Then I'll see what I can do. I have a friend who is a doctor. I'll probably have to see him anyway. He might be able to help. He has a friend in the police.

'Go now. But remember, not too far.'

We rush out, leaving the door open behind us in our hurry.

We go as far as we dare, in all directions, but no sign of Matt.

Feeling nothing as we all come back. It is like nothing is happening. Leastwise not to us.

When we get back to the flat the door is shut. We try to push it open but it is locked.

We knock.

There is no answer.

We knock again and again and again.

There is still no answer.

The door at the top of the corridor opens a fraction. A face peers out.

It is a woman's face. It is the face of one who is afraid.

I think she is about to say something but she don't. I think she is about to shut the door but she don't.

We are still not feeling but we think maybe Peter's worse and unable to open the door.

Hena walks up to the woman and asks if there's any other way we can get into Peter's flat.

The woman speaks in the language of the south. I don't speak it but I can understand a little. Enough to know what she says. She says we can't be right for nobody by that name lives here. In fact no one's lived in the flat for over a month.

We can't believe our ears. We tell her our story. About Mobu's death, about Peter's beating, about Mobu and Matt missing.

From her looks we can tell she understands, although we are speaking in the language of the valley.

From what I make of her reply she says we have a great imagination, but it's not a happy imagination. She says she's sorry for us.

She shuts the door.

We stand like statues.

The city has stolen Matt.

The city is stealing our mind.

Four

Black Balls Pink Balls

I have a dream.

I'm not asleep, but I still have a dream.

We're back in the hills of Bader, Hena, Golam and me, walking home.

It is more beautiful than I remember. There are rippling streams of blue water coming down the cracks in shiny black rocks. The breeze is cool and scented. The trees are green with leaves and monkeys dance on their branches.

Parrots of many colours fly and squawk all around us. A blue rhino offers me a ride.

Wild buffaloes play with the white spotted deer. The black cat raises its nose, sniffs, and goes back to sleep with a smile on its magic face.

Matt comes running from behind a tree. With him is a smart

young man wearing a pearl-white robe and a blood-red sash. The man lifts me off the rhino's back and puts me down on the dewy grass.

I immediately know the man is Mobu.

I also know why Matt had to go.

Most of all I know we have to do what we have to do, no matter what. Just as Matt has to do what he has to do, no matter what. And that he will be back when it is done.

And we'll meet when we are to meet.

All my worry is gone. There is peace in my heart.

But when I find myself in an empty box, hungry, with a dry mouth, and cold in spite of the heat, I am not so sure any more. There is no grass no water no rhino.

No Mobu no Matt.

Just a few empty and not so empty boxes. I'm in one of them.

Golam is in another. Hena in another.

Golam is looking very pleased.

'It was so nice to see Matt,' he says, 'and Mobu.'

I look at him in surprise. He is surprised at my surprise.

'You should know,' he says with his large eyes going straight into mine, 'you were there. So was Hena.'

I listen to him in silence. He speaks like in a dream, 'It was in this endless desert with golden sand and diamond stones.

'The sun was hot and the wind was hot and tall prickly trees with green bodies and green arms stood guard over us.

'There was milk in the trees and peace in my heart.

'I know now that Matt has to meet his fate and we have to meet ours. What will be, will be. But he'll be there to help us. I'm not afraid any more.'

Hena speaks. 'I saw Matt. And Mobu. You were both with me. But it wasn't in no barren desert.

'It was in this beautiful house with many rooms, each more wonderful than the other. There was even a television in one room, and magic cookers; and cupboards full of food; and trunks full of shawls and silk scarves and sandals, and gold beads and silver anklets.

'And I was happy. Happy to see Matt. Happy to see Mobu. And... just... happy...

I had everything.'

But she don't sound too sure.

The sun is out but it is dark on our side of the street. A man on a bicycle passes by, looking at us in our boxes, but not really seeing.

In a way I'm glad we haven't eaten since the last sunrise. At least I'm not wanting a shit. I wouldn't know where to go. The thought worries me even though I don't want to go at present. Not much chance in the future either. No input, no output – Leku used to say. Matt, on the other hand, says if you don't eat for long enough you start shitting anyway. More than usual even.

And he's right too, as ever. We smelt enough proof in the camp at Gonta.

The thought worries me. You bet.

Our food bags are in Peter's flat, as are our thick shawls.

Joti's photo and address are in my pocket. We are glad about that and decide to look for him today.

Hena says before we go we should make another try to see if

we can get into Peter's flat. She says maybe he was sleeping yesterday, or fainted from pain or something. She says maybe he needs help. We need help.

We walk up the stairs. It is hard work. When I was little I could've run up like the wind that is flying past us. Growing old is not easy. Take my word for it.

We are up there. At last.

We get in front of the door. We try to push the door. We try to turn the handle. Nothing. On both counts. And nothing again.

We're afraid to knock as we're afraid of the lady behind the door opposite.

But we knock.

We shut our eyes and pray to the Spirits. Hard. We shut our eyes hard. We pray hard. We pray that the door opens. We pray that Peter opens it.

We knock again.

Half our prayer is answered.

The door opens. But it is not Peter who opens it.

It is a young woman.

She looks at us wondering who we are and what we want.

Suddenly her face shows like she knows; but she don't seem too pleased about it.

'Wait a minute,' she says, shuts the door, and goes away.

At least she don't tell us to push off.

We wait.

She takes a long time to get back, but she gets back. She opens the door, holds out her hand, shoves a piece of old flat bread in our hands and shuts the door again, saying, 'What next, can't even have a bit of peace in one's own home.'

Hena looks like she's going to cry, but she don't. Golam does. I don't know what to do. But I'm happy about the bread. I've always been the first to crack when it comes to hunger.

When we're back out, I divide the bread into three equal parts, but Hena says she won't have it. Knowing her we know she won't if she's said she won't. We still try make her but, you've guessed, she won't! She's stubborn that girl.

Golam and I eat. It makes us more hungry. And thirsty. How I long to get near that magic tap. But, if wishes were horses beggars would ride, Grandma Toughtits always said.

Beggars. I'm suddenly struck with the word. That's what we just become. Well, there's nothing we can do about it. Leastwise that's what I tell Hena.

'Oh yes we can,' she says, her eyes lighting up with some new knowledge.

I wonder what it is. So does Golam.

She smiles in her old mysterious way, like she used to when she was a little girl – only she looked bigger then – and puts her hand in her blouse, like she used to put her hand in her bag when she was a little girl, and brings out some rotten old coloured paper. Our faces fall, till we realise it is the money that the white doctor gave us to keep.

I'm still not sure, not knowing much about money, but Hena says it should solve all our problems. Golam is not sure either. But we all know Hena, even if we don't know about money. So we believe that money will solve all our problems. At least for as long as it lasts.

We've no idea how long that will be. Even Hena don't know that.

Anyway, it makes us happy for now. We start our search for Joti in good spirits.

By now many people are walking on the footpath where we are. Shops are opening. There are quite a few bicycles on the road, and even some cars. We've seen two buses go by, one in each direction. We walk up to the place where the bus stops. On the way we see more boarded-up shops with empty boxes and tin drums full of rubbish outside.

When we get to the bus stop there is a large group of people all crowding there.

I go near some men hoping to speak to them but they don't pay no attention. I tug at one man's sleeve and show him the piece of paper with Joti's address.

'My cousin Joti lives there, sir,' I say. 'We will be much thankful if you tell us where it is.'

'And how to get there,' adds Hena.

The man looks at us in a strange way.

When he says nothing I speak again. 'We are come from our village to look for my cousin Joti. We will thank you very much and pray to the Spirits for your good health if you help us find him.'

'Your cousin works there?' he says at last.

Everyone in Gonta asked that. So did Mobu.

'He lives there,' I say, adding, 'I think,' when I see his face. 'Here is his photo.'

I take out Joti's photo, standing by his car I don't believe outside this house I don't believe.

I can understand when the man looks like he don't believe it.

Or us.

'The Regent,' he says, 'is the largest and most expensive hotel in Bader. In the whole country. Only white people or the very rich live there. They come and go. '

'Our cousin is very rich,' says Hena, 'and he comes and goes.'

The man don't argue.

He says, 'It is miles from here.'

'We can take the bus,' says Hena. 'We've got the money.' She takes our notes and shows them to the man.

The man's face changes. It becomes worse.

'Where did you get all that money from? Have you been stealing?'

The man has a long pointed nose which gets longer as he brings it down towards us. His deep round eyes look at us like pebble holes in the dry river bed, without water or kindness.

The man stretches a long arm towards us.

Golam moves back shaking. I try not to move back and stop myself from shaking by thinking of Matt. He wouldn't shake in front of any man.

'No sir,' says Golam, 'we don't steal, truly...'

'The white doctor gave it to us,' says Hena. 'We helped her with the sick.'

'She gave us vitamins as well,' I say, 'but they are with our food bags in Peter's flat.'

'And who is Peter?' says the man. 'And why doesn't he take you to your cousin Joti?'

'We don't know where Peter is any more,' says Golam. 'He wasn't well. All beaten up and covered in blood he was. We...'

'So you beat up Peter and took his money. Maybe even killed him.'

The man moves towards us. One slow long step after another slow long step.

'No sir, we don't...' Golam is saying through tears, but we don't let him say any more, Hena and me. We pull him away and run.

The man is going to run after us; but just then the bus comes.

Golam turns his head to look; trips and falls on his face.

The man is still trying to get to us but he can't. He is being pushed from all sides by people rushing to get into the bus. He is being carried forward, long nose, holey eyes and all.

We help Golam to stand up. Just then a big fat woman comes running from nowhere and bumps into Golam. He's flat again, this time on his back.

The woman stops, looking very sorry. She stops to pick Golam up. She also stops on account the bus leaves, leaving quite a few people behind.

Luckily the man with the long nose and holey eyes is gone.

The fat woman picks Golam up by the arm, nearly pulling it out of its socket.

Golam goes, 'Ouch.'

The woman goes, 'Dear, dear, dear. You're just a wire hanger.'

I know what a wire hanger is. Grandma Toughtits had one. She always kept her black silk scarf folded neatly over it. I don't know how she got one, but she had a wire hanger. Not many people do. I think the woman is right in calling Golam a wire hanger.

I smile. The woman bursts out in loud gusts of windy laughter. It wasn't that funny, but never mind.

Her big breasts jump up and down, her huge waist shakes. Her round stomach rolls out as she bends forward to clap her hands before slapping Hena and me on the shoulder, nearly flattening us on the footpath.

I splurt and cough. Hena shoots out her hand and grabs the woman's skirt to keep herself from folding and falling.

The woman stops laughing. She puts her arm round Hena. Hena lets go of the woman's skirt, but then holds on to it again as her head takes a circle in the air.

'Dear, dear, dear,' goes the woman with a worry note in her voice and a worry frown on her face. 'When did you last eat?'

'Only this minute,' I say truthfully.

'Are you sure?' she asks like she don't believe me.

'Well, Hena don't eat,' I say, bringing her share of bread out of my pocket. 'She don't want to eat like a beggar,' I explain. 'I've kept her share. Just in case she gets bad with hunger.'

The woman shakes her head sideways, cluck-clicking all the while.

'Is that *all*?' she says, dragging the all out for longer than I've ever heard a word dragged out. 'And when did you eat before that?'

Before I can think up an answer for that Golam says, 'Can I have some water, madam? We haven't had any for...' I kick him in the shin; Hena looks at him with eyes of fire.

'Why do you stop me asking?' says Golam. 'How can you get what you need if you don't ask, Matt says.'

'Matt is right, whoever he is,' goes the woman.

It seems like she is trying to make up her mind about something. She looks at her watch. On her wrist. Just by flicking it.

Matt never did get to wear a watch on his wrist. I don't think he's spoken of it in the last many months, but I know he did so want it, once.

This memory and Golam speaking of him makes me remember him and miss him. All of a sudden.

My heart is squeezed, splurting blood out of my eyes as water.

'Dear, dear, dear,' goes the woman. She thinks I'm crying on account I'm hungry for food. She don't know I'm crying on account I am hungry for Matt.

'Come home with me,' she says, 'and tell me your story while I get some food into your bellies.' She looks at Golam. 'And water. Some milk even.'

Golam's eyes shine with happiness. He smiles and his teeth show. For one moment he looks almost as pretty as he used to.

'And you, young lady,' she turns to Hena, 'don't you dare refuse any food I give you. Or you haven't seen trouble yet.'

'Now hurry,' she carries on, 'I've never been late for work in thirty years.'

She turns round to look at us. 'Never mind,' she says. 'Take your time. There's always a first time for everything. Or so Mama always said. So I'll be late today.'

I don't see anything funny in this but she starts to laugh again. Her huge eyes flashing her huge teeth flashing her huge mouth open so wide you could see right into her stomach.

*

We eat only a little bit and our stomach says: 'Thank you very much but I don't think I can have any more of it. I appreciate your concern but thank you. That's all I can handle for the moment.'

I am truly surprised. So is the big woman. Her name is Daisy.

'Is that all you can eat?' she says, dragging the 'all' again for a day and a half's journey. 'I thought you'd finish my week's ration for me.'

Golam drinks a gallon of water. So do we, even though we all feel sick after it. I thought we'd feel great after eating and drinking but we don't. We feel sick. Leastwise for the time being. Daisy says we'll start feeling good pretty soon.

She's right as well. After we've rested a while, and had a cup each of her 'special' tea, with about a whole bag of herbs in every cup, we start to relax and don't want to die that instant, as we did not too long ago.

The woman, Daisy, says we ought to have a bath as well, but there isn't enough water just yet. She has the magic tap, but she says the water runs for only an hour in the morning and an hour in the evening. Unless you have a storage tank 'up top', which she hasn't. She says we're in no position to go looking for our cousin Joti today. She says we'd better stay here and rest while she goes to work. She says she'll take us with her when she goes to work tomorrow and explain to us how to get to the Regent. She says that'll be best.

We say that's very kind of you Daisy – she don't like to be called 'madam' – and accept the offer.

Daisy rushes off to her work while we bundle up on her bed to rest, and before we know it are fast asleep. Leastwise I am.

When Daisy comes home in the evening she gives us all a good scrub down. We store all the water we can in buckets and cooking pots and even cups and glasses, so we can have some extra in the morning when the tap stops. It's great fun. I don't remember enjoying myself so much in years. I am a bit sad as I miss my Mam and Dada, and Matt, but I still enjoy myself. We all love Daisy. At night Daisy sleeps on the floor while we all get into the bed, sleeping sideways. My feet stick out a lot, on account I am taller than the others, but that don't matter. Especially if I roll myself into a ball.

Daisy lives in this little room, where she sleeps and cooks and everything. There is a little tap in a corner behind a little screen for washing up. Across the corridor is a tiny room for 'you know what' – that's what Daisy says about going for a s-h-i-t etcetera. She don't like us to say it straight out. Like the missionary bloke, though she's not the least bit like the missionary bloke in any other way.

She does believe in Jesus though. Which makes me think of Matt again.

Daisy don't quite understand about Matt, but she don't argue much about it when we say he'll be all right as he knows what he's doing.

Daisy's children are all grown up and live in the country next to us. She says they wanted her to go over there and live with them but she wanted to stay here.

However she's planning to go to them forever next month, when she's done full thirty years of service where she's working. She says she'll get a 'pension' then – not too much but enough to help her son out for looking after her in her old age.

Her eyes shine with happiness when she talks of her plans.

The next morning Daisy takes the money from us – all except a small note. She says it is best otherwise someone else might think we've stolen it. Or worse, steal it from us. She says some people kill for less. She says she'll leave us in front of the Regent Hotel before going off to work – it's the same general direction – and then meet us there at four o'clock in the afternoon. If we haven't found Joti, she'll bring us back with her and we can try again the next day. If we have found him she'll give us our money back and wish us luck and pray for us.

We stand in front of the Regent Hotel, full of wonder and worry and hope.

Two hours later we stand in front of the Regent Hotel full of nothing.

We don't quite know what to think, which is not unusual. Leastwise not for me. What is unusual is that we aren't even sure what to feel.
Leastwise I am not.
I am sort of numb.
I don't understand much of what I hear.

*

First we are not allowed inside the place or anywhere near the door even, which is not a very good beginning, I'm sure you'll agree.
When we, well, Hena kicks up a lot of fuss and I wave Joti's photo and address about, one of the men in hotel suits takes us to one side of the building and tells us to wait.

We wait, and wait, and wait, and wait, and wait...

Then comes this man, quite young, about Joti's age.

He looks at us and is not pleased at what he sees. But he comes to us and talks to us which is something we are grateful for.

He says Joti worked here once but does not any more. The way he says 'worked here' is strange and don't sound too nice.

By now we have come to accept that Joti most likely won't be living in such a grand place. Only working. But though it brings our pride down a bit, we don't think any harm in it. To speak the truth, once the first surprise is over, we are quite proud of Joti working there even.

But this man makes it like there is something bad in it.

We ask him what the numbers 317 in the address mean.

He says that is the number of the room in which lived a rich white man from some place called England. He says Joti was his 'fancy boy' for some time. But when the problems in the country became a bit bad, the white man left for his own country. Most other white men also left the hotel, and the country, so Joti wasn't left with much work.

He says Joti 'sold himself' to those who wanted boys, and arranged girls for those who wanted girls. He says the new Police Chief is very hard on such boys. And girls. He says the new Police Chief takes them to the Police Station and there they are 'shared out' among the police for free fun, and fines. So most of the boys and girls are running scared. Joti among them. There is no telling where he may be.

We stand in front of the Regent Hotel, full of nothing.

The sun is high in the sky. We've eaten the food Daisy put in a little tin box for us. We weren't too hungry but we ate it for it was there. Now we feel guilty about it. We could've saved it for the evening. That would've saved Daisy from making some more for us. We decide we won't eat tonight. We'll tell Daisy we're not hungry. Like Grandma Toughtits used to say when there wasn't enough.

It is still a long time before Daisy is to come. We are not allowed to stay in front of the hotel so we've moved away to one side. Far enough away to be allowed, but near enough to be able to see Daisy when she comes and to get to her before she starts wondering where we are. Behind a big old tree next to a lovely red drum for the rich people's rubbish. The men at the hotel can't see us here, but we can see them by moving our necks a little to one side.

We're wondering what to do with our time. I feel like walking around to see the city a bit, but we're afraid of losing our way. Golam says we'll ask someone if we get lost but I'm not too sure. I say look what happened when we asked the man at the bus stop. He says look what happened when we asked Daisy. We can't make up our minds.

Two boys, about our age but twice our size – more than twice our size – come walking towards us with heavy steps. They are wearing dirty brown shorts; no shirts. They look poor but they've got shoes on their feet. And they are properly formed like rich boys. Their bodies are nicely shaped and covered with meat. Their faces are full, their hair shines. It is good to look at them.

I remember seeing them when the young man in the hotel suit was talking to us about Joti. They were sort of circling round; not too close, but not far either.

They come and stand right on top of us as we sit resting our backs against the tree.

They say nothing, just stand there. Then they start circling round the tree – and round us.

They keep on going round and round till our heads swim just thinking of it. But we say nothing.

They finally come to a stop, again in front of us, legs wide apart, hands on hips.

Both looking down upon us.

After a while one of them raises his arms, spreads them out, bends his elbows, brings his hands to the back of his head and joins his fingers. At the same time he raises his head and starts looking far away into the distance. He moves one leg in front of the other, bends a knee and starts tapping a foot.

He has hair under his arms.

I don't have any.

Actually I had started growing some, many months ago. Under my arms, and on my balls, and round my dingus. They were spreading too. Then they stopped spreading. Then they stopped growing.

Then they disappeared. Nothing. I am left with smooth underarms and a bald dingus hanging over bald balls.

Golam never even started growing hair. Not properly.

I look, feeling real jealous, at the hairs under the big boy's arms.

They are soft and curly. They shine in the sun and move ever so gently in the wind. They are alive.

Now that I'm looking for them I can even see hair under the arms of the other boy, standing hands on hips, glaring down at us.

I bet they have hairy balls too.

I feel a strange feeling rise in me and I'm ashamed. I hang my head down and try not to look at their hairy underarms or think of their hairy balls.

'Well well well,' says the one staring down at us, 'look what's crawled out of the rubbish bin!'

The one looking far into the sun slowly moves his hips up and down, saying nothing.

'Shall we put them back in?' says the first. 'My boss always says, "If you see litter lying about, always put it away in a bin."' He says this in a funny sort of a voice.

'It's lucky then,' the other now speaks, still looking far away, 'that there is a bin so close by.'

He has a beautiful voice. But it is also frightening.

I try to shrink into a ball. But then I think of Hena and Golam.

I am still the biggest of us. I want to protect them but don't know what to do or say.

The first boy moves forward and lifts the lid of the red tin drum, looks at us and says, 'Crawl back in, litter.'

We huddle together.

'Wait!' the other goes suddenly, bringing his arms down and looking at us directly. 'Wait,' he says. 'This bin is much too clean for them lot. We must take these creatures to the backstreet where the *real* rubbish lies.'

'What a good idea!' goes the first, smacking his lips. 'And I always thought you was the beauty and me the brain.' They move closer, taking one long slow step.

I freeze, ready to fight if necessary but afraid to start it. I think perhaps I should at least stand up, but don't.

Hena stands up, all quiet and mysterious. 'Well all right then,' she says.

Golam and I stand up after her, without thinking.

The two boys look very surprised, but try to hide their surprise.

'All right then what?' says the Beauty.

'Yeah, all right then what?' says the Brain.

'All right then, let's go to the backstreet where the real rubbish is. If that's where you're more at home,' Hena says, cool as the desert sand at dawn.

'Yeah, let's go,' say I.

'Yeah, let's,' says Golam.

By now the boys have sorted themselves out a bit.

'OK then,' says the Beauty, 'if that's what you really want.'

'Don't blame us afterwards,' says the Brain.

'That is what we really want. And no we won't blame you. But you may blame us. Afterwards.'

We think Hena's pushing her luck too much.

'Go on then, what are we waiting for? Surely you know the way to your home.'

'Who says we're taking you to our home?' Brain pushes his big chest forward.

'Isn't that where all the rubbish is?' goes Hena, looking all innocent.

I say to myself, Oh boy, that's done it. We're in for big trouble now.

I say to the boys, 'Yeah, that's where the rubbish is, isn't it?'

Beauty and Brain look at one another. I can tell they are having a conference with their eyes.

Beauty speaks: 'We'd better be careful man.' He winks at Brain.

Brain looks like he don't know what's going on. I am beginning to think it is Beauty who has the brains as well.

'You know the film we last saw,' Beauty speaks quickly, before Brain can say anything stupid. 'Sinbad, I think it was called.'

'Yeah?' says Brain, slowly.

'Did you see how the wicked skeletons fought in that? I think we've got three of them here.'

I see Hena flinch for the first time. She always likes to look pretty. I don't think she likes being called a skeleton. Particularly as it happens to be a little true.

'Yeah. Them skeletons were ugly, weren't they?' Brain gets in on the act, pleased with himself.

'Not half as ugly as this lot,' Beauty carries on.

I don't think we like this line of attack. It seems to've put even Hena out of joint.

But not for long.

'At least we'll look all right once we've got some meat on us. There's no hope for you lot. Is there?'

Which isn't exactly true, for they look fine as it is. But that don't stop them from feeling foolish at what Hena says.

I think they are going to hit us.

I see their eyes go to the hotel entrance. I realise they will not start a fight here where they can be seen by men in hotel suits.

It makes me bolder, but I'm still not taking any foolish risks. So I say nothing. I feel a lot better though. I think they can tell the change in me.

'We don't hit girls,' says Brain at last, pleased with himself for finding a good excuse not to start a punch-up.

'Can't you come up with a better reason? Or is your think-box jammed with gristle? This girl can take care of herself.'

Both Golam and I look at each other. We wish Hena would give it a rest.

'So you want a better reason?' says Beauty with a new anger in his voice. I'll give you one. We don't kill those who are going to die anyway. How's that, crumbling bones?'

'And you think you'll go on forever, like the smell of shit?'

The silence is so hot you could bake your bread in it.

'Come come,' I hear Golam's voice, 'this is not getting anywhere. 'If you want to hit us, then hit us. If you want to go away, then go away. If you want to stay and make friends, then stay and make friends. I think we'll like that on account we've no friends here. That is except Daisy, but she goes to work.'

'And who is this Daisy bird? Is she like you lot or is she normal?' says Beauty, then adds with a mix of comedy and sorrow: 'I mean, is she likely to remain among the living for another day or so, or has she got her quick getaway ticket from this plain of pain ready and stamped for the next flight out, like someone we see before us now?'

I don't think it's funny, what I understand of it. I get angry.

'She is tall as a tree and big as a buffalo,' I say. 'She could arrange your instant burial in the hole you creep into at night.' I move a little to one side where the hotel men can see us clearly.

'My Pa was right,' says Beauty, 'when he said, "They have nothing to fear who are ready for death."'

'Better to die without fear,' says Hena, 'than of fear.'

'What does she mean?' Brain goes, looking both pale and angry, 'I'm not sure I like what she means.' He makes fists of his hands and bends forward as if to attack.

My short spell of bravery seems in danger of wearing off.

'Don't get your fists ready to fight,' says Beauty to Brain, all cool and calm, 'get your hands ready to pray. And don't crouch, kneel.'

'What'ya talking about?' Brain has a worried look on his face. 'Why should I kneel before these skellies?'

'To say prayers over their bodies, why else? Don't your Mama teach you to show your respect to the dead?' Beauty is enjoying himself.

I'm getting a bit fed up with him treating us like we are ready for the bone soup.

'I wish Matt were here,' I sigh to myself.

I must've sighed louder than I thought I'd sighed.

'And who is Matt?' Beauty sounds a bit wary.

'Matt can deal with the likes of you with the whiff of his breath.' I say this with full belief.

My belief gets through to Beauty.

'I thought you didn't know anyone here except this Daisy character.' He is sounding nervous now.

'We don't know Matt here,' I say. 'He came with us from our village. To look for our cousin Joti.'

'Joti!' both Beauty and Brain go together. They look at one another, then at us.

'Joti,' says Brain again, on his own this time. 'You can't mean the Joti? The one who...' he don't finish the sentence.

I take out Joti's photo and show it to them. 'Do you know him?' I ask all hopeful.

Hena don't seem too pleased about my asking them, but she don't object either.

Beauty and Brain look at the photo, then at each other, then at us. I can tell it is the same Joti they know.

I'm truly happy about it. I don't care what he did. I want to know where he is. I want to see him.

I want to see him like I've never wanted to see anyone before. Except Matt.

Beauty and Brain take us to what they call a 'safe' place. Hena is not too happy about it, but all things considered we decide to take the chance.

Behind the backstreet, beyond a forest of rubbish bins in an enclosed area for use by the hotel people, on the side of an empty building waiting to be rented, is a shed in a warehouse connected with the empty building. That is where we end up. The 'safe' place. If Beauty and Brain think of beating us up here we'll put up a good fight, but I won't bet on the result.

Come to think of it, I'm not even sure of the 'good fight' bit.

All Beauty and Brain want to know is our story. At least to start off. We tell it to them, backwards. First about Daisy, who she is and why she is coming to see us in front of the Hotel; then on to the death and disappearance of Mobu, along with Matt; and of course how and why we happen to be here in the first place. To look for Joti. Full circle, our story takes. Beginning and ending with Joti.

Beauty and Brain are known as Kagu and Tony, but we start calling them Beauty and Brain which they quite like.

Beauty likes being called Beauty on account he is a show-off. Brain likes being called Brain on account he is stupid.

Anyway, the point is that Beauty and Brain or Tony and Kagu or whatever, they show many strange emotions and make many strange faces as we tell our story.

At first I don't think they believe us. But then they look at our faces as we speak and listen to our voices as we speak. Then I think they believe us.

When we finish they go to a corner and talk, looking our way now and then. It seems they're arguing, but quiet so we don't hear.

They walk back to us.

'We don't believe you,' says Beauty, looking worried.

'Pull the other one,' says Brain, looking sideways.

'Pardon,' says Hena, looking puzzled.

'You tell great stories,' says Beauty, trying to sound sarcastic.

'You don't believe us!' I say, trying to sound amazed.

'That's what I said in the first place,' goes Beauty, pushing his chest forward; but it falls back.

'Yeah,' goes Brain, turning his eyes at us then turning them away.

I think: Either they don't believe us but are not sure; or they believe us and are not sure.

I soon find out.

'You say Mobu was killed, full of holes?' Beauty half says half asks, half believing half disbelieving.

'Yes we do,' says Hena, 'for that's what happened.'

'I saw Mobu this morning,' Beauty carries on. 'We both saw Mobu this morning.'

'How do you know Mobu?' I ask.

'Everyone knows Mobu. He's the rider on the bus. Everyone knows him. He was known even before he became the rider. Then there's what happened to his wife. Everyone knows Mobu.' Brain looks at us, from one to the other, then says, 'Everyone knows Mobu,' for the umpteenth time.

Beauty says, 'Mobu came to see my brother this morning. My brother, he's an idiot. Does nothing but write poems. He used to work once, now no one will have him. So he writes poems no one will have. Mobu came to see him this morning.'

It's our turn to show strange emotions and make strange faces.

'If that's so, then you shouldn't believe in us at all,' says Hena after some thought, 'but you don't sound too sure. Why's that?' There is a little silence.

'With Mobu was a skelly boy,' says Brain. 'Like you, only worse. His name was Matt.'

Beauty adds, 'So we think as there is a Matt, maybe what you say is not all lies.'

We are all quiet for a while, though we're truly pleased to hear about Matt.

'You've told us what Matt looks like,' I say. 'Describe Mobu.'

Beauty thinks. 'I don't know. Nothing special I remember. Just like any grown-up, I should say.'

'How grown-up?' asks Golam.

'Oh, thirty maybe; maybe less. Can't be any surer than that.'

'The Mobu we know looked like an old man,' I say.

'But not the Mobu I saw in the desert with Matt,' says Golam. His eyes shine.

Hena's eyes shine. 'Nor the Mobu I saw with Matt in the house with the many rooms.'

I remember. My eyes shine. 'And the Mobu I saw with Matt in the hills of Bader was young too.'

By now Beauty and Brain believe we've come from the fruit farm.

In all these surprises we forget about Joti. And Daisy.

We mention this.

'Your bodies may have a day or two to go yet,' says Beauty, 'but your minds've already gone.'

Brain finds it very funny, but we don't.

They say if we rush up, find Daisy and get the money from her, they'll tell us about Joti.

They nudge each other in the ribs, wink and grin.

We start back towards the front of the hotel.

Beauty and Brain say they will come with us to the Main Road, but no further. They say they'll wait there for us to come back. With the money. They say we must have money in order for them to take us to where Joti is.

We're not plain dumb as they might think. We know they are after our money. But we also know we have no choice. If we want to find Joti, they are our only hope left. On account we are sure of one thing. They are not lying about knowing Joti. Whether they will or even can take us to him we don't know again.

But we have to take the chance.

We are still many shadows away from the Main Road when we

see about ten, fifteen boys and girls in dirty tattered clothes come running out of nowhere.

They are not skellies like us, but they are not big and healthy like Beauty and Brain.

'Don't go out there,' they shout in twos and threes, pushing past us. Brain grabs hold of one of them with big strong hands.

Beauty says, 'What's up?'

'Police,' says the thin little boy.

'Raid?' asks Brain.

I am surprised to see him all pale and nearly shaking.

'We don't think so. It's more like a riot in town The police is blocking the Main Road so that the crowds don't come that way and bother the VIPs in the Regent or the embassies nearby.'

'Are you sure they're not looking for us?' says Beauty, still cool.

'I'm not sure of anything,' the lad pipes back, 'but I don't think so.'

Beauty pulls him out of Brain's grasp and pushes him away, aiming a kick at his backside. It's not too hard a kick but it sends him stumbling ahead like shot out of a gun.

'What's all this riot about?' I say.

'It's poor people who can't get enough food and things led by idiots like my poetry-writing brother,' says Beauty.

Hena is surprised. 'We thought everybody had food in the city.'

'Well you thought wrong then, didn't you.'

Just then we see police coming that way.

Beauty and Brain disappear so fast I don't see them move.

I know I have been having trouble seeing recently, but this is more than that! This is speed. I feel quite jealous.

I don't think I want to say much about the next few days. To tell the truth there is nothing much to say about them. Nothing really happened. Nothing you'd find interesting.

As you'll have guessed by now, we weren't able to meet Daisy that day on the Main Road as it was blocked out. Nor could we find the building where she has her room. We couldn't even get to the general area. The bus man wouldn't let us get on the bus. We did have some money, but he took one look at us, looking the way we do and on our own, and told us to get out.

We were brave enough to ask for some food with our money, and lucky enough to get it, with the help of a kind man. But it didn't last long.

Since then we've been finding some to eat from street bins at night, where the dogs or the city kids let us.

Hena would rather do that than sit on the road and beg. The city kids don't let us do that anyway. They have divided up their 'patches' and they don't want no one else there. Least of all us. We look worse than anyone living they've seen before and they think we'll take their trade away, on account people will pity us more.

To tell the truth we don't care any more.

We wish Matt was with us. We remember our village and our families, and call to the Spirits. Leastwise I do.

Without really thinking we keep stumbling back to the street behind the Regent Hotel. Maybe we hope we might still meet Joti there; or at least Beauty and Brain, who might help us in finding him. Maybe because there are cartloads of lovely food in the hotel bins – only it is impossible to get at, what with the high walls and the guards.

We're there again today.

It is our lucky day. We see Brain and Beauty, actually looking for us!

They say they'll take us to a place where we just might meet Joti.

Even if we don't, the person who lives there, a white man, will give us money and food if we do as he tells us.

They say he makes photos.

They say we might have to take our clothes off.

They say he make photos of naked skelly children to send back to white countries to help get food for our country.

He shows us a newspaper called *The Guardian*. It has the picture of an ugly naked skelly, worse than us, asking for money. We can't tell if it's a boy or a girl, even though it's naked. We are ashamed of him, or her. And of ourselves. But we go along.

We stand naked in this large magic room. There are lights all over the place. Lights, high and low; lights, soft and bright; lights, still and moving; lights, plain and coloured.

The carpets and walls move and change patterns and shapes and colours along with the moving lights.

In the centre of the room is a tall funny-shaped thing with three tin legs. There is a camera on it. All around there are sofas and chairs and tables and pictures the like of which we've never seen nor dreamed of.

My head reels as I look round me. Things become sharp and clear and then turn hazy again. The whole room moves one way, then suddenly swings in the opposite direction.

Brain is standing beside the diamond-shaped windows, staring at our naked bodies. His mouth is open, showing small sharp teeth. They look funny in his big blunt face.

Beauty has gone into the next room to talk to the white man about us and to arrange for some money and food for us.

It is the first time I see Hena naked. I try not to but I can't help it as the room is full of mirrors. She looks funny. Most likely because everything is moving, bending and twisting her bones into peculiar shapes.

Brain moves closer to us. I can see more of his teeth now, but less of his eyes.

He comes closer still.

'I'll tell you a secret,' he says.

It looks like he's trying hard not to laugh.

I don't blame him. We do look a bit screwy. Golam and I with our bald little balls and a little meat roll on top; Hena with her dry little nipples and a smooth little slit between the legs; all three with little cheekless assholes.

'I bet you're dying to know what the secret is,' he says. Then his eyes shine. 'Dying,' he goes, clutching his stomach and bursting into a laugh, 'dying, that's a good one. If only Kagu was here to hear it. Dying...' he's killing himself with laughing. 'You're dying to... Good one, Tony, that is a good one for sure.'

He controls himself at last, to give his best slingshot yet, 'I'll tell you the secret you're *dyyiinng* to know: it's not your photos being took for *The Guardian*, it's your bodies being took for fucking.'

He doubles up with laughter hiccups, pointing to our bodies.

'Bodies,' he says, 'bodies... bodies...' He's practically rolling on the floor, slapping his thighs, saying, 'Bodies... bodies... bodies...'

If he means to scare me, he does.

'I never thought I'd start my fucking life like this,' I think to myself.

I must've thought aloud for Brain replies, 'More like end your fucking life like this, seeing as what's in store for you.' He can hardly speak for laughing, all the while slapping his thighs in quick short slaps. 'I'm too good today, I am. If only Kagu was here. He won't believe me now.' He's actually rolling on the floor.

I think I'm going to cry.

I don't know much about fucking. Haven't thought of it much in the past few days. I don't think I can do much with my little bald dingus and my cheekless ass. Especially tired as I am with the long walk down here and the long climb up the stairs on top of it.

I can't think what I'll have to do.

I wonder if I'll get my food if I can't do it, whatever it is.

The more I think about it, the more I think I can't, whatever it is.

By now I'm feeling so ill with worry I don't think I want to eat anyway.

I just want to go home. Only I don't know how.

I don't think Golam and Hena know what's going on. By the look on their faces I don't think they bother.

They just stand there, hands by their sides, not caring to cover their bits and pieces – like I am – all quietly waiting to have their pictures taken or their bodies fucked or whatever.

Beauty comes out of the room. He has some notes in his hands. He winks at Brain and waves the money about. He says, 'Let's get out of here. Quick.'

He hurries towards the door. The door which opened with a

magic button and some pretty music when we came in.

'Hey, wait a minute,' said Brain, 'I want to see what happens. I sure want to see Whitey's face when he sees what we've got lined up for him.'

'That's exactly what I don't want to see. Hurry. He'll be coming any second.'

'I won't miss it for the world,' goes Brain. 'Boy, it'll be some fun.'

'OK stupid,' says Beauty, 'I'm off. I'll give you your share this evening. If Jimmy the Boy don't kill you before then.' With that Beauty is out. We hear the music of the door.

A look of worry comes over Brain's face. He's about to follow Beauty, but it's too late.

Jimmy the Boy comes out of the other room.

Jimmy the Boy is all big and white and naked. His dingus is all red and purple and hard; wobbling heavily from side to side and up and down as its owner walks in with a swagger.

He takes one look at us and his face turns like his dingus: all red and purple and hard.

He eyes Brain like he's going to kill him, just as Beauty said he would.

Brain sees his changing face and makes a dash towards the door.

Jimmy the Boy then runs after him, balls clattering between tree-trunk thighs.

Just as he nabs Brain by the shirt collar I shout to Golam, 'Look, he's only got two balls!'

Jimmy the Boy freezes, and turns to us with hurt eyes. 'How many did you expect?' he says.

I'm surprised he understands our language.

Brain takes the opportunity to run out, faster than a bean fart.

'Matt was wrong after all,' I say.

I look at Golam.

Golam looks as if he don't agree.

Jimmy the boy looks confused.

I hear a light thud.

Hena is lying on the floor; blood red carpet spilling out of her bones.

Five

Hena the Whore

Before Jimmy the Boy can say or do anything, there is this little music again and a fat black man comes in.

'You are all primed. Well, half primed,' he says, looking Jimmy the Boy over. Beginning and ending with the middle.

Jimmy the Boy is not quite as hard between the legs as he was.

'I came as soon as I got your call,' the fat man carries on. 'Now what have we...' He stops quick when he sees us. Then speaks again, 'Well, well, well, what do you know... I never thought you...'

I can't see clear enough to say if he's happy or angry or just about to laugh.

'It's all a mistake,' says Jimmy the Boy, shifting his weight from one foot to the other, upsetting the balance of his balls. 'They said young, but...' He looks like a dog that's bitten its tail. 'It's that bloody Kagu. Wait till I get my hands up his asshole.'

The fat man just smiles. He walks past me standing by the wall, hands over my little ones; past Golam standing in the middle of the room, half bent like a question mark, looking down at Hena; and stops on the other side.

'Don't tell me you've turned into a paedophiliac necrophile?' he says.

'Don't tell me she's dead!' says Jimmy the Boy looking worried, dingus downcast.

The fat man kneels on the carpet and passes his hands over Hena's body.

'She's warm,' says the fat man, rubbing his hands against Hena's little nipples.

Golam hides his face in his hands. His body shakes a little every little moment.

The fat man is passing his fat tongue over his fat lips. I don't like his face when he does that.

'You won't... I mean, don't...' Jimmy the Boy moves up next to the fat man. 'She's just a child.'

He squats beside her, shaggy balls scratching the shaggy carpet.

'I can see,' says the fat man. 'I can see she's a child.' He passes his hands over Hena's stomach.

'Watch it,' says Jimmy the Boy. 'She's half dead.'

'Yes,' says the fat man, tenderly, 'she does look half dead, doesn't she.' He's rubbing his hands on Hena's thighs.

'She probably is dead,' says Jimmy the Boy. 'And even if she isn't she won't last your...'

'I'll bring her to life,' says the fat man. 'Stop fussing.'

'You're not doing anything here,' says Jimmy the Boy, 'not with her.'

'Stop fussing,' says the fat man. 'Stop fussing.'
His hands go on working on Hena.

Jimmy the Boy goes back into the other room.
While he's gone Fatso picks up a camera from the shelf and makes some 'instant photos' of us.
Jimmy the Boy soon returns wearing clothes and carrying some food. He tells Golam and me to put our robes back on, then wraps a shawl round Hena and gives her a drink which he gets from a large cabinet.
She moves a little, comes to life.
Jimmy the Boy – he says to call him JB – goes back to the cabinet, which opens out in all different ways, and takes out of it many coloured drinks. He calls them orange and Coke and Pepsi and goodness knows what-all. I like mango juice best.
He then gives us fruit bread and cakes and biscuits. And chocolates.
We've never seen so much to eat and drink in all our lives.
He says, 'Never mind about the crumbs on the carpet,' and gives us a smile. He has a good smile.
Once we've finished eating and drinking and Hena can sit up straight and I can see straight, JB says, 'I'll show you some magic you've never seen before.' He looks serious. 'Well I think you've never seen it. Have you seen TV?'
We say 'No, sir.' We still don't know him enough to call him JB.
He's pleased to learn we haven't seen TV before.
He 'switches on' this 'magic box' as he calls it.
It's all sort of black and grey on a shiny plate.
A man in uniform is talking of all the trouble in the city. He

is saying how the Government is doing such wonderful things and how troublemakers are making it difficult for all the decent people everywhere.

JB says, 'Fucking shit. I'll show you something more interesting. I've got video films, but most of them – ' as he is saying this he is looking through a whole stack of packets of some sort – 'are not for kiddies.

'Wait a minute, here's something you might like, A Fistful of Dollars. Most people like that. A fistful of dollars.' He laughs, looks at us, then says, 'Never mind. The Guns of Navarone, Gone With the Wind... Can't make up my mind. Here, that's it. Mary Poppins.' He takes it out. 'Or,' he laughs again, 'Dallas.'

He is making as if to show us Mary Poppins when Golam stops him.

'Please, sir, can we see Dallas?'

'Yes, sir, can we?' I say. We remember our old friend Kofi and his friends Jon and Donna.

'Call me JB,' says JB, looking puzzled. 'Why would you like to see Dallas?'

We say nothing. It would take too long to explain.

He puts it on for us. He says it is not a proper video film, but taped from TV back home.

We're not sure what he means.

He says: 'It will have ads in it. You know, advertisements. Things to buy. You understand?'

But we don't. Not that it matters.

Fatso has taken Hena in his arms. He is cuddling her and stroking her hair.

Golam and I sit with our back against the sofa.

We watch *Dallas* with open eyes and even more open mouths. It is in such beautiful colour. With such strange people doing such strange things.

And the 'ads'! We can't believe the things we see.

When Dallas finishes the local TV comes on by itself.

This time there is another man talking.

He is saying there is a new group of troublemakers starting up. A real dangerous group. They look like they sit around and do nothing. But, he says, they are more dangerous than the other lot.

They show a picture of this new dangerous group.

They are standing on the roadside in front of a Government building.

Behind them is a very large crowd.

In the centre of the group is young Mobu.

With him is my friend Matt.

I don't remember nothing after that on account I fall asleep.

When I wake up I'm in this strange room on this beautiful soft bed.

Golam is next to me, fast asleep.

I can't see Hena anywhere.

I get up from the bed.

I am worried about Hena.

I am dying for a shit. My first in a long time.

My mind and stomach are both in a boil.

There are many doors in the room, some with mirrors. I open one of these. It is full of fancy clothes for women.

I open another door.

I see a large room, with a glass floor and mirrored walls.

There is a blue stone sink, matching the blue glass floor, with blue stone magic taps.

Part of the floor is sunk in the shape of a flower. There is a blue stone seat with a large hole in it.

Could it be... I wonder.

It is a bathroom, I can tell. So the seat must be for... I wonder.

Daisy's little room had a little hole in the floor.

This is a hole too, even if it is half way up in the air, even if it is fit for a queen to sit on.

I don't care if it is or isn't.

I sit on it and let myself go. You could've heard me back in my village.

There is paper here which I use like stones and sand back there. The relief is true happiness.

Everything is sort of floating in there but I don't know how to get rid of it. I try pulling whatever I can pull, push whatever I can push and turn whatever I can turn. Nothing.

Well, not exactly nothing. I get a fountain coming out of the sunken floor, I have all sorts of music come on. But nothing that moves the shit.

Then, suddenly, without any warning, whoosh. Water starts pouring out of the sides of the seat like streams down the hills. Water circles in it like an eddy. Water winds round my shit, whirls and swirls till all is sucked down with the music of the rapids.

I think it all happens when I step on a small grey circle on the floor.

I wash myself in joy.

But then I remember Hena.

I come out of the room more worried than before. Now that my stomach is at ease, my mind can worry better.

Golam is still sleeping.

I open another door. It leads to a long wide corridor with a red floor.

I walk along it.

'You've been sleeping for more than a day and a night,' says a voice.

I nearly jump and hit the hanging lights above my head.

It is Fatso.

I ask him about Hena.

He tells me not to worry. That she's fine. He says if I go back to the room and bring Golam with me, he'll take us to the eating room. He says Hena will be there.

I wake Golam up and show him the shit trap. He needs it too. Then we go to the eating room. It is like something out of *Dallas*.

Hena is there.

But she don't look like our Hena.

She has this red and white silk dress on. She has gold on her fingers, gold round her wrists, gold round her neck and gold in her hair.

And shining stones – red and white. With red and white shoes which make her a hand taller.

We look at her. Her face seems hard and cold and old. She says, 'You took your time coming.' She's still our Hena, no matter what.

Fatso says Hena is going to stay with him now, on account he's sort of adopted her, like a niece.

He says both he and Hena feel we should go back to our village now. He says we should go back so that we can take food and gifts and money for our families which he will give us.

'What shall we tell our folks?' I say.

'Tell them Hena sends you gifts.' Hena speaks in a hard voice.

'Yes, tell them Hena sends you gifts and money. Gifts and money which she's not stolen nor begged.

'Tell them she'll send more, and keep sending. Tell it specially to my Mam.' For the first time I feel like her voice is going to crack, but it don't.

'But we've yet to find Joti, and meet up with Matt before we can go,' says Golam.

'I don't know of Matt,' says Fatso. 'But I know Joti well. Hena's told me about him. I'll see if I can help you find him. The last I saw him he was trying to hide from the police. I'll ask my chauffeur if he knows something.'

'Surely you can do more than that,' Hena snaps at him, all angry.

'Sorry, love. I'll try.' He turns to us. 'I'll take you to the Regent and ask around for you. There are some waiters there who might know. If not, I'll ask a couple of police inspectors. Is that better?' he looks at Hena again.

'We'll see how it works out,' she says.

When we've finished eating, Fatso claps his hands and a servant girl comes to clear the table.

'Don't throw any of the food away,' Hena tells her.

The servant girl looks at Hena in surprise and what could be hate. Fatso looks at Hena in surprise and what could be love.

'What'll you do with it?' he says. 'You're not still hungry, are you? And if...'

'Not me. Not any more,' she goes, looking through him. 'But I know many that are.'

'How will you find them? And how will you get it to them?' says Fatso with a weak laugh. 'Surely you're being...'

Hena stops him with a look. 'How will I find them?' she goes. 'How will I find them! How can you not find them? As to how will I get it to them. Simple. I'll take it to them.'

Fatso says nothing.

The servant girl changes her look, but she don't seem too sure what to change it to.

*

That evening Fatso takes us in this mile long car to the Regent, to enquire about Joti.

He asks the chauffeur to park in a sidestreet.

We stay in the car as he walks to the Hotel. The chauffeur goes away for a quiet smoke.

While we wait we see Beauty and Brain standing by a lamp post, not far away, looking at us.

We could drive our car, huge though it is, through their mouths if we could drive.

Slowly they come towards us. They look around to make sure that we're alone. They come right to the window. They look at me in my new black robe. They look at Golam in his new white robe. They look at Hena in all her finery and gold and stones.

Brain says, 'Wow, look at her. Just look at Hena.'

'I don't believe it. The little whore.' Beauty speaks so softly we hardly hear him.

They start going round the car. First slow; then fast, then faster and faster still, chanting, 'Hena the whore. Hena the whore. Hena the whore. Hena the whore. Hena the whore...'

Hena opens the car door and steps out.

Beauty and Brain stop, like hit by a bullet.

'I'm sure you know many hungry city kids,' says Hena, a little to my surprise. Beauty and Brain are a little surprised too.

'We what?' says Brain.

Beauty just looks at her.

Hena repeats herself.

'We sure do,' says Beauty, still puzzled and very wary.

'Gather them tomorrow in the shed where you first took us and tell them Hena the Whore will bring them food. Six in the morning. And six in the morning every day from now on.'

'Six in the morning!' says Brain.

'You heard,' says Hena, 'six in the morning. Every morning. I have other things to do as well. But do warn them – they might have some work to do.

'And by the by, I know you don't need food, but there will be something in it for you, too.'

Beauty is about to speak, but stops, turns and runs. So does Brain.

The chauffeur is walking towards us with quick long strides.

Hena gets back into the car.

'Why the city kids?' I ask her. 'They were horrible to us.'

'Maybe because they were hungry,' says Golam.

Hena don't say nothing on account she's crying.

I look at her face. I have never ever seen her cry before. She don't hide her face or hang her head down.

Soon Jak is back. Jak is Fatso's name.

There is no sure news of Joti; but one waiter says the last time he met Joti he was planning to go back to his village. Partly to escape the 'city heat', but also he was worried about his folks at home, what with the news of famine and raids. He was even hoping to bring his Dada down to the city, if possible.

When we make the unhappy chauffeur take us to the warehouse shed at six the next morning, with our baskets of food, there, among the hungry city kids, is Matt.

Part IV

SPIRITS OF SHIT

(the journey back)

One

Tunnel Trouble

We are in this blue and yellow jeep specially painted for our trip home.

It is painted blue and yellow so as to look different from the dirty green of the Army jeeps. So no one attacks it thinking it is an Army jeep. It is also painted blue and yellow on account Jak's chauffeur likes it painted blue and yellow.

Jak's chauffeur – he's called Reza – is so fed up with taking Hena to the warehouse shed at six every morning he'd rather drive us back to our village.

He says – under his breath but we hear it – that Hena'll have to find some other mug to do her running around at that hour of the day.

In the village we're used to starting our day even earlier, but I reckon these city people are soft.

Anyway, here we are, Matt, Golam and me, all loaded with food and gifts to take home. As much food and gifts as our blue and yellow jeep can hold. And it sure can hold a lot.

It is some weeks later since our meeting up with Matt. Hena and Jak made us stay on and put some meat on us before starting our journey back.

I don't recognise myself any more. I am beginning to look almost as big as I was at nine, three years ago. Golam is getting his smile back, his hair is starting to bounce again and his shoulders are stronger and fuller than a wire hanger.

We're sorry to leave Hena behind. Hena don't say much about how she feels. She does look pretty, though, in her new clothes; even if she is mostly bones. She don't seem to be putting on flesh like we are.

Jak adores her. He calls her his favourite niece, his long-lost cousin, his nearest and dearest little relative.

Some believe what he says, many don't; but they don't say nothing except to say she's a dear little girl and remarkably clever. The way they say it I'm not sure what they mean. The words are nice but somehow they don't sound nice.

Hena don't seem to bother. Or if she does, she don't show it.

We are told to say we're friends of the family, from a far-off village fallen on hard times.

Although we'll miss watching TV and seeing our shit whirl and swirl down the shit trap, and other such luxuries, we're truly looking forward to getting back home.

We don't take the road used by the bus company, but go on the road through the hills of Bader.

We are allowed to use it on account Jak is some 'high-ranking official connected with the Defence Department' of the Government.

I am very happy about it. I know that in the end we'll have to come out in the plains, but in the meantime it is lovely to be here.

We are going at a slow speed, partly because the road is bumpy but mainly to enjoy the scenery as we go along.

Reza is acting strange. He's friendly and kind one minute, and shouting down our ears the next. We don't know what to make of it. But then you never know with him. There are many things he always does but always complains about doing. There are many things he never does but always says he'd like doing. But then again most grown-ups are like that.

Reza had a nice face and a good body. Best of all, he has a thick sleepy voice that wakes you up when he sings sad songs that make you happy.

We loved to hear him sing while he waited when Hena gave out food to the hungry children.

I won't mind being friends with him, but it's not easy. There's no telling what he'll say or do.

We pass many groups of soldiers on the way, some of whom stop us. Reza shows them something called a 'Military Pass', and they wave us on. One or two ask us a few questions, but mostly they do nothing except stare at us rather oddly. I expect we still don't look too good. Or perhaps they're just surprised to see poor country boys going about in Jak's jeep.

I wonder if that's why Reza is acting strange. Even stranger than usual.

It is nearly night now. There haven't been any soldiers for some time. Leastwise no one has stopped us. I am just saying this to myself, almost in my sleep, when the jeep suddenly stops with a hard jolt.

I look up, half awake, and I see this tall man in a sharp uniform, khaki instead of spotty green, with a few stripes and ribbons added on.

He is standing in front of the jeep.

He has this big gun hanging down by his side, and a revolver in his hand.

He asks to see our papers, same as the others.

He looks at them, then goes and talks to two other soldiers waiting in a jeep nearby.

He comes back to us and tells us to follow the other jeep.

Reza asks him if there's any problem; he's all polite, but we can tell he's nervous and afraid.

The officer says not to worry. He says there's some trouble on the road ahead so he's leading strangers to the outside road. Not the bus route which runs to the right of us down by the plains, but another road which goes round the hills from the upper end.

Reza asks if there is some explosion or a terrorist attack, but the officer don't answer, just tells us to follow the other jeep.

To my surprise, and to Reza's surprise as well, the officer jumps on to our jeep instead of going on his own jeep.

We get off the road and on to a hilly tract of land. We carry on like this for some time, then we are stopped by another group of soldiers. Reza is looking more and more worried, though he's trying not to show it. He's good at it too, and if I didn't know him I wouldn't've guessed he's worried.

But, among other little things, he's not smoking. And he don't smoke only when he's upset. Otherwise he loves to lie back or lean back – depending on where he is – and light a smoke. Also he's smiling a lot, and talking a lot. That's not him either.

More surprising, the officer with us don't seem too happy to be stopped. I can tell even though I don't know him well. Don't know him at all really, you know.

Anyhow, this group of soldiers let us pass on, and everyone seems like saved from a falling boulder.

We carry on. We pass some more soldiers, but they cheerfully smile at us and wave their hands and we wave our hands and no more than that. By now I am getting more worried. For no particular reason I can tell. Except perhaps that Matt looks strange.

When we'd started he was laughing and telling jokes and pulling our legs like he used to when we were kids, all excited about going home to our village. But now he's tense again, like he is most of the time these days.

I can't dare to ask him as whatever it is, if it is anything at all, no one seems to want to talk about it. And I am surely not going to be the one to open my mouth and fall into it.

Golam is the only one not seeming too bothered about anything.

We go up and down the bumpy hillside till we are on a sort of a flattish land. On one side is a high mountain, and on the other is a low valley.

It is all black now, especially under the shadow of the mountain.

Suddenly it is pitch black, like Grandma Toughtits' silk scarf.

I can't see the palms of my hands, nor the whites of Golam's eyes. Also it sounds peculiar.

'Don't be frightened lads,' I hear Reza's voice, sleepy again now, 'we're in a tunnel.'

After that we hear nothing except the rumbling sound of the jeeps closing in on us from all sides.

And we see nothing. Except a flash of light and then the red end of a cigarette.

Reza's worries seem to be over.

The tunnel don't end.

I miss Hena. I, who spent a lot of my life wanting to be rid of her, I miss Hena.

We are out of the tunnel; and in trouble.

We've been kidnapped.

The officer and the two soldiers who brought us here are not real Government Army people, but guerrilla fighters dressed up. It seems Reza works for them.

They are thinking of demanding hundreds of thousands of American dollars for our 'release'.

I don't know whether to laugh or cry.

I mean, who'd pay five dollars for us?

Mam and Dada would, but they haven't got five dollars.

I mean, 'It's not like we are real people even,' I say out loud.

'What d'you mean, "real people"?' asks Golam.

'Real people... You know... Proper people. People other people care for I don't know... Smart sort of people...' I am having difficulty in saying what I mean when I get this idea: 'Like in *Dallas*. Y'know.

Proper people.'

'What do you think we are then?' Matt says in sudden anger. 'Spirits of Shit?'

'You tell me. You're the smart-ass,' I shout back at him.

'None of your squabbling,' says Reza. 'We know someone who will pay for you lot to be free. Fatso Jak.'

Reza thinks he'll pay on account of Hena.

Hena would want to pay, says Reza, not only because of us, but also because she'll sympathise with their 'cause', seeing as she's so concerned with the hungry people.

And if Hena wants to pay, as she will, then she'll make Jak pay.

Reza says Hena can make him do anything. He says he don't know how that little Miss Bones can do it, but she can do it. He says. He says Jak oughtn't to mind much as it isn't his money anyway. It is part of the money which some countries send to our country to help our people, but which never gets to our people. It is used by people like Jak and the Government for buying guns and bullets and bombs and fighter planes to keep the people down. Instead of feeding them, as it is meant to do. So the people have a right to it.

We ask him what they'll be doing with the money.

He says they'll be buying guns and bullets and bombs and fighter planes to fight the Government.

We look at each other on account we don't understand. Leastwise I don't.

'You want to take their money – sorry, the people's money – so Jak and the Government don't buy guns and things with it. Then you want to buy guns and things with it. Don't make sense,' says Matt.

'But these guns are to support the people, not suppress them. Surely you can see the difference,' says Reza.

'No, to tell the truth, we can't,' says Matt.

Golam just shakes his head from side to side.

I think I am beginning to understand, but I'm not altogether sure.

'You are too young to understand, perhaps,' says Reza, 'but you should start. The sooner the better. It is your world and you have to change it. And you can change nothing by sitting on your backside hoping. By the time you grow up it may be too late. Now is the time to do something about it. Let me tell you that...'

'Don't tell them anything. They are bad news.' I hear a voice.

A voice I think I've heard, but I can't remember.

I look up. I remember. I remember the face that goes with the voice. It is the man in blue jeans who took us to and from the caves near our village. When the white folk were taken. When Kabir was killed.

He had a smiling voice then. It is a hard voice now.

I think he thinks we are to blame for Kabir's death.

I think we are in more trouble than I think.

Two

The Miracle

It is our third night in the mountain hide-out of the guerrillas; and the second after Reza is roughed up a bit, drugged a bit, and left as close to the power station as possible with a ransom note pinned to his shirt.

The guerrillas – they call themselves RAFFs which is short for Revolutionary African Freedom Fighters – are hoping that Reza will soon be spotted by the soldiers and taken to Jak, along with the ransom note.

Reza's story will be short and simple: while driving us through the hills he stopped when he saw a man lying across the road; he got out, was hit from behind, and remembers nothing after that.

There is a risk that Jak might suspect him; but then it is a risky business and risks have to be taken.

Leastwise that's how Jabbar sees it. That's how Reza see it too. With the lives of their people in danger, they're not afraid to put their own lives in danger.

We're all waiting to see if Jak shits out the money or not.

Golam can't make up his mind. One minute he thinks Jak will, and the next he thinks Jak won't.

I think he will on account I believe, same as Reza, that our Hena can make him do it.

'I think Jak will give the money,' says Matt. 'I hope Hena won't pay it out.'

We don't get a chance to learn what happens. Not now at least.

We don't even find out if Jak gets to see the ransom note or not.

We are all in this large kraal between the rocks. It has the bum of the squatting mountain as its sky and the thighs and feet of the squatting mountain as its boundaries.

There is a big enough crack in the bum to let good enough light through. The opening between the legs runs into a tunnel at the one end, and expands to a wide bush covered entrance at the other.

Boulders and trees help to hide it from sight. There is water from a trickly waterfall, which keeps animals and unwanted human beings out as well. To make sure of this a particularly thorny kind of bush has been specially planted by the RAFFs. It looks quite natural and stops anybody from straying in by accident.

Inside, the area has been divided into two halves. One half has three sleeping areas and a cooking area. The other half is a large meeting area. Hidden behind this is another large area used for storing guns and bullets and bombs. Most of these are in huge wooden boxes covered with hessian and straw mats to keep them dry as well as to hide them.

This part, and the entrance, are always well guarded; so is the tunnel.

It is in the tunnel that we first hear the commotion.

Leastwise that's what Matt says, on account he was the only one awake at the time. The only one among us there, that is.

Soon everyone is awake.

Someone says to put the lamp on to see what's going on. Someone says to put the lamp out for Heaven's sake.

We all sit huddled close, not knowing what to say or think.

Jabbar holds on to his big gun with the bullet belt, tenses up like a cat ready for the kill, and moves forward in quick soft steps to see what it's all about.

Jabbar is Kabir's friend, the man in blue jeans from the caves near our village; the one with the smiling voice turned hard.

Some follow him; some hide between rocks, ready to attack any unwelcome visitor.

Soon three of the guards come in, bringing a struggling man along with them.

Jabbar is behind them, big gun held in the right position, ready to fire.

We hear a deep sleepy voice. 'It's only me, for God's sake.'

We see Reza, still struggling to free himself from the guards.

Everyone relaxes. Their shoulders go down and they breathe easy.

Jabbar's eyes are still hard and his gun is still held up.

'What are you doing back here?' he says more than asks.

Reza says the Tabiris are in great danger and he's come to warn us.

The Tabiris are a tribe that live in clusters of straw huts a little to the north, where the mountains and the desert and the bush country meet.

They are supposed to be great friends of the Freedom Fighters.

They hide their men when necessary and generally give them every kind of help possible.

They once owned a whole tract of land to the south, in the greener part of the country, and were ruled by their own Chiefs.

The new Government under General Tako took their fertile land and their cattle, drove them north to the bush country, and killed or arrested their Chiefs. Now they are ruled by the Government.

But the Tabiris are hard working, and with a little bit of luck plus a little bit of water and a little bit of good soil from the mountains they manage to survive.

They learn to hate Tako and his soldiers, and make friends with the guerrillas.

I didn't know all this before, but I know it now.

Reza's story goes like this.

He's been lying around waiting to be found, hoping it's going to happen soon as it's getting cold and he's feeling bored and miserable.

Although he really hasn't been beaten up, not much anyway, his limbs are aching and getting stiffer by the minute. The wind is sharpening up and cutting right through his bones.

Jabbar tells him to cut the poetry and get to the point. He says he don't believe in playing violins. Wouldn't know how even if he wanted to.

I'm not sure what he means, but I don't reckon it's of much importance.

Reza looks a bit hurt. I mean in the mind, his body's hurting anyway.

He comes to the point.

'The Tabiris are going to be wiped out by the BASTOs,' he says.

BASTOs stands for the Bloody Awful Soldiers of Tako.

'When?' asks Jaffar.

'Tomorrow night. At least the BASTOs plan to start out of here tomorrow, just past the midnight hour. They'll get to the Tabiri settlement some time after dawn, in their jeeps.'

'How do you know all this?' Jabbar carries on, still in a harsh-ish voice.

Reza says that while he's waiting – he don't go into any details now – he sees this group of soldiers come towards where he is. He is pleased. Pleased but scared.

The soldiers don't see him. He is about to groan a little to attract their attention, but stops dead when he hears what they are saying. They are talking about their planned raid on the Tabiri settlement.

They think the Tabiris are storing arms and ammunition for the RAFFs. Perhaps even actually buying arms on their behalf from the white traders.

They – the BASTOs – think it is high time the Tabiris were 'permanently' stopped from doing this. In the process they also hope to grab a great deal of welcome 'material' which the Tabiris are keeping for the RAFFs. According to the BASTOs, that is.

When Reza hears this he prays the opposite of what he was praying before. He prays they don't see him.

They don't.

He unpins the ransom note and ties it with a string round a small stone. While crawling back here, as quietly and carefully as possible, he leaves the stone with the note in one of the Army jeeps scattered around the power station.

He hopes the stone will keep it from flying away, and someone will notice when it is daytime.

There is a lot of loud talking and discussion after Reza has finished speaking.

They think the 'only possible course of action' is to attack the soldiers first. Before they can get to the Tabiris.

To wait for them at the lower end of the upper mountains and charge when they get there on their way to the Tabiri settlement.

'On the positive side,' says Jabbar, 'we'll have the advantage of surprise.

'On the negative side, we'll be on the BASTOs' home ground. If they can get quick reinforcements, we'll be surrounded and could be in a very difficult situation indeed.'

'We all know the hills better than the BASTOs,' says Reza. 'They are all from different parts of the country. Some are even foreigners.

'Most of us were born and bred here. If necessary, we will be able to spread out and hide. Especially at night.'

'On the other hand, if they follow us here, they could get hold of all our ammunition,' says one RAFF. 'It's losing that that worries me more than losing my life.'

'If only the good Lord made a miracle,' says Reza in his deep sleepy voice, 'and our stock of arms was increased manifold, we could wipe out the entire colony of BASTOs.'

'If only we could get some money for those skelly boys, that would help more than your Lord can,' says Jabbar.

'I know Kabir, may peace be upon him, thought of you as his right arm, and I also know we could well do with the money, but I do wish you hadn't spoken like that – ' Reza's voice is more awake than we've ever heard before – 'of the boys, or of the Lord.'

Jabbar is quiet for a long time, then says, 'You are right. I shouldn't have.

'And I promise if your Lord can work this miracle, I'll join you in your faith.' He says this with a smile in his voice. This is the first time I hear a smile in his voice since that time long ago when Kabir was alive.

'I'll say Amen to that,' says Reza.

'Amen,' say some others, a few seriously, a few jokingly.

'Amen my foot,' says one RAFF. 'Say Amen to the God who allows half of mankind to die in pain and shame just because they happen to be black, when it is He who is supposed to have made them black in the first place! You must be joking, and joking in very bad taste.'

'Here, here,' say quite a few.

'Down with tyranny,' says Jabbar.

'Down with tyranny,' say all.

'Down with Tako,' says Jabbar.

'Down with Tako,' say all.

'Down with BASTOs,' says Jabbar.

'Down with BASTOs,' say all.

'Long live the people,' says Jabbar.

'Long live the people,' say all.

This goes on for some time.

Everyone is so excited and worried about the situation that they forget to send anyone to guard us in our sleeping area.

'Now is the time to run away,' I say, nearly as excited as the RAFFs.

'Now is the time not to run away,' says Matt, more excited than the RAFFs.

We don't sleep much that night.

Well, to tell the truth, I do. But from what I hear most others don't. Even though Jabbar orders everyone to their straw mats to sleep and rest as much as they can in order to be fresh the next morning to prepare for the attack.

When I say Jabbar orders everyone to their straw mats to sleep and rest, I don't mean absolutely everyone.

There are some he sends out under cover of the night to gather together as many men as they possibly and safely can. He says those living in and around Bader can, with any luck, be here before tomorrow night, before the planned attack on the BASTOs, before their planned attack on the Tabiris.

The next day is worse than school. Everyone is being told not to do this but to do that. Or this and that while preparing for the other as well.

Men are coming and men are going. Women too.

Orders are being given, and changed.

Plans are being drawn, and redrawn.

'Vantage points' and 'strategic points' and 'collision points' are being thrown around so fast that everybody is full of points.

All are tense and nervous, which I can understand. Afraid and unafraid at the same time, which I can also understand.

What I can't understand is that they seem almost happy.

After everything has been organised to the satisfaction of most – at least to Jabbar's satisfaction – it is time to 'launch the attack'.

It is planned to sneak out in twos and threes; and to crouch, creep or crawl up to the craggy rocks where it is agreed they will ambush the BASTOs.

As the final and most important act, Jabbar takes a few of his trusted men to the rear cave where the gun boxes are kept, to share out the guns and things.

He comes out looking like a white man.

It looks like he's seen his gun boxes multiply in front of his very eyes.

As it happens, that's exactly what he has seen.

And so have the others who went with him.

They all come out looking like white men. Leastwise like Chinese. Only more tanned. And with large round eyes rather than slit slanting eyes.

It takes them a long while to explain what they have seen.

One or two say they actually saw the gun boxes increase in number while they stood in front of them. Others say the cave was full of boxes even as they went in.

However or whenever it happened, they can't agree upon; but

they are all agreed that the boxes are many times more than they were.

Other people rush in, one by one and in groups. They all come back with the same story: the cave is full of boxes, right up to the ceiling and along the walls and in the centre.

One of them says even the walls of the cave have moved in order to make room for more boxes.

'Yes. The cave did seem much bigger,' say some others.

The rest are too dazed to say anything.

Jabbar is the first to recover his cool.

'Does this mean I too cross over to Jesus and Mother Mary?' he says to Reza, 'Like you.'

He looks calm, he is even smiling, but his voice is like a leaf in the wind.

I am surprised as I didn't think Reza was a Mother Mary and Jesus believer. Leastwise his name don't show that.

Reza is one of those too dazed to say anything. All he can manage is to sway his head, half way between shaking and nodding.

'Now we can take on and destroy all the BASTOs this side of Bader,' says Jabbar, with a new passion in his voice. It still quivers, but is deeper and stronger, like water in the wind.

His face is a mating snake; his eyes, glass in the sun.

'Let's go get 'em,' he shouts.

'Don, Mutabe, Kalu, Lebu...' he carries on, getting more and more excited, 'go get the boxes out and let's see what we've got.

'And you, Marilu, Andy, Len, Kuru... choose your men. Go as far north, south, east or west as you can and round up all the men you can.

'We'll launch an all-out attack on the BASTOs.

'I'll have to start drawing new plans for a three-pronged attack...'

'Wait a minute, wait a minute...' Reza's sleepy voice finally wakes up. 'What about our attack tonight?'

'That would be frittering away our resources... I know I know I know... I know what you're thinking. About the Tabiris. But we have to see to the greater good of all. Even if it does mean sacrifices...'

'Sacrifices my foot. It's only too easy to sacrifice others. We decided to...' Reza's voice is wide awake.

'And why did we decide what we did decide? On what you told us. How do we know it is true? How do we know you are not leading *us* into the BASTOs trap, while making us believe it is we who are trapping the BASTOs? We've only your word for it.'

'How can you even...'

'I've never really trusted you. Leading a life of super bourgeois luxury with the ruling classes. How do we know it hasn't tainted your vision of working class supremacy. How do we...'

'I think you'd better not say any more. I don't want to be forced into doing or saying anything I might regret later.'

'How do we know,' Jabbar carries on as if he hasn't heard a word Reza has said, 'how do *we* know you're not working for Jak to spy on us, rather than the other way round...'

'I'm warning you...'

Before Reza can say any more, Don, Mutabe, Kalu and Lebu come running out of the other cave.

We can't make out from their faces what they're feeling. We

can't make out from their words what they're saying.

We can make out by their gestures they want the others to go into the other cave with them.

Reza jumps up and goes. So does Jabbar. I think they are both a bit pleased to get out of the argument.

Many more follow.

Golam and I sneak in between their legs.

Some of the boxes are lying open.

They contain grain and powdered milk. We can tell for we've seen plenty of it in the camp at Gonta.

Like mad Spirits one and all pull all the boxes down, push open their lids, and look.

They all contain either grain or powdered milk.

One of them has apples.

'You and your bloody Lord and your bloody miracles,' says Jabbar.

'The Tabiris are done for now.'

'A minute ago you were coming over to my blo... my Lord.

'A minute ago you were going to re-draw your whole plan of attack.

'A minute ago you were quite happy to sacrifice the Tabiris...'

'Do not worry for the Tabiris,' says Matt very quietly in the middle of all the noise.

There is a sudden silence.

'Do not worry for the Tabiris,' says Matt again. 'Miracles have wings. They go everywhere.

'All you need is eyes to see them and minds to use them.'

Everyone looks at Matt with new eyes.

Jabbar finds words, 'Oh yeah! Then what do we do? Sit on our ass and wait for them to happen.'

'No,' says Matt, 'get off your ass and make them happen.'

'Oh yeah!' says Jabbar. 'So I go about changing boxes of guns into boxes of grain. And how do you suggest I do that?'

'Easy, just change your shopping list.'

'And where do I get the money to shop?'

'By changing hearts.'

'Into what?'

'Back into hearts.'

Everyone stands in silence; not speaking, not moving.

'It's time for me to go now,' says Matt.

He takes Golam and me by the arms and leads us out towards the big opening. When he is half way there, he turns round and says: 'It will be good if you follow.'

'God Almighty!' We hear Jabbar's voice come at us like a scream as we are nearly at the bush-covered gap, on our way out. 'Now I know what has happened.

'The bloody idiots who transported the boxes must have got them from the wrong warehouse. The one where Kari hordes the Aid food for police black marketeers...

'Phew! And to think I nearly... Very nearly... Phew!' Then suddenly, in a different voice, 'After them. Don't let them get away.

'I have a fat ransom to collect. For the people... Hurry, hurry. What're you looking at me for like that? Get going, get going. Fast...'

We don't know if the RAFFs hurry and get going or not. But we do.

Down the trickly waterfall is a thin crack in the rock.
Only skellies like us can squeeze through it. We do, and wait,
hoping for the hoo ha to die down before making a move.

Three

The Black Cat

It is almost dawn when we dare to squeeze ourselves out.

We walk downhill along the wall of the mountain. Firstly because we think it will lead us to the plains that spread between the mountains and Gonta. Secondly because it is safer: there are many cracks and corners to hide in.

We have to watch out for BASTOs as well as RAFFs.

We just want to get back home now.

When it is light we gather some tender leaves and roots and fungi; and hide ourselves to eat and rest a while.

Before we know it we're asleep. Leastwise I am.

When I wake up it is nearly dark again. Golam is still sleeping. Matt is sitting up hugging his legs, chin resting on drawn-up knees. He looks so much like the thing in *The Guardian*. Only he's not all naked.

We wake Golam up, make sure there are no BASTOs about, and start our walk again.

We haven't gone far when we hear this sudden silence.

Matt stops dead in his tracks and holds us back with his arms. All the noises of the night are completely gone.

It's only when we practically stop our breathing that we hear this other breathing. It is heavy and comes and goes in quick short gasps. More like panting than breathing.

It is the black cat in search of food.

She is in front of us, not far off. We can see two green stars in the blackness of the earth.

We hear a twig crack.

It is behind us, not far off.

We wonder whether to walk ahead towards the cat, or back to whatever is behind us.

To the left is the mountain wall; to the right, a long fall.

We decide to stay where we are. Well, I don't think we actually decide to stay where we are. We just do. More through not deciding than deciding. Leastwise as far as I am concerned.

We're not moving one hair's breadth, but the cat's eyes are getting closer, so I reckon the cat must be moving towards us. You don't have to be a genius to figure that one out. Little wonder I figure that one out.

We can now just about see the slim muscled form of the animal. Blacker than the night, and as beautiful.

I wonder what the cat makes of us. She certainly gives us a thought, for she stops in front of us and looks us over.

There is a rustle of leaves behind us.

The cat's eyes jerk away from us in half a flash. In the next half she leaps into the air, flies above us and lands on whatever is behind us. There is a scream and a roar.

Golam and I run the other way. Matt leaps up in the air, like the cat; and follows the cat.

We stop, Golam and me, look at one another then, very frightened, turn round and slowly make our way towards the cat and Matt.

By the time we get there the cat is gone, leaving Matt holding her victim in his arms.

It is another boy like us. Only not skinny like us. Quite fat really. Filled out.

When we get near we find out it is not really a boy at all, but a grown man. A small grown man. A midget man.

A midget man we know quite well.

It is Kofi.

He don't recognise us. At first. But when we tell him who we are, he remembers. He remembers very well, though he is surprised. He is surprised to see us, and he is surprised to see us looking the way we do.

But then he says he shouldn't really be surprised, seeing the lack of food and the state of sickness in the country.

Luckily he's not badly hurt. He says he can't believe he's still in one piece.

It seems Matt rushing over to him frightened the cat away.

As it happens he's only got claw marks on his arms and chest. They are quite deep, but not too deep. They are bleeding, but not heavily. We take him to the nearest place where there is some water. We wash his wounds and bandage him up as best as we can.

He don't seem to be in too bad a state after we've taken care of him.

When Kofi asks what we're doing here, we tell him we've left the RAFFs' hide-out and are making our way towards our village.

He says that's funny on account he is looking for the RAFFs hide-out.

We ask him if he was going up or down when the cat got him.

He says down.

We tell him in that case he's missed the place for it is a fair way up.

He says oh bother and what have you and other words and phrases, some polite, some not so polite.

We tell him not to worry on account we know where to go and will lead him there, provided he don't tell Jabbar where we are.

We say Jabbar is not too pleased on account he couldn't ambush the soldiers last night – or was it the night before? – on their way to the Tabiri settlement.

Kofi gives us a strange look and asks us what we know of the BASTOs' plans for the Tabiris.

We tell him what we know.

He says my word and what have you and other words and phrases, some polite, some not so polite.

He says he was with the Tabiris on the morning the soldiers got there.

He says a white reporter and his camera team were there at the time. In fact they'd only got there the night before, but they planned to stay some time as they are doing a long 'documentary' on the past, present and likely future of the Tabiris – and their relationship with the Tako government.

He says when the Tabiris see the soldiers they think they've come to kill them and to burn their huts.

But the soldiers say they've come to help them, as they've heard they've fallen on hard times.

He says at first he don't believe them, and think they've quickly made up the story on seeing the white TV people.

But when the TV people ask to look into the camp which the BASTOs have set up a little to the north, they find grain and powdered milk instead of weapons.

The TV people say they'll be coming again to make a follow-up programme.

The soldiers say they'll try to see that the Tabiris get their supply of food.

The soldiers' behaviour was very strange, Kofi says. They also looked very strange. Like they weren't quite sure what to say or do. If it hadn't been for the grain and milk, Kofi says, he'd never have believed them.

Four

The BASTOs

We're having this quiet chat with Kofi and making plans for taking him to the RAFFs' hide-out when we are surrounded by many pairs of big black boots.

Five

Spirits of Shit

We don't know how many hours or days the BASTOs keep us.

At last they take us in their jeep and throw us out.
They spit at us through their teeth as we fall. Some of it gets us, some of it don't, but it don't matter as we don't have no clothes to worry about.
It is a long fall. We fly through the air, arms and legs spread out, whirling and twirling, the wind cutting through our eyes, blinding us with sharp blades.
Maybe it is the darkness of the night that blinds us.
Maybe it is fear.
Though I don't remember feeling afraid.
I don't remember feeling anything.
Leastwise I don't remember feeling a feeling for which I have

learnt a name.

We whirl and twirl, like shit caught in rushing winds instead of flushing water; going down, under, sucked into the gutter of the Earth.

Any minute I expect bits of me to start falling off, melting in the clammy night air.

I can feel them falling off, but I don't think they melt away.

I hear an owl hoot. My head drowns in the joy of it. I want to live.

With the want to live comes the pain, thumping in every drop of blood.

I fall with a dull thud onto something both soft and hard, both wet and dry.

I hear another thud. Is it Matt, or Golam? I can't be sure.

Something falls on me. It is heavy and wet. A part of Kofi, maybe.

The black of the night turns stark white before turning to nothing.

The stark white returns.

It burns its way through my lids into the core of my eyes.

I try to see but can't. It's not easy to see through eyelashes thick with dried blood.

Kofi's blood? My own? I can't say.

I try to rub my eyes but can't, on account my hands don't move.

I try again. Harder this time. Praying with all my Spirit to the Spirit of Grandma Toughtits.

She answers my prayer and comes to me.

I'm happy to find out she's not in Pasadena, California, USA.

She lifts my right hand and brings it to my eyes.

Even she can't move my left hand as it is under something, or somebody, and she was never very strong.

She gently breathes on my eyes, like she used to when I was a baby, blowing the good Spirits into my heart through my eyes.

My lids tear apart, slightly. It hurts. The pain brings tears. The tears soften the dried blood.

I can almost see now. I see red. I see white. I see black. I see all colours of the rainbow.

But I don't see shapes.

I open my eyes more. They hurt more. They bring more tears. They loosen more.

It is funny. I can't see Grandma Toughtits now. Not with my eyes open, when I saw her clearly with my eyes shut.

The colours I see begin to separate themselves and form into groups and take on shapes.

The blue is the most far away, yet somehow the nearest. It is like a spot. A spot that grows bigger and turns smaller with every throb of the heart, every beat of the head.

The green hangs about here and there. The brown and black juts out everywhere.

Black moves against black. This time much too close, bringing it warmth and comfort.

It is the black form of Matt.

He rolls a weight off my arms.

I look up at his face.

I can see now.

His hands and face are covered in blood.

There is more pain in his eyes than there is in the world.

I wonder why. Matt wouldn't let some blood on his face and hands worry him like that.

I can move now.

Matt sits down by my side. He raises my head and puts it on his thigh.

I am a bit surprised as I felt his thigh on the other side.

I jerk my head to look that way.

It is a thigh, but not Matt's.

I look up, not understanding. I see another thigh. And another. And another. Loads and loads of thighs. And arms. And torsos. And heads.

I am lying on a silent wave of bodies. Matt is sitting on a shaky mountain of bodies.

Out there, in front of me, Golam is standing in a sinking pit of bodies.

To my left is Kofi is a body.

The scratches made by the cat are now wide enough and deep enough for boots.

It is not easy to walk on rotting bodies. Even if you are in the best of condition.

It is worse trying to walk on rotting bodies with your own body cut about and burnt from feet up to asshole up to head.

It don't smell too good either.

Golam don't say a word.

Matt and I don't say a word either, but it's different.

It's like we don't want to speak so we say nothing. Golam looks like he wants to speak but says nothing.

We are trying to climb out of the living bog of the dead that circles us on all sides, onto the dead rocks of the living that circle us on all sides.

We're in a huge cave. The only way in, or out, is at the top where the roof has come down, or cracked, or perhaps never was.

There is a bright shaft of light coming in from the hole in the roof.

It is making one part of the cave, where I was lying when Matt found me, very bright. The rest of the cave looks strangely dark. Once our eyes get used to it, we try to see what we can see.

It is hard to look at the bodies. It is hard to look away from the bodies.

Bodies with arms. Bodies without arms. Bodies with legs. Bodies without legs. Bodies with heads. Bodies without heads. Bodies with burns all over. Bodies without burns all over. Bodies with holes in them. Bodies without holes in them. Bodies with their insides out. Bodies with their outsides in. Bodies without flesh. Bodies without bones.

We manage to force ourselves to look at the walls of the cave in the hope of finding a way out.

Leastwise Matt and I do.

Golam just stares ahead of him. I don't think he's seeing. I think he's just staring.

There are old tree-roots sticking out here and there; there are sharp or blunt edges of rocks everywhere; there are even a few cracks and holes about.

We can haul ourselves up by any or all of these.

We try.

It is cold and damp. Our hands are either too stiff to hold on to anything firmly, or they just slip off on account of sweat.

I wonder why we're sweating when we're so cold.

We've to keep pushing Golam ahead of us, and tell him to do this or not to do that. It don't seem like he's listening, but he must be for he does what we tell him – even if we have to tell him it more than once.

We go up from here, and fall down.

We claw our way up from there, and come crashing down.

We end up more bloodied than we started.

We don't give up.

But we don't get anywhere either.

Matt is the only one who seems to clamber up, but he won't go without us.

I say maybe he should get out on his own, if he can; and then maybe try to get help for us. But he don't want to take the chance on account there may not be no one outside – except maybe BASTOs, and we know the help we'll get from them.

I am glad he don't leave us, though I suppose he should go, if he can.

We sit down for a rest, taking care not to put our asses on any faces, or balls and thingies. Not that there is much left of people's faces or balls and thingies. But we're still careful.

Another thing to avoid sitting on is sharp bones. There are plenty of these about.

While we're deciding where to sit, Matt has an idea.

Some of the bodies are naked. Some are not.

If we take the robes off of the not naked ones, and tie them together, we'll make a sort of rope. Matt can then clamber up and lower this rope down for us to pull ourselves up.

We try this.

Unfortunately most of the robes are too tattered or mouldy to be of any use.

Then we think of jeans. They are made of a tougher material, and it looks like some of the new dead ones have quite strong ones on.

It is not easy to pull them off. They are sticking to the bodies – either because of the cold and the damp, or dried blood.

After a great deal of search and struggle we get a few good strong ones.

When I say we, I mean Matt and me, Golam just stands and stares.

With jeans it is easy as we can use one of the legs to tie a knot, while the other leg hangs to form the rope.

When we've got a long enough stretch we put the plan into action.

Matt ties one end of a leg round his waist with a belt we found round someone's neck.

He begins to climb up.

It's not easy and many times he slithers down, but he carries on.

When he gets to a little ledge on which he can sit he ties the rope round a jutting bit of rock and tells Golam to come up.

To my surprise Golam listens to him the first time and starts up.

I shut my eyes for I can't bear to look.

It seems years after when I hear Matt shout, 'Now you, Kimo.'

I look up. Golam is sitting next to Matt on the ledge.

It is my turn.

I'm so nervous I keep slipping down each time I'm anywhere near the ledge.

I am close to crying.

Matt tells me to stop a while, shut my eyes, and breathe slowly and deep.

I try that.

I then try climbing up.

I make it this time.

The ledge is bigger than it looked from below. We all rest on it for some time.

Makes a change from sitting on dead bodies.

Matt starts off again.

He hasn't gone too far up when he gives a shout of happiness.

There is a crack up in the wall. Like the ledge it is much bigger close up than we thought it would be.

Matt shouts to us and says if he can squeeze through it we may not have to haul ourselves all the way up to the top.

But first he has to see what lies outside the crack. If there's nothing but a long drop it's of no use. If there's another rock or a ledge nearby, we'll be free.

He leans out of the crack and looks.

There is a ledge running on the outside leading to some flat rocks leading to the main hills. There are even some trees and bushes to cling to or hide in, if necessary.

I'm afraid once again I don't remember much what happened after that.
I think we dropped off to sleep, somewhere among the bushes, half way between the cave of the dead and the main hills.

When we wake up next it is another night.
We go back to sleep.
When we wake up next we don't want to wake up.
Leastwise I don't. Nor does Golam.
We just want to lie down and go back to sleep again.
I don't so much as want to move the little finger of my right hand.
I'm sure Golam feels the same.
But Matt won't let us rest.
'Rest?' he says. 'You've done nothing but rest much too long as it is.'
He pushes us and pulls us and shouts at us till we are fully awake.

He says he's found a place where there's some water, and we should wash ourselves.
He's also collected some roots and leaves, and even some sort of fruit, which he says we must eat.
We don't feel like opening our mouths, much less swallow; but Matt forces us to.

We're feeling much better.

Tired, but better.

Golam is still not saying a word, though even he's looking a little less wild.

Matt has given up trying to make him talk. He just holds his hand every now and then, and puts his arms round him and gives him a hug.

We keep on walking for many a day. Or rather night, as we sleep during the day.

At last we're out of the hills, and out of the BASTO area.

Leastwise that's what we hope.

It'll be even more dangerous for us if they are here as now we are in the sandy plains we've nowhere to hide.

Our only cover is darkness.

Our supply of food and water is no longer sure.

Water specially, as there are still some roots and bushes we can eat.

We gather leaves of thick juicy desert cactus-like plant which hoards some water in it and hope for the best.

There is not much else we can do.

It is just another night.

We started walking not long after sunset, rested for some time around midnight, and are now on the march again.

The thought of our village and families keeps Matt and me going.

Matt and me keep Golam going.

Suddenly we find the sandy even land under our feet become a bit lumpy, hard and roundish.

We look down.

In the dark before dawn we can just about make out logs of tree trunks under our feet.

We're a bit surprised to see logs in the plains, but then we're still quite close to the hills so we think someone's been cutting timber and storing it away till the river is full again and it can be floated off.

As we walk on we see logs everywhere. All around us and as far as the eye can see.

They are hard and shaky to walk on. We try to look for some open space but can't find any.

So we just grit our teeth and walk on, on account we don't want to turn back.

Soon the dawn light begins to filter through the desert haze.

Just then I nearly fall over as a log moves beneath my feet.

I hear a sort of a moan, like a wind through the trees.

We look around. There are no trees, except dead ones.

Nor is there any wind.

But there is a moaning sound.

It seems to increase and starts to come at us from all different angles.

Gradually it develops a broken rhythm of its own.

Above the weird sounds rises a piercing scream.

A hollow scream.

A scream of pain.

A scream of such pain that even the dead trees come to life and move restlessly.

The scream rises again.

It is Golam.

His face is all twisted up.

'I see them,' he cries, 'I see them, I see them.'

'See who?' I say, happy that he speaks but worried at the way he speaks.

'Spirits,' screams Golam, 'I see Spirits. The Spirits of Shit.'

As his words cut through the air some of the moving trees sit up.

They are not trees after all, but bodies.

We've been walking on bodies again. Only this time on dying bodies rather than dead ones.

Matt says, 'It would have been good if they had followed.'

Golam starts to run.

As he runs his body bends forward sharply: his arms bend sharply at the elbows, his legs bend sharply at the knees; his stickly bum sticks out sharply.

He looks utterly ridiculous.

He screams as he runs.

He runs and screams, screams and runs, runs and screams; running and screaming all over bodies; bodies of men and women and children, bodies dead living and dying.

We run after Golam.

We are all running. Golam screaming, I shouting, Matt saying, 'Oh God, my God, why have you left us and gone away?'

It's like the camp at Gonta, but nothing like the camp at Gonta.

It stretches all round the belt of the world, over and over and over again.

Everywhere are ugly twisted bodies making fun of human beings.

Golam keeps running and screaming.
I keep running and shouting.
Matt is running and weeping.
We make so much racket that some real people come out of nowhere to see what's going on.
They are somewhere in the distance, in the centre of the rotting wounds of the self cut world.

The real people come towards us, picking their way delicately between the bodies.

Part V

MY FRIEND MATT

(a beginning of another sort)

One

An Old Friend and Some New Plans

We all get taken quite ill after we're found by the people who look after the refugee camp.

They clean and bandage our wounds and burns, give us some medicine for our fever, and make us rest.

They also give us some porridge and milk.

It seems they have 'limited supplies', and if we don't 'respond' pretty soon, they'll just let us 'live out our time'. They can't 'afford' to do more than that, even for 'special cases' and 'excellent examples'.

We're not sure what it all means, but we sure are grateful to them. They make lots of pictures of us, especially of our cut and burnt parts.

They also 'record' a talk along with the pictures, which ends '...
by the time you see these pictures, these children will almost
certainly have died...'

They are quite upset when they find out we understand English,
but Matt tells them not to worry. If we have to die, then we have
to die.

That's what Grandma Toughtits always said.

We've been lying around for a week or so, sometimes knowing
what's going on around us, sometimes not knowing what's
going on around us.

They seem to have given up hope on us. Leastwise on Golam
and me.

They are puzzled about Matt. One minute he looks the weakest,
one minute he looks the strongest.

I'm whirling and swirling downwards when I feel this cool
gentle hand on my forehead.

I recognize it at once.

When I say I recognize it, I don't mean I recognize whose hand it
is. I mean I recognize it is a hand I know, even if I don't exactly
know who it is who has this hand.

But I do know it is a good hand. The hand of a friend.

Suddenly I feel better.

But I'm still not sure who it is.

I hear Matt's voice. 'Hello, Alberto.'

Even then it takes me a while to figure out who Alberto is.

Of course now that I know it seems unbelievable that I didn't
know at once who Alberto is, but when I didn't know it didn't

seem unbelievable that I didn't know.

Anyway that don't matter.

What matters is we are truly happy to see Alberto.

We soon start feeling all right too.

Everyone is surprised.

Golam is still not himself, though.

His fever is gone and his wounds are better, but he is still not himself.

Alberto asks how we happen to be here, and in such a state.

We tell him.

We ask him if he knows if the BASTOs have found out where the RAFFs' hide-out is.

We truly don't remember what we told the BASTOs when they were making us talk about it.

He says he don't know anything about that, but he does know that there is something big going on among the soldiers.

There are many rumours going about, and they can't all be wrong.

He says he's visiting different camps, big and small, and will soon be going to Gonta. He says he'll take us there with him, and if we're willing to wait here for a couple of days he'll drop us at our village before going onto the next camp.

We're full of joy to hear this.

Matt asks him if he knows anything about Tom and his miserable wife.

Alberto says they are in Pasadena, California, USA.

I am truly shocked to hear this.
Matt is not.
He says he always knew that.
Smart-ass.

The next day Alberto goes to visit the sick and hungry to see if he can help in any way. He takes Matt with him.

Alberto comes back alone.

We don't see Matt again even though we look for him everywhere, tripping over bodies and slipping over shit.

Many days go like this for it is a big camp with more people in it than I've ever seen in my whole life; and Alberto wants to spend as much time with them as he can. He is pleased that more of the sick are getting better than he had hoped.

When the time comes for us to leave, Matt comes back and says, 'The time has come for us to leave.'
He says this with tears in his eyes and a strange look on his face the like of which I've never seen before and which I've never forgotten since.
We sit down and have our last meal together.

While scooping my last bit of porridge I ask Matt how he knew it was time for us to leave.
He says, 'I know what I know.'
I look at him, then I look at Golam and his face with the lost

smile and his once dancing hair which now lies more on where he rests his head than on his head; and I ask Matt if he's such a smart-ass how come he don't know how to help Golam.

Matt says, 'I am not the sun, but the Earth. I shine only when it shines. I have no light of my own. I can't make it bright just because I want to, no matter how much I want to. He has to want it too. He has to want it first.'

I can see it's not easy for him to say this.

Alberto is quite taken aback at Matt's words and calls on Mother Mary to help us all.

Then he says to Matt, 'Make of it what you will. You are older and wiser than I am. I only shine when it shines.'

All the while Golam stares straight ahead, eating only a little, not seeing what he's eating.

Two

Hena Rules

We say our thank yous to all for their food, medicine and robes,
and walk out of the camp with Alberto.

We haven't gone far when Golam suddenly turns into a tree and
refuses to walk any more.

His feet are rigid, his eyes are fixed; his body is shaking like a
rattlesnake's tail.

We follow his gaze.

There is a khaki jeep standing there.

We know that if Alberto is planning to take us in that we'll never
be able to get Golam into it.

Golam thinks it's the BASTOs.

Luckily the jeep belongs to the camp.

Alberto says he likes to travel in a van on account he has to carry
sick people in it sometimes. Also, he says, Golam is not the only

one with a horror of BASTOs and their jeeps. So he avoids all jeeps.

So into the van we get and on to Gonta we go.

All along the way we see lines of people dragging their feet, their children and their few belongings in search of food and water.

We keep driving off and on for more than a day and a night.

At last we are within sight of Gonta.

What we see makes us come to a sudden stop.

The road is blocked by many jeeps and a number of soldiers are standing around checking everyone going in or out.

It is lucky that Golam is in the back of the van with the sunblinds drawn to stop his fever coming back. So he doesn't see the soldiers. To tell the truth Matt and me are scared stiff too, but we can handle it.

Leastwise I hope we can.

Alberto don't want to take the chance. He quickly makes both of us get into the back as well. Then he carries on. He thinks it will be worse if we turn back now and they decide to follow us.

Soon we are stopped by the soldiers.

My own heart is going ding-dong, but I'm more worried about Golam. For his sake as well as our own. If he starts screaming we may get into more trouble than otherwise.

Matt puts his arms around him and holds him down.

We can see through a chink in the curtain that Alberto has got off and gone away with the soldiers. They seem to be having a serious talk.

It goes on and on for such a long time that we get truly worried.

By the time he gets back Golam is asleep.

We drive on as we are still some distance away from the actual old village of Gonta, and even further from the camp, which is on the other side towards our village.

There are soldiers everywhere.

I've never seen so many soldiers in all my life.

I'm almost getting as bad as Golam for fear of them.

I'm only too happy that Alberto is with us. I don't know what we'd have done otherwise – or, more important, what they would've done. Alberto stops in front of the little building which is part of the little hospital.

We get out, looking all around us to make sure the soldiers can't be seen. Golam is awake now and we don't want to make him frightened any more than he is already.

On our way into the building Matt asks Alberto why there are millions and millions (you know how Matt goes on!) and millions of people in the camp where we've just come from, when the hospital here seems much better.

Alberto says that camp is near Bader where the main airport is and where all the food and medical supplies first came. So everybody tries to get to it. No one is allowed to go any closer to Bader so they just camp there. Every day it gets bigger and bigger. And the bigger it gets the worse it gets.

By now we are inside the first room on the left.

There are one or two people there, but none that we know.

After Alberto has greeted them and so on, he takes us to one side and says, 'Now tell me truthfully, what've you been up to?'

We're surprised that he asks us that, and we tell him we're surprised he asks us that.

'We're surprised you ask us that,' we say.

Well, I say.

Matt just looks at Alberto in surprise.

Golam stares at nothing with no surprise.

Alberto is quiet for a long while, looking at our faces and into our eyes as if trying to make up his mind if we are really surprised or just pretending.

He can tell we're truly surprised he asks us something like that.

'Some of these soldiers are especially looking for you.'

The moment he says that Golam's face turns like burnt wood.

He begins to shake like a rattlesnake's tail.

'Oh Lord,' says Alberto, 'I shouldn't have said that.'

But it's too late for that.

Still, we manage to calm Golam down by giving him a drink of precious water, and holding him in our arms.

While we are doing that we're dying to find out what it's all about and why the soldiers are looking for us.

Matt says, 'Now that you've said some of it, you best say the rest. If Golam knows this much he might as well know all. It's often better than knowing half.'

'But I don't know much else. That's the whole point,' says Alberto.

'That's why I asked you. I thought you must know something. After all, the soldiers wouldn't be wasting their time looking for you without some reason. They even had your photos.'

We can't think of nothing to say.

'It can't possibly have anything to do with the coup,' says Alberto after a long while, almost to himself.

'What coup?' says Matt, jumping up from the floor in his corner.

'What is a coup?' say I, without jumping up from my corner on the floor.

'Change of Government, sort of,' says Alberto, looking at me. Then to Matt, 'Nothing exciting. One General has taken over from another. Happens all the time in the world. I doubt if there will be any real changes.'

'I think there will be,' says one of the men in the room.

'Who is the new General?' Matt asks as he sits himself down again, his excitement dying down.

'Some General Dnomo,' says Alberto. 'The name is vaguely familiar but I don't think I know anything about him.'

'Not much is known about him,' says another man. 'He's always been a pretty powerful man, from the little I've heard, but behind the scenes. Something to do with defence.'

'What else!' says the first man.

'Left wing?' asks Alberto.

'No one knows. That's the trouble,' says the second man. 'Already there is a four-way split in the air. The soldiers who still support Tako and those behind Dnomo on the one hand; the hardline rebels led by Jabbar and the Peace Piper rebels led by Mobu on the other. These last want to meet with Dnomo to see if they can come to an arrangement, but with Tako supporters and Jabbar supporters both dead set against it, it's going to take some doing.'

'It's funny, the two who hate each other are most in agreement for once,' says the first man.

'Isn't that often the case,' says the second man, 'sadly.'

'And while all this is going on,' says Alberto, 'the world will sit back and wait to decide whether or not to give aid to the starving, depending on which side Dnomo takes.'

'True.'

Matt's been listening to all this, becoming more and more excited.

'Hena,' says Matt softly.

I don't understand. I say so.

'General Dnomo is Jak,' explains Matt.

I still don't understand. But nobody cares.

'Who's Hena?' asks Alberto.

'You know her,' I say to Alberto, 'our Hena.'

Alberto looks like he don't believe us.

'Hena,' says the first man, 'known among the city kids as Hena the Whore. A little chit of a girl who frightens big men. Or so we hear.'

'You're joking,' says Alberto.

'I'm not really sure of anything,' says the man, 'except one thing. I most certainly am not joking.'

'No wonder the soldiers were looking for us,' says Matt. 'Hena must've got our ransom note. She must've also learnt from Reza that we're no longer with the RAFFs. So she's sent the BASTOs to look for us. She must've given them the pictures Jak made of us. Strange.'

'They're not BASTOs no more,' I say, trying to be clever, cleverer than Matt. 'BASDOs perhaps, but not BASTOs.'

'What on Earth are you talking about!' says the first man.

'How well do you know this Hena?' says the second man.
'Only too well,' I say.
'Not well enough,' says Matt.

'Wow!' I say after everybody's dropped the subject. 'Just think, all those soldiers – looking for us.'
'I hasten to disillusion you,' begins Alberto, 'but...'
'You what!' I go, without really meaning to be rude.
'I am sorry to disappoint you,' he begins again. 'Oh sorry. Forget it. I mean they are not all looking for you. Most of them are there to see there's no trouble over the new Government.'
I *am* a bit disappointed to hear that. Disillusioned even, whatever that may be.
But I'm glad as well.
The thought of hundreds of soldiers looking for us is a bit frightening; even if they are sent by our Hena.

We've now to decide what to do.
Golam being the way he is, he won't go with the soldiers.
Truly speaking I am none too keen to go with them myself. Who knows, the Government might change again. Or something. I wouldn't want to take a chance with the soldiers.
We could go on to our village, but it is likely Hena's got in touch with our folks and maybe called them to Bader.

Although we are truly pleased that we've got rid of Tako and our Hena has a hand in looking after our country, we are also a bit lost about what to do next. But I expect you've gathered that by now.

Matt says it would be best to stay here and somehow get a message to Hena so she can send Reza or some non-soldier to fetch us.

The plan sounds good, but there are two problems.

The first being how to get the message to Hena without getting the soldiers involved.

The second is that after all this time we are so keen to see our families we just want to go ahead and see them. I'm even dying to see big sister, whom I hate.

But then again they may not even be there.

We are back full circle.

Alberto says to sleep on it tonight and decide the next day. When you're rested and refreshed you think better, he says.

As it happens we don't get a chance to rest and get refreshed.

Not a proper rest, on account we're woken up by smoke and fire in the middle of the night.

Three

Dust, Ashes and Dallas

Matt is the first to get up and see what's going on.

He tells us to hurry up and move out – us being Golam, me and two of the people who help around the camp: Madru and Dano. We are in this open shed just outside one of the rooms where the medicines are kept.

A part of Madru and Dano's job is to see the medicines are safe and not stolen or anything. Not that anyone would do something like that, but still, it is best to play safe – as the doctor says.

When we are out and fully awake we see the strangest and most beautiful sight we've ever seen; and hear the strangest and most frightening sounds we've ever heard.

Leastwise me.

It's like you've left your old life and come to a new life to see the whole world burning away the traces of the old life and preparing for a new life.

It's Grandma Toughtits' vision of the big night of fire come true.

The real thing. Not the kitchen fire or the big bangs in the copse all those years ago.

There are flames as far as the Spirits can fly, and further – only there is no further.

The dust that rises from under the screaming feet of the half-dead running from the dead mixes with the flames and burns; its fairy dots flicker and flash and dance, and dance and flash and flicker, like stars gone mad.

The smell of burning bodies is the smell of baking bread.

Some say the fire started in the little shack by the bus stop where the petrol is stored. Some say it started in one of the little straw huts.

Some say it started in the room where the medicines are kept.

All we know is it didn't start in the room where the medicines are kept.

Some say it was started by the 'new' soldiers to show their power.

Some way it was started by the 'old' soldiers to show their anger.

Some say it started by itself.

Some even say it was started by the Spirits annoyed at people for their sins.

All we know is it started somehow, somewhere, and is now everywhere.

While I'm still too dazed to do no more than wonder – it happens.
So quickly I don't know it's happening till it's happened.
So slowly it's still happening.

Matt lurches forward, from neutral to top in no time flat.
He is in the fire of the burning huts, with the burning people.
I try to rush after him; to stop him, to hold him, to bring him back; but Madru and Dano grasp my arms so hard I can't break free.

I remember the heat, the loneliness and the beauty.
Strange, for I was shivering with cold, surrounded by people, and swallowed by ugliness.

After Matt has brought many people out he starts to burn.
He tries to rush back to see if he can do more, but realises half way he can't make it.
Then he turns, as if to come to us and say his last farewell, but can't.
He stands there, fixed on the burning sand, burning.
His arms rise as if to embrace us, his whole body glowing with flames.
It is then I start screaming.
I barely notice a crowd of men in white robes, their heads covered in white hoods to save their faces from the blowing flames, standing around to watch Matt burn.
Dano is still holding me back, but Madru lets go and says in total disbelief: 'Where on earth did they come from?' his voice is hushed and full of fear.

I keep on screaming and Matt keeps on burning and the hooded men in white keep on watching.

Golam turns to Madru and says, 'Dallas.'

The word sounds so unreal in the middle of all this that I turn round to look at him.

Suddenly there's no one there except Golam and me, ashes and dust. Golam again says, 'Dallas.'

The red in the sky is not just the glow of the fire.

The wind whirls and howls. A dust storm of the greatest power starts up as all the Spirits of the Desert sigh and moan and wail, angry at being disturbed by the fire.

No wonder anyone who can run away has run away.

Four

End of the Line

We've been travelling – Golam and me – with the lost caravan of the sick and the burnt and the hungry.
We are going somewhere. We don't know where.
We're just walking. Dragging ourselves bit by bit.
We don't know where Alberto is. We don't know where anyone we know is.

To tell the truth I don't know where Golam is.
I look at the skelly next to me.
He is bald. On his head, instead of thick bouncing hair, is a big many-mushroomed boil. In his mouth are rotting gums instead of flashing teeth. His silky black skin is dry and flaking in parts, wet and leaking in others.

We are not walking any more.

Golam can't take a step any longer.

To tell the truth I can't take a step any longer.

I'd rather be anywhere than here – even Pasadena, California, USA – but I can't make the effort to go anywhere.

Poor Tom.

He had only two balls after all.

I try to look at my balls. It seems like I haven't got any.

Funny that.

Leastwise I think it is.

I try to smile, but my face is too stretched and hard. I think it will crack and fall to bits if I smile.

Golam lets out a little squeal and a little shit and dies.

I thank the Spirits.

I want to carry Golam's body to hide it under a bush, but I can't.

I try to drag him. I can't.

But it's not easy. I have to first lie down and drag myself – it's easier than walking – then pull him across the sand.

It is an ocean of sand. I can see a bush. Like an island. It is always the same distance away, no matter how near I get to it.

I give up.

There's not much point in getting to the bush anyway.

It is better if buzzards get Golam here. At least he'll provide food for them.

I take his robe off, tidy its tatters and place it over his body.

The wind blows it away.

I wish I could mark a little cross next to his body.

I know Golam hasn't had his soul saved, but I think he'd like that.

Leastwise that's what Matt would've done.

There is nothing to make a cross with.

I lift a handful of sand and sprinkle a cross on Golam's chest.

The wind blows it away.

Then I have an idea.

I wipe some of the shit off Golam's thighs. It is still warm and fresh.

I make a shit cross on Golam's chest.

It stays there.

The blood in the shit makes it look real pretty.

I put my head on Golam's chest, a little to one side, so as not to disturb the shit cross. I put my arms across his waist and lie down next to him.

I remember wanting to do that years ago.

I go to sleep truly happy.

Five

My Friend Matt

I am woken up by my friend Matt. 'Wake up,' he says in the gentlest voice I've ever heard. 'Wake up. The time has come.'

I stretch and curl at the same time, like a cat; contented and happy.

'The time has come for you to take over,' says Matt.
'You are now the Earth; and the Earth is yours.
'I'll shine on you when you are dark.
'I'll rain on you when you are thirsty.
'I'll smile on you when you are happy.'

He ruffles my hair and smiles.
His tears fall like dew on my face. The dew turns to rain. Gentle rain.

Like dew. Like Matt's tears.

I look up at Matt. It is raining a gentle rain outside.
It is falling on everything I can see.
My stomach fills with joy.
I smile at Golam, at Matt, at Hena.
Dada puts his arms around me. Mam gives me a hug.
I feel like a flower.
I feel like grass.
I feel like a tree.
I feel like a tree again. And why not? After all, our family are
Spirits of trees.

Ask Grandma Toughtits if you don't believe me.